The blood-red gld from the eye socket with
ever-increasing int   s
face being dragged   s
head back. Then it   d
loose from the bon   t
to meet and touch tl

And then the fac   e
eye sockets blinded   e
could feel the slimy flesh of the creature's face pressing
against—and into—his own.

His nostrils were filled with the stench of corruption, his
tongue smothered in its hideous taste as the moldering flesh
enveloped him. He tried to scream, but his mouth and tongue
and throat were filled by a suffocating putrescence that was . . .

. . . himself.

Ravenloft is a netherworld of evil, a place of darkness that
can be reached from any world—escape is a different matter
entirely. The unlucky who stumble into the Dark Domains
find themselves trapped in lands filled with vampires, were-
beasts, zombies, and worse.

Each novel in the series is a complete story in itself,
revealing the chilling tales of the beleaguered heroes and
powerful evil lords who populate the Dark Domains.

BOOKS

Ravenloft

BOOKS

King of the Dead

Gene DeWeese

For the eldritch Brothers Duane and all the minions
of SSR and Shanadu, particularly Robert E. Briney,
W. Paul Ganley, and Brian J. McNaughton

KING OF THE DEAD

First Printing: March 1996
Printed in the United States of America.
Library of Congress Catalog Card Number: 95-62198

9 8 7 6 5 4 3 2 1

8071-XXX1501
ISBN: 0-7869-0483-6

TSR, Inc.
201 Sheridan Springs Road
Lake Geneva, WI 53147
U.S.A.

TSR Ltd.
120 Church End, Cherry Hinton
Cambridge CB1 3LB
United Kingdom

# PROLOGUE

Helpless, he struggled through the suffocating mists with aimless desperation.

Where was he? What was this place, and how had he come to be here?

There was a time when he had known, of that he was sure, but now he did not. He could remember only that he *had* remembered, and this knowledge was even more terrifying than the mists themselves. It was as if he were himself being eaten away by whatever powers lurked just beyond his vision, hidden in the endless, blinding whiteness.

And perhaps he was.

For all he knew, that was precisely what was happening, and he was helpless to combat whatever manner of creature was doing this to him. Helpless even to know if such a creature existed.

Or if *anything* existed beyond the imprisoning fog.

For now, he had no goal other than survival and the increasingly desperate hope that the impenetrable fog, like the fog that cloaked his mind, must somewhere have an end.

For what seemed like eons, he forced himself to continue

moving through the silence, the only sound the muffled thud of his feet against the unseen and unnaturally even ground, a punctuation to the litany of unanswered questions that echoed endlessly through his mind: What is this place? Why am I here? Will my torment never end?

Abruptly he stopped. From somewhere came the distant sound of rumbling laughter, and the thought appeared, unbidden and meaningless, in his mind: the shadows.

And a face, that of a young man, barely beyond boyhood, flashed before his eyes and was gone, swallowed up by the mists. The features were achingly familiar yet utterly unknown.

And a second face, this one lingering, at first distorted and half concealed by the cloaking mist but quickly becoming so frighteningly, loathsomely vivid that he threw up his arms to ward it off. It was not truly a face, but what had once *been* a face. Now it was rotting, virtually fleshless, as if it had been dragged from a month-old grave, decaying and utterly lifeless.

Except for the eyes.

Eyes that were not eyes but glowing coals recessed deep within sockets so cavernous they must have been rooted in whatever remained of the creature's brain.

But eyes that burned with some perverted form of life.

And eyes that seemed to radiate pain and horror.

Shuddering, not only at the repulsive features but also at the thought of what the soul trapped within such a shell of corruption must endure, he was relieved when, finally, the image was swallowed up by the mists. Whatever it was, whatever that tortured soul had done to be meted such punishment, it was none of his concern.

His only concern was—

Was what?

Panic clutched at him anew. For a moment, the images had driven his own fears from his thoughts, but now they came flooding back. He was trapped and helpless, remembering nothing, not even his own identity. He had no past, no future, only a fog-shrouded, terror-filled present!

As if to taunt him anew, the grotesque, meaningless images returned to swirl around him. The rotting face, now perched atop a decaying body wrapped in kingly robes that mocked and made ridiculous their pathetic contents.

And the young man's face, now haloed in golden curls, becoming even younger than before, until it was no longer that of a young man but that of a boy, the eyes pleading, the lips working soundlessly, desperately, and all the while the muffled laughter mocked them both, and—

Suddenly the mists and all their imagined contents were gone, not parting or swirling away but simply vanishing, leaving only an echo of silent laughter.

And utter darkness.

But only for a moment.

Even as the distant laughter faded, a world formed around him, a world of chill night air and faint starlight and a wall of massive trees rearing up before him. For a long moment, he luxuriated in the feel of the cool breeze on his skin and the damp odor of the night as he hungrily drank in the sight of the stars in their unfamiliar patterns and the rugged, corrugated bark of the trees, the delicate tracery of veins in their many-pointed leaves, even the individual blades of grass at his feet. It was as if his senses had been starved by the suffocating mists, and now . . .

But then he wondered how he was able to see such details when the only light was from a scattering of stars in a moonless sky. Was he a sorcerer, to be capable of such things?

The thought did not startle him. It seemed almost natural. It was the implications that were disturbing.

If he were a sorcerer, had he run afoul of one more powerful than himself? One that had robbed him of his mind and cast his helpless shell of a body into this alien plane?

His back was suddenly atingle, and he turned sharply from the forest.

It was as if his fears had been pulled from his mind and given form. No more than a quarter of a mile distant across a treeless plain stood a hill—no, not a hill but a massive outcropping, a jagged heap of flinty rock that thrust up through the earth as if from some subterranean pit.

And perched atop the misshapen mound, covering it like a grotesquely magnificent crown, the towers and turrets of an immense castle stabbed high into the alien sky, its sheer walls unscalable, unassailable. A single narrow road wound its precarious way to a massive door, the only visible entrance, in a section of wall between two joined towers. Other than that door, there were only narrow slits in the rough-hewn stone of the walls, slits through which archers could loose barrages of arrows and spears against anyone foolhardy enough to approach.

Whoever was master of this place obviously did not welcome visitors and certainly would not welcome *him*, especially if the one who dwelt there was the sorcerer responsible for his present predicament.

If . . .

He knew no reason to think thus, but nonetheless he could not shake the thought.

Irritably he turned his attention once again to the forest. Random speculation was pointless and did nothing but waste precious time. What he needed was knowledge. Facts. First of all, now that he had at last escaped—been released from?—that featureless limbo of mists and found himself in what appeared to be a real world, he needed to know what that world was.

But most importantly, he needed to know what and who *he* was and what powers he possessed. For, no matter where he was, something deep within him seemed to say, he could rely only upon himself, upon his own abilities, his own strengths, whatever they might be. Once he learned their nature, there would be time enough to discover and challenge his enemies, whether they dwelt conveniently in this forbidding castle or elsewhere.

He listened, puzzled at the silence. Surely a forest as dense as this would be filled with life, and yet the only sounds were faint rustlings of the leaves in the chill breeze and the distant rush of water past the banks of an unseen river. If there were night creatures of any kind, their voices were silent.

Except . . .

From somewhere deep in the forest came the faint sound of whispered voices.

So. There were others abroad in the night.

Focusing on that sound alone, he blotted everything else from his seemingly preternatural senses until he had a direction pinpointed in the darkness. With no thought for concealment, he plunged into the dense undergrowth of the forest, brushing the leaves and branches and vines aside as if they had no more substance than the mists he had just departed.

He was, he realized after a hundred yards, approaching the source not only of the whispers but of the rushing water as well.

And of a faint, greenish glow that originated not in the sky but in the depths of the forest.

PART I

DARKON

 **ONE**

579, Barovian Calendar

Silently Balitor hooded his lantern and motioned for Oldar to do the same.

"You knew we must hide ourselves in darkness," Balitor said in a soft whisper when the younger man hesitated. "Not that darkness alone could shield us from his eyes," he added, fingering the minutely inscribed medallion resting beneath the coarse weave of his peasant's shirt.

Oldar shivered in his ragged woolen cloak but nodded and complied, nervously brushing his fingers against an identical medallion suspended, like Balitor's, from a leather cord around his neck. The cover on his lantern clicked into place, and darkness closed around him so completely it made him sway. Only by spreading his feet and planting them firmly, as he had so often braced himself against the tug of horse and plow, could he keep his balance in those first moments of blackness. He had not imagined anything could be this dark.

"This must be what it is to be blind," he murmured, his voice soft but still startlingly loud in the silence of the forest.

For a long time, they stood perfectly still. Finally, like half-formed shadows, the trees took phantom shape around them. To Oldar's eyes, Balitor was distinguishable only because of his nearness and the faint susurrus of his breathing.

Silently, gingerly, they moved forward. Behind them they heard the occasional chirrup of an insect, the flutter of a night bird or a bat as it sought out a morsel. Ahead there was no sound of any living thing, only the faint rush of water where there should have been none. The canals of Il Aluk were ten miles distant, the waters of the Vuchar no closer.

Oldar shivered again despite his efforts to keep himself under control. The warnings about the darkness and the lifeless silence had not prepared him for the reality, any more than warnings of the pitfalls of leaving his tiny village for the teeming streets of Il Aluk had prepared him for that reality. It was as if the still-unseen castle—or its master, the rarely seen Lord Darcalus—exuded darkness and silence, making dim the light of the lanterns even before they had been hooded, muffling their footsteps, dulling even the internal sounds of their own breathing and heartbeats.

Until the last few hundred yards, all had been normal—as normal as night could ever be in this land where doors were sealed and windows shuttered virtually from sunset to sunrise. There had at least been occasional sounds of life, occasional rustlings in the high grass and brambles, the sight or sound of a snake or rabbit darting for cover at their approach. Here there was nothing but the looming presence of the cursed castle somewhere beyond the forest that surrounded them.

"The woman was mad," Oldar whispered, suddenly

despairing of ever seeing his father again, or the tiny patch of land he had called home for his first eighteen years.

Balitor chuckled silently. "Was she, now? I wonder. She is doubtless safe in her goose-down bed, while we are abroad and helpless in the night, in the very shadow of Avernus, doing her bidding."

"So we are even madder than she. That is scarcely a comfort."

"Then take comfort in the fact that, so far, she has been right in everything she told us. You can feel the shadow she predicted would envelop this place. You can, I imagine, hear the stream ahead of us, a stream that has neither source nor destination outside this forest. And we will soon see if, as she believes, it emerges from the nether regions and returns without ever being exposed to open sky. We may eventually even learn if its magical curative powers are as great as she hopes."

"If her rightness is so comforting and makes us so safe, then why would she not come herself? Why should she hire the pair of us?"

"That is the way of ladies such as she. If anything smacks of work or hardship or discomfort, they have it done for them. Would you have it otherwise? And deprive the likes of us of a livelihood?"

Oldar sighed, knowing he would never best his friend in a battle of words or wits. Even minor skirmishes such as this were lost before they had even begun. "A lot of good it will do us in our graves," he muttered, "provided we are whole enough to even require graves after this night."

Balitor laughed softly. "We have no choice but to remain whole, friend Oldar," he whispered back. "She has already paid us more than either of us could hope to earn in a year—more than either of us ever *have* earned in a year—and if we are successful, she will pay us even more. We must remain whole if we ever expect to spend those generous bounties."

"*If* we are successful. *If* we survive. I am beginning to doubt both outcomes."

"Then leave," Balitor said with a shrug. "It will mean that much more for me. Only do it quietly, and do not show your light until you are well outside the shadow."

Oldar stood silently, irresolutely. With each passing moment, he more desperately wanted to turn tail and flee, even if it meant crashing blindly into tree after tree as he caromed back the way they had come. Scratches and bruises were a small price to pay for his life.

But he could not run away. He had given his word, and he had no choice but to honor that word, even though he had not been entirely sober when it had been given.

In the end, he sucked in his breath, the sound as muffled as everything else in this place, and moved slowly, deliberately forward, shoulder to shoulder with Balitor. With even the stars blocked by the roof of leaves high overhead, they had no way of marking the passing of time. At best, they could count their steps and thus take measure of the distance they covered.

And listen to the only sound that was not muffled or silenced: the growing rush of water.

Slowly it grew louder, until finally it sounded more like a gushing mountain falls than a stream.

The underbrush thickened, now laced with heavy vines that reached up and gripped the branches of the trees and had to be forced aside like the flexible bars of a surrealistic prison. The ground softened and became ominously springy, as if they were walking on the poorly supported sod roof of a huge cavern.

And then, to their surprise—this was *not* something the lady had predicted—they forced their way through one last curtain of vines and found themselves bathed in a dim, greenish glow. The source of the stream was fifty yards in front of them, beyond a stand of waist-high marsh grass. The water didn't bubble up as if from a spring. Instead, it rushed out of an unseen opening, like a miniature river racing down a mountain slope, only it was racing *up* a slope, then leveling off for no more than a hundred feet before it vanished once more into the earth.

The water, almost frothy where it emerged, glowed a sickly green, but faded back into darkness barely halfway along its course, as if overcome by the darkness radiating from the opening through which it returned to the underground.

"I would say," Balitor breathed, "that this water does indeed have some unusual properties."

Oldar found himself laughing nervously as his partner took one of two metal containers from the small leather pouch suspended from a strap over his shoulder. Like the medallions, its leaden gray surface was inscribed with intricate, incomprehensible symbols. Uncorking it, Balitor cautiously eased his way into the thicket of marsh grass, grimacing as the ground became even more unsteady under his feet.

But finally he was there, within arm's reach of the glowing cascade. Kneeling slowly, he lowered the first container into the rushing water.

And gasped as he pulled back.

"Stings like the devil," he said with another grimace. "I do not believe I want to know what it feels like inside a person. That I will leave that for the lady to learn without my help." He looked back at Oldar. "You collect some from the other end, where the darkness takes it. And some from the middle."

Oldar swallowed, saying nothing, only nodding reluctantly. Even more reluctantly, but knowing he had no choice, Oldar took a cautious step into the waist-high grass and onto the springy, almost quivering earth beneath it.

He took another step.

And yet another.

He stifled a scream as something gripped his ankle. Instinctively he jerked backward, trying to pull free. Instead, he fell, his back crushing the thick grasses onto the resilient ground.

Whatever it was released its hold or was torn loose, and Oldar scrabbled backward and lurched to his feet . . .

And gasped and fell backward again as sheer terror froze his mind and his muscles into immobility. Rising spasmodically out of the grasses in front of him, a skeletal figure in a tattered, dirt-encrusted shroud lurched toward him, its decaying shreds of flesh a hideous green in the water's glow. Its hands, patches of bone and ligamentless joints plainly visible, reached out for him as it lurched forward another step, this one less unsteady than the first, as if it were gaining strength and coordination with each moment of its existence.

A scream shattered the silence, his own scream but not born of any conscious thought. The sound—and the sudden rasping pain it inflicted on his throat—shattered his paralysis, and he lurched to his feet, no more gracefully than the creature before him.

"Run!" Balitor shouted, his voice seeming to come from a great distance, but despite the soundness of the advice, Oldar found that he could not follow it. Nothing visible was gripping him, unless it was the glow itself, but he could barely move. It was as if his limbs had suddenly been submerged in water or in something even thicker and more viscous.

And as he turned slowly, ponderously, he saw that Balitor was no better off. The older man had returned the now corked and full containers to his leather pouch, but his legs were moving no more rapidly, no more freely than Oldar's. His face was a mask of terror, mouth wide, eyes bulging.

Vainly Oldar strained to run, the terror cutting through him like a knife as he managed only a single, dragging step, then another. If it weren't for the frantic beating of his own heart, muffled though it was, he would have thought time itself was coming to a stop. He should never have listened to Balitor or to any of the other fools he had fallen in with in Il Aluk! He should have stayed with his father and tilled the land and not tempted the fates with his foolish desire for adventure and excitement. He should have—

The remnants of a hand clamped tightly on his shoulder, and an overwhelming odor of decay assaulted his nostrils, almost choking him. He would have screamed once again if only he had been able to.

Several yards behind Balitor, Oldar saw the curtain of vines writhe and part, and he could only wonder what new horror this cursed place was about to loose upon them.

* * * * *

He was still dozens of yards from the source of the glow when a scream of terror drowned out the sound of rushing water and sent him racing ahead.

The ground grew spongy beneath his feet. Grass and brush were replaced by vines that seemed to grasp the trees like prisoners it feared would escape, but they didn't seem to hinder his passage. It was as if they sensed his coming and writhed aside, causing him to wonder once again if he were a sorcerer of some kind, but still no answer appeared in his mind.

Suddenly the last tangle of vines and underbrush parted, and he found himself emerging into a clearing. He lurched to a stop, his eyes taking in the grotesque tableau in an instant: The source of the glow was a torrent of water rushing up out of the ground, an underground river suddenly coming to the surface.

And there, in the tall marsh grass that spread out from the water, illuminated by the sickly green glow, a creature like the one whose rotting features had pursued him through the mists loomed over a young man in a ragged woolen cloak, the young man seemingly frozen, incapable of meaningful movement as the creature's skeletal hand reached out and grasped his shoulder. An older man, almost within the emerging rush of water, strained to run as well, moving as if some force held him to an inch-worm's pace.

Without thought or hesitation, he charged forward, an incantation—nonsense syllables to his conscious mind, but obviously far more than that to whatever part of him it was that had produced them—forming on his lips. Though he felt resistance, as if the air had suddenly thickened to liquid consistency, it barely slowed him as he felt strength surging through his entire body. Even the marsh grasses, like the vines, seemed to part before him, and he was upon the creature in seconds, his own hand grasping its arm and tearing its ragged hand from the young man's shoulder.

For a moment, its unblinking gaze remained on its lost prey, but then it turned its almost fleshless face toward the intruder. Its eyes, like those of the creature in the mists, were coals looking out from deep within its skull.

And behind those eyes . . .

For just an instant, terror clutched at him. It was as if he were being sucked into those eyes, into the mold-encrusted skull. For just an instant, he saw the creature that was actually in control, felt its chilling touch. Like the creature before him, its features were those of one long dead, its glowing coals of eyes the only sign of some perverted form of life animating the putrefying flesh. Unlike the creature before him, it was dressed not in a tattered shroud with clumps of dirt still caught in the folds but in majestic robes of velvet and fur with jeweled medallions suspended from gold and silver chains about the decaying flesh and exposed bone of its neck.

And on its head, perched atop a skull with patches of stringy hair sprouting at odd angles, was a crown studded with jewels of a dozen varieties and colors.

And then the image was gone, leaving behind only a startled impression of sudden fear, though what such a creature could fear was beyond his comprehension.

But whatever it was, it inspired the puppet creature before him not to retreat but to snarl in a soundless parody of rage and to lunge at him, grasping him in a crushing grip and going for his throat like a maddened dog.

Without thinking, with only a moment's amazement at the strength the incantation of moments before had temporarily granted him, he broke the hold, forcing the creature's jaws away from his throat with a force that would have broken any normal neck.

But this one did not shatter, though he could see the vertebrae through the flesh in half a dozen places, could see there was no flesh or muscle worthy of the name to hold them in place.

As he stood, holding the creature at arm's length, the marsh grasses stirred a dozen yards away. A moment later, a second creature lurched to its feet and began to shamble toward him.

His fingers biting into the creature's undead flesh, he braced himself and lifted its writhing form high over his head. For a moment, he prepared to throw it with all his might directly at the approaching creature, but something stopped him. It would do no good. Obviously creatures such as these could not be killed, even if he snapped their spines in two. They were already dead, their disintegrating bodies being held together and controlled by the sorcery of the thing he had glimpsed behind the creature's eyes.

Still holding the creature aloft, its frantic struggles dislodging clots of dirt that fell from its shroud onto his head and shoulders, he lurched to the water's edge, not at the point of its glowing emergence but near the other end, where darkness seemed to reach out and suck the water in.

With all his newfound strength, he hurled the creature into the water, almost precisely at the point where it vanished into the earth.

For a moment, the darkness seemed to deepen, as if it were a living thing, gaining strength from the horror it had just devoured. Even the glow where the water emerged from the earth seemed to fade.

As he turned to face the second creature, it had already lurched to a halt and stood swaying, as if its distant master had lost control. Then it turned, not toward him or either of the two men standing nearby but toward the water, toward where its lost brother had just disappeared.

And it followed, reaching out with seeming eagerness as it approached and half fell into the swiftly running, darkening water, and was swept away, unresisting.

* * * * *

As if totally paralyzed by the creature's grip, Oldar could only watch through terror-filled eyes as something appeared where the vines had parted. For a moment, while it was still in the shadows of the forest, he thought it was another horror like the one that already gripped him. Its eyes had seemed to glow redly, but as it emerged into the clearing, into the sickly green light cast by the water, they faded, and the face was revealed to be that of a hawk-nosed man of about Balitor's age. His clothes were simple peasant's garb like their own, while from the forest shadows, they had seemed otherwise.

Then the newcomer was racing across the intervening space, obviously not slowed by either fear or whatever devilish power gripped himself and Balitor.

The hand of the creature was ripped from Oldar's shoulder, the creature itself lifted and thrown, struggling, into the water, where it disappeared into the underground darkness. Moments later it was followed, willingly, even eagerly, by a second creature, which had apparently risen from its nearby grave only moments earlier.

Suddenly, as if the power that had gripped them had vanished with the creatures, Oldar realized he could once again move normally.

"Whoever you are, sir," Balitor's voice came, "we thank you most profoundly, but I suggest we remove ourselves from this place before discussing the matter further."

Their rescuer hesitated only a moment as he cast an eye up and down the brief length of the river.

"You would know better than I," he said, and he followed as Balitor led the way at a brisk trot, reentering the forest where the two of them had emerged only minutes before, though it seemed to Oldar an eternity must have passed.

Balitor continued, maintaining his silence as he retraced their steps as best he could through the nearly total darkness. Finally they passed out of the muffling shadow of the place, and the sounds of the night resumed.

Balitor unhooded his lantern and Oldar followed suit, turning curiously toward their rescuer as he did.

"Again, sir," Balitor said, "we thank you most deeply. I am Balitor. My young friend is named Oldar."

 **TWO**

579, Barovian Calendar (continued)

Until the moment the two men turned toward him, the newcomer realized that, despite the clarity of his vision, he had not looked—had not dared look?—directly at the young man's face. As he had approached and torn the creature's hand from the man's shoulder, his attention had been riveted on the creature, not on its victim. Once the creatures were disposed of, his attention had turned to the older man, and from that point on, the two of them had had their backs to him as they led the way from the clearing, retracing their steps fumblingly through what was obviously, to them, utter darkness.

But now . . .

Now the younger man's face seemed to leap into sudden focus, as if whatever had been forcing his attention elsewhere had abruptly withdrawn.

For a moment, he thought it was the face that had haunted him in the mists, the young, slender, helpless face that had at once been achingly familiar and entirely unknown.

But it was not quite the same face, he realized. There

were differences. The face in the mist, even when it first appeared, had been younger, on the verge of becoming a man, while the one who stood before him, the one called Oldar, had already undergone that transition. And there on his unlined forehead was a diagonal scar, the mark of some past battle or accident, while the face in the mist had been untouched by injury.

Untouched by *physical* injury, that is. There had been pain in the eyes, a pain he could neither understand nor alleviate.

And at the thought of that pain, he remembered: The face was that of Irik, his son, and that other rotting travesty of a face was that of his son's killer.

And the mist . . . it had appeared out of nowhere and swallowed the killer up, and he had followed, plunging recklessly into the fog on the creature's heels, but the creature was gone, and a moment later his whole world was gone, and then even the *memory* of that world, the memory of *everything* was gone, until . . .

Until now.

Without further warning, a flood of memories bore down on his mind, crushing him beneath their unbearable weight.

* * * * *

For a moment, the image of their rescuer seemed to shift before their eyes, as if a distorting lens had passed before him, but before Oldar could even begin to catalogue the changes, the image was steady once more. The man's eyes, which had seemed briefly to glow with more than the reflected light of the lanterns, had fastened on Oldar with an unnerving intensity.

"My name is Firan," the man said, an uncertainty in his

voice, as if he were trying the name out for the first time.

"We are most pleased to meet you, friend Firan," Balitor said. "Now I suggest we be on our way again," he added, "and quickly. We have a long way to go and only our feet to carry us."

Firan did not disagree, nor did Oldar, who was only too glad to be moving once again, as long as it was away from Avernus.

For nearly an hour, they picked their way silently through the forest, the only sounds the swish and crackle of their feet through the underbrush and the increasingly frequent night sounds of insects and birds. Finally Oldar heard Balitor draw in a long breath.

"Considering the fact that we owe you our very lives, friend Firan," Balitor began, only a trace of uneasiness evident in his voice, "the last thing I would wish to do is offend you. However, I must ask how you came to arrive at such an opportune moment. Did you, like us, have business in the area?"

For several seconds, there was no reply as Balitor seemed to hold his breath.

"In a manner of speaking," Firan responded at last. His tone was firmer than when he had announced his name so tentatively, but it still did not have the confidence that one would have thought would be possessed by one capable of such deeds. "Tell me, if you know, whose creatures those were."

"I can only assume they were in the service of Lord Darcalus, the master of Avernus," Balitor said quickly, "indeed of all Darkon. He is reputed to be a wizard of no mean abilities."

"These names mean nothing to me," Firan said, a touch of pettishness entering his voice. "This Darcalus lives where? In the castle beyond the forest where I encountered you?"

"Castle Avernus, yes," Balitor said cautiously. "You are from afar, then, friend Firan?"

Firan seemed to consider his answer for some time as they continued to walk. The forest was thinning now, and soon they would be emerging onto the narrow cart path that led eventually to the main road to Il Aluk.

"Truth be told," Firan said finally, as if having come to a decision, "I do not know. I suspect I am the victim of some form of sorcery myself, perhaps performed by this same Darcalus you speak of. Until I spoke it to you minutes ago, I could not put a name even to myself, let alone my origins."

"I see," Balitor said, though to Oldar, it seemed obvious that Balitor saw nothing. But Oldar was used to such behavior. "Then you do not know how it is you had the power to move freely while the two of us were nearly paralyzed? You do not know how you were able to overcome those creatures, almost certainly raised from their graves by Lord Darcalus?"

"I do not." Firan's face hardened. "You say he is a powerful wizard? And that he rules this land you call Darkon?"

"So it is said. I personally have never seen him, nor has anyone of my acquaintance."

"He rules unseen, then?"

"As far as the likes of us are concerned, at least. It is said that those he appoints to rule in his stead have seen him, have even spoken with him. Each year there is a grand ball at Avernus, to which all such are invited."

Firan seemed to shiver at the words. "He has been your master for some time, then?"

"For as long as anyone can remember," Balitor said, his

face momentarily clouding as if he were trying—and failing—to remember a time before the coming of Lord Darcalus.

"And no one has challenged him?"

Balitor snorted. "Some have tried. The creatures you saw earlier this night could easily have been among such challengers. Lord Darcalus is said to be neither generous nor wasteful with those he defeats."

"Nor, I would think, with those who trespass upon his grounds, as I must assume the two of you were doing."

Balitor did not reply, and Oldar pulled his ragged woolen cloak more tightly around his shoulders, as if such a futile gesture could ward off the dangers they had courted that night.

The younger man was relieved when, at last, the rutted cart road appeared before them, but his relief was short-lived. They had gone no more than half a mile when the sound of distant voices reached their ears. Oldar stiffened, casting his eyes about in the faint light of a rising quarter moon. Far ahead, around one of the many bends in the forest road, a light flickered in the shadows of the trees. Lord Darcalus's men? Now that the three of them had eluded Darcalus's magical defenses, had he sent his earthly forces to pursue them?

Oldar looked apprehensively to Balitor, who only shrugged and sighed. "Whatever it is, we cannot flee it." He glanced toward Firan. "Can we, friend Firan?"

"They are travelers, camping for the night," Firan said, not indicating how he knew despite a questioning look from Balitor.

Slowly they continued down the road, the light growing brighter with each step. Rounding a bend, they saw it was, as Firan had predicted, a campfire. Half a dozen men and

women in colorful Vistani garb sat about the fire in a clearing a few yards from the road. A luxuriantly mustached
man tended to a pair of horses tethered next to the round-
roofed, elaborately painted wagon that served as their
home. Oldar watched apprehensively as they drew near the
clearing. He had heard of these gypsies who called themselves Vistani but had never, on his father's patch of land or
in Il Aluk, actually seen even a single one.

Nor had he wished to. His father had spun tales of Vistani curses visited upon innocent peasants who had, all
unknowing, offended one of their tribe. It was even
rumored, his father often said, that an offense was not
always required. There were times, he had been told, when
they cast minor spells—a rash that would not go away, an
odor that repelled even one's mate—simply for their own
amusement or to promote commerce in their remedies and
charms.

The Vistani looked up, their eyes glistening in the firelight as the trio approached, but no greetings were called
out, and Oldar was not going to be the first to speak.

The three were abreast of the clearing, their shadows
looming and lurching as the Vistani campfire flared and
faded and flared again, when the gold-trimmed door at the
back of the wagon swung open silently, and a woman easily
twice as old as any of the others emerged. All Vistani eyes
turned toward her as she moved precariously down the
steps.

"I have been awaiting your arrival," she said in a voice
far stronger than her appearance would have indicated.

Oldar's heart raced as he glanced toward Balitor for
guidance. The older man swallowed audibly but managed a
smile as he slowed, then stopped. Frowning, Firan followed
suit. Oldar barely suppressed a flinch as he looked back at

the Vistani camp and saw that all had risen and were moving about purposefully.

But instead of blocking the road, they soon stood in an almost geometrically straight line from the wagon to the campfire, as if forming an honor guard for the old woman, who now haltingly approached the fire.

"I would speak with you," she said, her voice still strong despite her unsteady gait.

"I would be honored," Balitor said quickly.

"As would I," Oldar added, while Firan remained silent.

"Come, warm yourself at our fire," the old woman said. "It is rare that a *giorgio* ventures out in the Darkon night, yet here are three in its deepest folds."

"We have been on a mission for the Lady Karawinn," Balitor said. "We are returning to her even now."

"Ah!" The wrinkled features folded into a smile. "She whose husband would be baron of the grandest city in the land."

"We know nothing of Lord Karawinn or his ambitions, my lady," Balitor said earnestly. "It is only the Lady Karawinn whose bidding we follow."

"Just so. But surely the lady follows the bidding of her mate."

"Perhaps. His name, however, was never mentioned, nor did we so much as see his face."

"It would be surprising if you did. But tell me, what was the mission? To fetch a potion of youth, perhaps?"

"How—" Oldar began, but Balitor's hand on his arm cut him off.

"The nature of the mission is between the Lady Karawinn and myself," Balitor said quickly. "She paid dearly, and I will not betray her trust."

"Which is as it should be," the old Vistana said, another

smile folding her features, "and I would not ask you to do so. However, I would warn you: Take care when you meet her again. Accept from her hand only that payment to which you have both agreed."

"We thank you," Balitor began, but the old woman had already turned from him. Her eyes now focused intently on Firan, who had stood silently, utterly motionless, throughout the exchange.

"You are new to this land," she said, echoing Balitor's words of only minutes before.

"Perhaps."

For a long moment, she studied him, frowning thoughtfully. "There is a familiarity about you. Have our paths crossed in other lands?"

"I am not aware of any such crossing," Firan said carefully.

"Can you be certain you would be aware of one had it occurred?"

"You would, I imagine, be difficult to forget. Unless you so desired it."

"As would you, though I sense that you are not entirely as you seem."

"Nor are you, I daresay."

The old woman laughed, a dry, raspy sound in stark contrast to her vibrant speaking voice. "We all have our secrets, good sir."

Firan nodded slowly, studying her. "Assuredly. It would be a dull existence if that were not so. Yet there are some secrets I would learn—*must* learn."

"If they are mine to impart, they are yours for the asking."

"At what price?"

The old woman shrugged. "None for now, and none ever

that you will not yourself assess."

"I hope your secrets are revealed less cryptically than their price."

She laughed again. "I can reveal to you only what has been revealed to me. I do not pretend to understand its meaning. The gods of these dark lands are not known for their forthrightness and clarity."

"You receive your information from the gods, then?"

Another shrug moved her seemingly frail shoulders. "They do not introduce themselves, nor even show their faces, and I do not ask. It is enough that their words on occasion touch my thoughts."

"And have any of these words concerned the one called Darcalus?"

"The lord of all Darkon? The gods would be remiss if they did not now and then concern themselves with the mightiest in the land."

"They have spoken of him, then? Are you aware that you are camped virtually within the shadow of his zombie-guarded castle?"

The old woman smiled with perhaps a touch of contempt. "Your question underestimates both the Vistani and Lord Darcalus. The shadow of Avernus lies over all of Darkon. Now tell me, what secrets of his do you seek?"

"Only one: Is he responsible for the death of my son?"

"The son whose likeness you see in this boy before you?" The old woman's eyes darted to Oldar, whose skin prickled at her words.

"There is a resemblance," Firan admitted.

"In time, there may be more than that. Give me your hand, young Oldar."

The prickling intensified, making Oldar shiver beneath the woolen cloak and wish even more fervently that this night had never begun.

Yet he held out his hand. One did not deny a Vistani request.

As her hands took his, they were strangely warm, but that warmth did nothing to banish the chill that now had him fully in its grip.

"You fear the Vistani, young Oldar?" she asked, her eyes startlingly youthful in her ancient face as she looked up into his own.

"I—I have heard tales, my lady."

She laughed, her brittle hands caressing his. "I have no doubt you have. Some may even be true, though I would wager little on the likelihood."

He swallowed the parching dryness in his mouth but said nothing. Her eyes seemed to burn into his, as if she could see into his very soul. His father's tales had spoken of this as well, how the Vistani could find in your thoughts secrets that even you did not know you possessed.

"You have nothing to fear from me, young Oldar," she said, lowering her eyes to the hand she held, "unless you fear the truth."

His eyes darted to his two companions of the night. Until tonight, he would not have admitted to such a fear, but now he feared almost everything.

"This rambling is getting us nowhere," Firan said sharply. "You said you would reveal what secrets you possessed, yet you have revealed nothing."

A stirring among the other Vistani at such disrespectful words sent new fears coursing through Oldar's body. This Firan may have saved them earlier, but now he seemed intent on endangering them all.

"Do not be impatient, old man," she said, though he appeared no more than half her age. "Secrets do not reveal themselves without coaxing. Is that not right, young Oldar?"

He blinked at the words, words he had heard often from his father. "I imagine it is," he said.

Her eyes rose to meet his again. "You would be with your father tonight, would you not?"

"I would, my lady," he said, a lump forming in his throat, "but I know not if he still lives."

"He does, young Oldar, and he thinks of you often." Her hands pressed his more tightly for a moment. She smiled. "You see, young Oldar, we Vistani are not always so frightening after all, nor is the truth."

"I am sorry if my fear has offended you."

"It has not." Her face sobered. "Fear and its helpmate caution are often required for survival, as they will be for you and your companion before the night is out."

"What—"

"Heed my words, young Oldar, and be cautious in your dealings with Lady Karawinn. If you do not, you will not see your father again in this life."

Still gripping Oldar's hands, she turned abruptly to Firan, her voice turning harsh. "And you, old man—that which you seek is indeed where you believe it to be, in Avernus. But be even more cautious than young Oldar in your quest for secrets, lest you find a truth more terrible than you can imagine."

As if dismissing Firan from her thoughts, she turned back to Oldar, her hands tightening on his, her eyes seeming to peer into his very soul.

"Heed my words, young Oldar," she repeated, her voice softer now but more intense. "Heed my words and your own good sense. It would not sit well with your father were you never more to grace his humble table."

For a moment, a translucent image of his father seemed to float in the air between them, and he felt a phantom pair of hands wrapping comfortingly about both his own and the old woman's. A Vistani trick, of course, he told himself, but his conviction could not keep a lump from forming again in his throat as he felt—remembered?—the familiar scars and calluses of those work-worn hands.

And then the illusion was gone, his father's hands last of all, and she was releasing him and drawing back.

"Now begone, the lot of you," she said abruptly, turning her back on them all. "I would rest, and you have business in Il Aluk."

Like a wraith, she flowed from the campfire to the wagon, her steps hidden beneath the colorful skirt that skimmed the ground but somehow never touched it. Only when she mounted the steps was the normal physical nature of her motion obvious.

Firan took a half step after her, but he was instantly confronted by a shoulder-to-shoulder line of the Vistani men, as if they had anticipated his move. His gaze locked with theirs as he seemed to consider treating them as he had the creatures in the marsh grass, but as the door of the wagon closed behind the old woman, he lowered his eyes in seeming submission and turned silently back to the road.

"Come," he said to Balitor and Oldar. "The woman speaks the truth. Business awaits us in the city you call Il Aluk."

Oldar, relieved to be free of the Vistani yet reluctant to leave, stood looking at the wagon for a long moment, hoping for he knew not what. Perhaps for a last glimpse of the old woman through one of the tiny windowlike openings, perhaps for some sign that the image and the touch of his father had not been entirely the illusion he believed and feared it to be.

Then Balitor's hand was on his arm, nervously urging him away from the campfire and the still vigilant line of Vistani men.

They walked in silence until the light from the campfire was lost in the distance, hidden by several bends in the cart road. Only when they emerged from the deeper part of the forest and rejoined the main road from Il Aluk to Rivalis did Firan speak.

"Tell me more about this Lord Karawinn, whom you have never seen. Was the old woman right in her assessment?"

Oldar, who had not even known of Lord Karawinn's existence until this night, said nothing but turned an inquisitive look on Balitor. If he were to follow the Vistani's words and exercise caution in his dealings with the Lady Karawinn, part of that caution would be to learn what he could of the woman and her family.

"In all likelihood she was," Balitor said. "Karawinn is cousin to Lord Aldewaine, who became Baron of Il Aluk not many years past. Their relationship, never the best, was not improved by Aldewaine's good fortune."

Firan smiled, his eyes going to the small leather pouch suspended by a strap from Balitor's shoulder. "Would you wish to know the nature of what you have collected for the Lady Karawinn?"

"I will not say I have no curiosity," Balitor admitted, "but I am more interested in delivering it to her intact and receiving the balance promised us."

"And so you shall, I guarantee. I need only briefly hold one of the vials in my hands."

"And from that you can divine the nature of the contents?"

"If it is what I suspect, yes."

"Give it to him, Balitor," Oldar said nervously. "You heard the Vistana's words warning us to be cautious in our dealings with the lady."

Balitor laughed, but the sound was tinged with uneasiness. "You worry too much, Oldar. Do you expect her to betray us once we give her what she wants?"

"Your young friend is right to be concerned," Firan said, holding out his hand. "When power is at stake, betrayal is the rule, not the exception."

Balitor frowned, then shrugged and produced one of the stoppered, faintly glowing vials. Placing it in Firan's outstretched palm, he felt a chill sweep over him, and he glanced back in the direction of the Vistani camp.

"Hold your lanterns close if you wish to see," Firan said, cupping the unopened vial in both hands.

The glow, never nearly as bright as the rushing water from which the liquid had been taken, disappeared entirely in the light from the lanterns. Firan held his cupped hands directly in front of himself, chest high. After a moment, his lips moved, but the words—if words they were—seemed to be absorbed and muffled by the very air. For nearly a minute, he continued, his eyes focused intently on the vial, as were Balitor's and Oldar's.

Slowly the liquid began to darken, and Balitor cried out, "What have you done? The lady will see that this—"

"Do not concern yourself," Firan said. "When it comes time to deliver it into her hands, it will be as it was. Now watch."

For a minute, the liquid continued to darken, but then it began to churn, as if trying to escape its tiny prison. Next it grew lighter, as if it were dissolving whatever had darkened it. But it didn't lighten to the transparency it had possessed before. Instead, in the light from the close-held lanterns, it developed a sharp crimson hue, brighter than the freshest blood.

Firan sighed. "It is as I suspected, a poison deadlier than nightshade and as undetectable as the air to anyone not versed most thoroughly in the magic arts. The heart simply ceases to beat, and no one is the wiser."

"*Poison*?" Balitor's mouth was agape. "But it was flowing from the earth like a spring!"

Firan laughed derisively. "Have you already forgotten where that spring was? And what creatures guarded it? Both were within the shadow of Avernus. Its master, Lord Darcalus, is almost certainly capable of many things, few of them good."

He uncupped his hands and offered the vial, the crimson of its contents now rapidly fading, to Balitor, who took it gingerly, remembering how the flowing liquid had stung his hands. With great care, he replaced it in the leather pouch.

"If it is truly poison," Oldar began, "we should destroy it, not—"

"We will deliver it to Lady Karawinn as promised, Oldar!" Balitor snapped. "Whom she uses it on, if anyone, is her business. Or Lord Karawinn's. She doubtless has many ways of disposing of her enemies without resorting to this, and if we do not keep our promise, do you think we would long be counted among her friends? Or among the living?"

"But if she knows that we are aware that it is poison she paid us to fetch . . ." Oldar stopped in midsentence, shivering.

"There is no reason she should know," Balitor said. "And if you fear you will let the information slip while we conclude our business with the lady, I suggest you remain behind. I will go to her alone."

"That would not be wise," Firan interrupted. "With only two vials—you were asked to fill more, were you not?— and your partner missing, she would be a fool not to be suspicious. I cannot imagine that she or Lord Karawinn is a fool. Nor can I imagine either of you withstanding the kind of interrogation she is doubtless capable of, either magical or physical." He smiled. "Keep in mind the nature of the substance she is paying you to bring to her. Also consider that she would not be paying a bounty as generous as you describe unless she had a powerful need for that substance."

"Then what are you suggesting, friend Firan?" Balitor demanded angrily. "Should neither of us go to her? Should we depart Il Aluk and never return? If she is as powerful and clever as you suggest, would she not easily hunt us down?"

"In all likelihood, yes. That is why I suggest that you keep your appointment, both of you. However, I also suggest that you allow me to accompany you—for your own safety and my edification."

Reluctantly they agreed.

 **THREE**

579, Barovian Calendar (continued)

It was still full dark when the three approached the huge oaken gates that kept all but a favored few from Lord Karawinn's mansion in the Desolatus Highlands beyond the North Canal. Looking back to the south, they could see all of Il Aluk spread out below them in the faint light of the moon, now well up in the cloudless sky. Miles to the south of the city, Oldar thought he could still see the towers of Avernus, but he was no longer sure his senses weren't playing tricks on him, as they surely had in the Vistani camp.

As Lady Karawinn had promised, a tiny door within the courtyard gates themselves yielded to the key she had bestowed upon Balitor at their last visit. Sucking in his breath, Balitor stepped through, followed closely by Oldar and then Firan. No lights showed at any of the three rows of windows.

"Come to me the moment you return from Avernus, regardless of the hour," she had said, and Balitor was not about to depart from her instructions, particularly after what Firan had shown them.

Still, his heart seemed ready to leap out through his

throat as he led the way up the sweeping carriage drive to the massive front door. Swallowing audibly, he lifted the huge eagle's-head knocker and let it fall with a startlingly loud thud.

Almost immediately a tiny port opened in the door, and an eye peered through. The door itself yielded a moment later, after the sound of chains being released had quieted. Lady Karawinn herself, her thin face flushed, a velvet nightrobe belted closely about her tall frame, stood in the opening, motioning them inside.

Her eyes widened when she saw the third member of their group. Frowning, she blocked their way. "What is this, Balitor? There was no mention of a third person involved in our venture."

"If it were not for Firan here," Balitor said, following the line the three of them had agreed upon while they had journeyed on from the Vistani camp, "there would be no people involved at all. No living people, at least."

Her frown deepened. "My price will not go higher, no matter what dangerous adventures you invent, no matter how many street vagabonds you choose to recruit."

"We ask for no more," Balitor said. "We will share the agreed upon sum three ways instead of two."

She scowled at them for a moment, then shrugged and stepped back from the doorway to allow them to enter. "As you wish. Come." She held out her hand as she led the way through the dimly lit, luxurious entry hall toward an open door near the far end. "Give me the vials and I will fetch your payment."

She evinced no interest in what role Firan had played in their adventure, only in the results. As they entered the room, a small but no less luxurious sitting room lit only by an ornate, wall-mounted candelabra, she opened the leather pouches Oldar and Balitor had laid in her hand as they walked.

"What is this?" she scowled at the four empty vials. "Have you found another market?"

Balitor managed a grin. "For water, my lady? No, the truth is, the spring was guarded more thoroughly than you led us to believe. If it were not for the lucky arrival of friend Firan, we would have obtained not even the two. We would most likely not even have retained our lives."

For a moment, a flicker of curiosity played across her features, her lips parting in the start of a question, but then her attention seemed drawn back to the two full vials.

"No matter," she said. "I will fetch your payment. You may wait here." Her eyes went to a bottle of wine on an intricately carved table beneath the candelabra. A pair of already filled glasses, the finest cut glass, sat next to the bottle. "Have a touch of refreshment while you wait," she said, producing a third glass from a small ivory cabinet and filling it. "You have had a long night, I suspect."

"Thank you, my lady," Balitor answered for the three of them. "I perceive it is of a particularly fine vintage."

"In the House of Karawinn, nothing less would be tolerated," she said. The pouches and vials held closely, she walked quickly but gracefully from the room.

As the door closed behind her, Firan held up a hand. "Before you partake, I suggest you wait a moment."

Oldar swallowed nervously, nodding. He had no intention of drinking the offered wine, not after the Vistani woman's words of warning and Firan's discovery regarding the nature of the liquid in the vials.

Moving quickly, Firan took one of the glasses and cupped his hands around it as he had the vials, the stem of the glass extending downward, pressed between the edges of his hands. As he had on the road, he murmured a series of sounds, words that Oldar suspected he would not recognize even if he could have heard them clearly.

The wine, already a deep red, stirred into motion even though Firan's hands remained motionless, but it did not spill from the edge of the glass. After a moment, it settled once again into stillness, but the color was now neither the deep red of the wine nor the bright crimson of the vial.

It was a putrescent yellow, the color of an infected wound's discharge. Oldar grimaced, while Firan only smiled.

"As deadly as the other," he said, "though easily detectable. But that is not surprising. After all, there would be no need to take such pains to dispose of the likes of us. Found at the side of the road, left to rot in the marshes or be devoured by the waters of the Vuchar, who would question the means of our death or disappearance?"

Balitor darted a glance toward the door, then turned back to Firan. "You said you accompanied us for our safety. How do you propose to make us safe? If we refuse to drink, she will surely have other means ready and waiting. If we run, you have already said she will track us down."

"You forget, I am not entirely powerless. I suggest the two of you leave. I will deal with the Lady Karawinn."

"As you dealt with those creatures of Darcalus?"

"Not precisely, but—"

The door to the hallway opened, but it was not Lady Karawinn who entered. Instead, it was a pair of ruffians, the likes of which would have been more at home in the foulest back alleys of Il Aluk than here. Or so their filthy and ragged clothing indicated. Their clean-shaven, scowling faces, however, Oldar noted, were a different matter, and after a moment, he recognized the larger of the two as the coachman who had brought them to their first meeting with Lady Karawinn.

"You have not tasted your wine, gentlemen," the smaller one said.

"Nor will we," Firan said, "unless perhaps you would care for a sip before us?" He picked a glass from the table and extended it toward the two.

"It is not our place," the man said, waving the glass away.

"Nonetheless, I insist," Firan said, his eyes locking with those of the other man.

The man shook his head and started to step back but froze in his tracks a moment later. Firan crossed the few feet between them at a deliberate pace and placed the glass in the man's motionless hand.

"Now, drink," he said, his voice taking on the same muffled tones it had assumed when he had murmured the incantations over the poisons.

The man's eyes widened in sudden confusion, turning to terror as the hand holding the glass began to slowly rise. The larger man only gaped.

As the glass approached his face, the man clamped his lips tightly shut. His eyes pleaded with Firan as every part of his body except the hand holding the glass began to tremble. Oldar, glimpsing once again the glow that seemed to come from deep within Firan's eyes, could no more move now to leave than he could when the undead creature had gripped his leg, nor could Balitor.

At last the rim of the delicate glass touched the man's lips. They were still tightly clamped together, but the jaw was beginning to vibrate, as if the teeth were chattering from an icy wind.

Abruptly Firan laughed, a harsh, grating sound. "You are

not thirsty enough, then, to die?"

An instant later, whatever forces had restrained the man let go. The hand holding the glass snapped back like a suddenly released catapult. The glass shattered against the far wall, a red blotch forming on its pristine surface. At the same moment, the man lurched backward, slamming into his larger companion, almost knocking them both to the floor.

"I would speak with your master, Lord Karawinn," Firan said quietly, watching the two men intently as they regained their balance and then held themselves motionless, eyes still wide in terror.

Suddenly the smaller man fell to his knees. "Forgive me, Lord Darcalus! If I had known it was you—"

"On your feet, fool!" Firan snapped. "If I were Darcalus or one of his minions, do you think that you or anyone else in this traitorous household would still be alive to perform such pitiful groveling? Now, impose no more on my patience, either of you! Go and fetch your master!"

Before either could comply, a faint sound in the hall outside the door attracted Firan's attention. He raised his hand in an imperious gesture that froze the two like trembling statues. As his eyes went to the door, a thin smile seemed to harden his features even more.

"If you wish to skulk about the corridors of your own home, Lord Karawinn," Firan said quietly, "that is your concern, just as it is your concern if you wish to trust your life to fools such as these. Neither practice, however, has much to recommend it."

For several seconds, there was only silence except for the rapid, raspy breathing of the two terror-stricken underlings. Finally a step sounded in the hallway, and the door opened once again.

This time a man of stately bearing, easily six feet tall in a dark, brocaded smoking jacket, his graying hair in loose curls, stepped into the room. Yet despite his seeming dignity, despite his look of belonging in this place, there was an air of uneasiness and uncertainty, even fear, about him. A scowl crossed his patrician features as his eyes touched those of the two cowering men. A brief nod of his head sent them scurrying from the room as he turned to study Firan and his two companions.

"I take it these two are under your protection," he said after a moment, distaste obvious in his voice.

Firan nodded. "And I was given to understand that Lady Karawinn owes them a fee for the services they performed this night."

Karawinn's scowl returned, but then he shrugged. From a pocket, he withdrew easily a dozen coins and held them out. "Will this be sufficient?"

Balitor nodded quickly, nervously, and Oldar followed suit. "Take it, then," Firan said to the two, "and be on your way. If I have need of your services myself, I'm sure Lord Karawinn will be able to direct me to you. And he will see to it that your health is at least as good then as it is now," he added, turning his gaze on Karawinn.

"Thank you, friend Firan," Balitor said, hastily pocketing his share of the coins. "Once again we are indebted to you for our lives."

Firan nodded a curt acknowledgment but did not take his eyes off Lord Karawinn as the two hastened from the room, the door slamming shut behind them.

"You have the advantage," Karawinn said after a moment.

"Indeed, Lord Karawinn," Firan said. "But I have no reason to keep either my identity or my purpose from you. I am Firan Zal'honan, and I would assist you in your plot against Lord Darcalus."

Karawinn stiffened. "There is no such plot."

Firan laughed harshly. "Little wonder that you employ fools to do your bidding. Like calls to like."

Karawinn scowled. "And what if Dendrite were right? What if you are either Darcalus or one of his minions?"

"You would not be alive to ask the question. Is that plain enough for you?" Firan glanced toward the two glasses that remained on the table and at the red stain that had now spread all the way to the floor. "It would be tiresome, but another demonstration is possible."

"No!" Karawinn twitched backward, then caught himself and swallowed audibly. "Very well," he said, his voice unsteady. "It seems I have no choice."

"Wisely spoken, my lord. Now tell me, is Baron Aldewaine your accomplice? Or your mentor?"

Karawinn's eyes widened. A denial was forming on his lips, but it faltered before it emerged. "Why would you believe he was even involved?"

"If this Darcalus is as I believe, no one but his hand-picked lieutenants would have the slightest access to him, and I am given to believe that your cousin, as Baron of Il Aluk, is such a one." Firan smiled. "When first I learned of the poison and your relationship to the baron, I suspected he was the intended victim, but your doltish henchmen's actions revealed the truth. Indeed, you would have far greater likelihood of success were your cousin the target of your scheme. In any event, I am pleased to have been proven wrong. The murder of your cousin would gain me nothing, while an attempt on the so-called life of the one you call Darcalus fits quite well with my own mission."

"And what might that mission be, Firan Zal'honan?"

"To see the creature destroyed."

"And after that? Would you take his place?"

"Beyond his destruction, I have no goal."

"I see." Karawinn eyed him suspiciously. "And why should I take you at your word?"

"Do you have a choice in this matter any more than in the last?"

Karawinn smiled regretfully. "I suppose I do not. But could you at least set my mind at rest and tell me why you would see Lord Darcalus dead, yet would not succeed him? Surely to be ruler of all Darkon is a prize to be coveted."

"Not nearly as coveted as to see Darcalus destroyed."

"And the source of this hatred?"

"I have reason to believe he is responsible for the murder of my only son, whose name was Irik. Is that sufficient motive?" The words were spoken evenly, but silent emotion crackled in the air.

Karawinn was silent a moment. "I suspect," he said at last, "that Lord Darcalus is responsible for the deaths of many, sons and daughters alike."

"Assuredly," Firan agreed, "and worse."

"You know him, then?"

"If he is the one who murdered Irik, I most assuredly do know him. If he is not, I still know much about him—about his kind—much that you will need to know if we are to succeed."

"We already know that he is a powerful wizard, that Avernus is guarded by myriad protective spells."

"And yet you believed he could be disposed of by a simple poison!" Firan shook his head pityingly.

"It is not a 'simple' poison. Its ingredients, only one of which your friends procured, are the most potent, and our own wizards assure me—"

"Then your wizards are even greater fools than you! Darcalus is no simple wizard! Tell me, have you or anyone you know ever observed him to partake of either food or drink?"

"Not I, certainly, but Aldewaine—"

"I will question Aldewaine, then, but I would be greatly surprised if he has observed such actions."

Karawinn squirmed uncomfortably. "Perhaps you are right. But what of it? It is said that Darcalus dines privately, and in fact is observed in public only rarely. But even wizards cannot divorce themselves entirely from physical sustenance. Certainly at the upcoming ball, which all the barons of Darkon are invited—nay, *required*—to attend less than a fortnight from now, the opportunity would arise—"

"The opportunity would arise," Firan interrupted harshly, "for your pathetic scheme to be discovered! The opportunity would arise for you and Aldewaine and likely all your households to regret the moment of their birth and long for the moment of their death! None of you has even an inkling of what you are dealing with!"

"Then tell me, wise Firan, what *are* we dealing with?" Karawinn's voice dripped sarcasm. "What kind of wizard is it that cannot be killed?"

"One who has already died, you fool! One whose soul can commandeer a new host as easily as you can summon a carriage!"

Karawinn paled, the sarcasm of a moment before obliterated and forgotten. "That is not possible!"

"Is it not? Do you deny such creatures exist? You who claim fraternity with wizards?"

"I would deny the existence of nothing the mind can imagine! But the creatures you speak of—" Karawinn shook his head. "They are solitary creatures of hideous aspect. One was run to ground in the wilds south of Karg when I was a boy. I have spoken with those who witnessed the foul creature's destruction. I have seen depictions of its form!"

"And have you likewise seen depictions of Lord Darcalus? Does a portrait hang in Baron Aldewaine's anteroom? In yours?"

"No! But the baron has *seen* Lord Darcalus!"

"Has he indeed? Or has he seen only what Lord Darcalus wishes him to see? Even a wizard is capable of illusion."

Karawinn shook his head again, this time with an edge of desperation. "But these undead creatures have no interest in worldly matters, only their own pursuits."

"And who is to say what those pursuits may encompass, my lord? Who is to say what interests may develop in a mind encumbered neither by mortality nor by acquaintance with others of its kind? And how better to insure that he is not distracted from his pursuits than by amassing all power to himself and then using it not for day-to-day rule, which is left to Aldewaine and his like, but to isolate himself in an impregnable, spell-guarded castle?"

"If you are right . . ." Karawinn shuddered.

"If I am right, you are indeed fortunate, Lord Karawinn, that I have entered your life, else it would have shortly ended, though your service to Darcalus would likely have continued for many years. I have seen the use he makes of his defeated enemies."

Reaching out, Firan laid a hand briefly on Lord Karawinn's forehead. As he withdrew it, the bloodlike stain on the opposite wall shimmered and flowed and gradually became the rotting face that had haunted him in the mists for he knew not how long, a face indistinguishable from those of the resurrected corpses he had encountered in the shadow of Avernus.

"Beware, Lord Karawinn," Firan said, "lest this be your fate as well."

Karawinn said nothing, but the bloodless pallor of his face was acknowledgment enough.

* * * * *

Firan slid between the silken sheets of Karawinn Manor with an unexpected shiver of pleasure, of vivid but unplaceable memory.

What is this? he wondered. His memories, he had realized on the long walk from the Vistani camp, were still far from complete, but surely the undiscovered portions did not include the likes of this. Sorcerer he might be, but not nobleman or royalty. Indeed, the one he hated most, the one who had slaughtered his son, had been self-proclaimed royalty.

But the meal Karawinn had roused his staff to prepare, Firan realized, had had a similar effect. His hunger had not been great, and yet it was as if no food had touched his tongue in ages, as if it were far more starved for taste than his body was starved for sustenance.

The mists? He remembered the hunger with which he had drunk in the sights and sounds and the feel of the night into which he had emerged, and he wondered once again if his entrapment in that timeless, sensationless limbo had so starved his senses that they cried out for stimulation and responded with puzzled ecstasy when it was supplied, whether it be taste or touch or smell.

And sleep? How long had the strange mists kept him from sleep?

He shivered again in pleasurable anticipation, this time at merely the thought of sleep, of the complete and dreamless rest that it could become.

How long . . . ?

Still wondering, still reveling in anticipation, he drifted into peaceful oblivion.

 **FOUR**

579, Barovian Calendar (continued)

"What new nonsense is this?"

Baron Aldewaine, a younger, more rough-hewn version of his cousin, paused in his pacing of his book-lined study and scowled angrily at Firan and Lord Karawinn. His green doublet was unfastened, his hand-embroidered vest barely restraining the beginnings of a paunch he refused to acknowledge. It had been two days since Firan and Karawinn had convinced Aldewaine to acknowledge the truth of the plot against Lord Darcalus and to grudgingly admit that they could use Firan's help. It was still obvious, however, that he was unhappy with the situation, never more so than now.

"It may be nonsense to you, Baron," Firan said, "but I assure you I have my reasons."

"Would it be too much to ask that you share them?"

Firan's irritation with having to deal with Karawinn and his recalcitrant cousin inclined him to refuse, to simply withdraw and let them flounder about—and die—on their own. But much as it galled him to admit it, he needed Aldewaine. Without him, without his *willing* cooperation, Firan would in all likelihood not be able to so much as cross the threshold of Avernus, so strong were the spells that doubtless protected it. The spell that had gripped the two peasants near the poison stream was as nothing compared to those that would shield Avernus itself, and those would be redoubled the night of the ball. Even if he were able to force his way through, a doubtful proposition at best, his efforts would certainly be detected, his presence noted, and his freedom to move about the castle nonexistent.

The intricately carved gold and silver amulet Aldewaine wore about his neck was Firan's only hope. It was not only Aldewaine's badge of office, indicating to all who saw it that, within the confines of Il Aluk, he spoke for Lord Darcalus in all things, but also, on the rare occasions he was summoned for an audience, the key that allowed him within Avernus. On the even rarer occasions that Darcalus "entertained" his barons and their guests, the amulet's protection was extended to those guests, to whomever—family or servant, friend or lover or jealous enemy—each baron chose to accompany him.

Without that protection, Firan's chances for gaining access to the castle were virtually nil, and his chances for success in his vendetta against Darcalus even less. It was a protection that would cease the moment Aldewaine decreed it, or the moment Aldewaine displeased Darcalus and was himself stripped of his office.

Firan mentally gritted his teeth and spoke. "As I have explained, Baron, my sole purpose is to destroy the one you call Darcalus and to prove to my own satisfaction that he is, as the Vistani woman confirmed, the one who murdered my son. Because of the remarkable resemblance Oldar bears to my son, I would—"

Aldewaine snorted with uneasy derision. "I will accept

your outlandish premise that Lord Darcalus is indeed one of the undead. In Darkon, no horror is impossible. But he has been Lord of Darkon for as long as I can remember. He could not be this creature you pursue, who ruled in this other land until you pursued him into whatever strange netherworld you claim led him—and you—to Darkon only days ago."

"You misunderstand, Baron," Firan said tightly, "I hope not willfully. For all I know, I could have been held captive in this 'netherworld,' as you choose to call it, for a lifetime, while the one I pursued may have passed through without hindrance. I suspect time does not pass there as it does in either Darkon or my own native land. It was obviously a place where normal rules of nature do not apply."

"Even accepting that as a possibility," Aldewaine said, "what do you expect to accomplish with your little prank? You certainly cannot believe that, if Darcalus is indeed the monster you seek, he will be startled into confessing at the sight of this Oldar?"

Firan winced mentally. The fool was right, and yet that knowledge, never far from Firan's thoughts, did nothing to diminish his determination to carry out the "prank." Perhaps he simply wanted the comfort of having the boy with him, so like Irik did he appear. Perhaps he wanted a reminder of what he had lost, a talisman to concentrate his power and determination when—if—he came face-to-face with the creature he sought.

"Nothing as simplistic or naive as that," Firan said flatly. "I only know that it is necessary if we are to prevail—if *I* am to prevail."

Aldewaine stared at Firan, shaking his head in angry resignation. "And I only hope," he said finally, "that there are more concrete reasons than that for believing Darcalus is vulnerable and that you have the key to that vulnerability."

As do I, Firan said silently. As do I.

*　*　*　*　*

Within a week, rich and ornate carriages began arriving in Il Aluk from all corners of Darkon. The barons were gathering. Most made believe the ball would be just that—a ball, an entertainment for their benefit, a reward bestowed by a generous Lord Darcalus for their sterling performances as his representatives.

For some, it might even be true.

Only the most arrogant, however, truly believed it. Most listened for the sound of a scythe and hoped desperately they would survive the festivities. All too often in the past, many who had entered Avernus as barons had left as powerless underlings to new barons . . . if they left at all.

But at least they had a chance, those who screwed their courage up to the breaking point and traveled to Avernus. Those few who did not, those who crossed their fingers and sent their regrets, soon had those regrets returned a hundredfold, delivered like as not by their impatient and well-armed successors.

For Il Aluk and its merchants, the gathering was both a blessing and a curse. Many would prosper from the coins of generous, often drunken visitors. Others would face ruin and worse at the hands of the less generous but equally drunken lords and their rowdy retinues.

Balitor, who had precariously survived four such previous gatherings, this time felt obliged to lie low and counseled Oldar to do the same. "Lord and Lady Karawinn's coins give us that luxury," he said, "and we would be fools not to take the advantage, as we would be fools if we were to reveal to any either the extent or the source of our temporary riches."

Oldar himself found it easy to accept Balitor's advice, since he had no intention of flaunting his supposed good fortune anywhere in Il Aluk. He had already decided, in fact, to go a step further and depart from the city altogether.

"The Vistani woman said my father is still alive and often has thoughts of me, as I do of him," the young man told Balitor. "These coins are more than he would receive for two years' harvest, and surely it is better that I use them to meet his needs and improve his fortunes than to squander them in this den of thieves and cutthroats."

Thus it was with mixed feelings that they received Firan's invitation—nay, his command—to accompany him to Avernus the night of the ball.

"Go to your father, young Oldar," Balitor said. "I will tell them you had already departed before the invitation arrived."

But Oldar shook his head. "We owe him our lives twice over. And there will be time enough for home when I have fulfilled my obligation as best I can. But you need not accompany me. It was my understanding that, while mine was a command, yours was truly an invitation."

Balitor shrugged. "I would not let my apprentice loose, unprotected, in that crowd of velveteened villains."

Oldar did not protest, though he perhaps knew he should. To enter Avernus was not something he wanted to do without a friend at his side, and Firan, though he had indeed twice salvaged their lives, would never be one Oldar could consider a friend.

 **FIUE**

579, Barovian Calendar (continued)

Baron Aldewaine's carriage was as luxurious as those of any of the visiting barons, its cushions the finest crushed velvet, its eagle-taloned crest fashioned of pure gold inlay punctuated by blood-red rubies. The baron himself, in lace cuffs and silken doublet, his paunch forcibly restrained within sturdy velvet breeches, cut a no less imposing figure as he stepped down onto the flagstones of the outer bailey of Avernus, followed closely by a similarly attired Lord Karawinn. On Karawinn's arm was Lady Karawinn, resplendent in low-cut green and gold, her hair loose and flowing, a far cry, at least externally, from the sharp-eyed matron who had grudgingly accepted the vials from Balitor.

Firan, in dark broadcloth without a touch of finery, emerged last, while Oldar and Balitor, outfitted in servants' livery, lowered themselves from the hard wooden seat they had shared with the coachman.

Firan had felt the tingle of competing spells wash over him as the carriage had moved sedately through the massive arched gateway into the bailey. Without the protection afforded by the baron's amulet, he suspected the tingle would have escalated into paralyzing pain within seconds, freezing him in place until Darcalus's minions could come and, if he were lucky, eject him. Even with the amulet's protection, he could feel the raw power behind the spells, which both encouraged and alarmed him. Encouraged because he was certain that only an undead creature like the one he sought was capable of such power. Alarmed because the underlying power was so great, even greater than had been wielded in that other world by the one who had killed his son. If indeed it were the same one, it had put its years in this land to good use. Either that, or the lands this side of the mists were more amenable to the creature's particular brand of magic.

But regardless of the reasons, could he withstand such power, even for the brief moments required? Or would he be defeated again, despite the knowledge he had gained from that other, ill-starred confrontation?

For a moment, his eyes rested on Oldar as the young man clambered down from the carriage, and the pain and hatred and revulsion that drove him welled up in him once again. He could not blot out the now inevitable image of his son, Irik, head bowed in the final obedience as the undead horror stood over him, massive jeweled saber held high like a headsman's axe in the rotting flesh of its bejeweled hands. He could only stand, frozen, controlling the ear-shattering scream that he could hear again and again in his mind, knowing that if he lost that control for even a fraction of a second, his only chance at vengeance would vanish the moment the scream emerged and the monster who ruled this land turned its attention to him and only him.

Finally it would come to that, just the two of them, but not yet.

Not yet. There was much to do before that moment if he

were to avoid utter disaster.

Then it was over. The pain and fury once again faded to a bearable level. Oldar's face, instead of evoking the searing mental pain of a moment before, now served only as a touchstone, something that constantly reminded Firan that not a second's laxity was possible.

"Stay close," he whispered to the boy, and then they were swept along with the crowd from a half dozen other carriages toward the entrance to the castle proper.

A gigantic ballroom, Aldewaine had said, and so it was. At least a hundred people already milled around, some eying the massive columns that dominated the thirty-foot-high room. One adventurous soul was even starting a tentative climb up the stairs that spiraled around the column, ending in a precarious-looking walkway that gave access to a balcony that ringed the room at the second-floor level, a good fifteen feet up.

Massive portraits, some three and four times life size, dominated the curving walls above and below the balcony. Did one of them represent their host? Firan wondered, but put the question out of his mind. It would not be Darcalus's true image, in any case. Any more than his appearance tonight, if he deigned to honor the assemblage with his presence, would be his true image.

In any event, what Firan sought would not be in this grand room. It would be somewhere in the farthest reaches of the castle, perhaps in the deepest dungeon, perhaps in the highest tower. But wherever it was, it would be protected as powerfully as the castle itself.

For not the first time, Firan wondered if he were simply deceiving himself, as those two fools Karawinn and Aldewaine had done with their fantasy of using poison on a creature already long dead.

But it didn't matter. He had no choice but to continue the pursuit and to lay down his life if he failed. Choice had been taken from him, on a world now lost to him forever, when the horror that had called itself Azalin had brought the blade down on the neck of a nineteen-year-old whose only sin had been to be born the son of Firan Zal'honan. In the battle that ensued, Firan's fury had made his own sorcery the equal of the creature's. His fury had given him the power to destroy the creature's body beyond even its ability to restore itself.

But destruction of the body, already long dead and decayed, had not been enough.

Too late, Firan learned the true nature of the creature. Too late, he learned that destruction of its body did not mean destruction of its evil soul. Too late, he learned that the true home to its soul was a magical vessel, crafted with infinite care even as the rituals that transformed the living mage into an undead horror were being performed.

Too late, he learned that the creature not only "lived" again but had also found the wizardry to open the way to another world to escape Firan's vengeance.

But the creature had *not* escaped, Firan told himself fiercely. Heedless of the danger, Firan had plunged through the opening Azalin had created. And had emerged here, in this place called Darkon, where Azalin's despised and corrupted face had leapt out at him, as if in challenge, from behind the burning eyes of one of the creatures that inhabited the shadow of Avernus, the lair of the mage the locals called Darcalus.

The lair of the creature that even the Vistani woman had confirmed was the one he sought.

"Did you speak, Master Firan?"

The voice was Oldar's, speaking softly only inches from

his ear. Firan brought himself harshly back to the present.

"If I did, I did not intend it," he said dismissively. A band of strolling musicians had appeared from somewhere and wended their way through the milling crowd, but few appeared to even notice, other than to wonder, as Firan did, if they were human or simulacrum, living beings or spirits given the illusion of flesh for one night. Others in servants' livery not unlike Oldar's scurried about with silver trays covered with delicacies of endless varieties, every one of which seemed to beckon to Firan, as if demanding to be sampled and savored, as had virtually every foodstuff he had been presented with since the mists had deposited him here.

Angered by the distraction and yet unable to resist, he snatched a delicate pastry from one tray, a redly spiced sliver of some exotic meat from another, a glistening yellow fruit from a third, consuming each in its turn, concealing as best he could the ripple of pleasure that each bite inflicted on him. All around him, murmured conversations blended into meaninglessness, but no eye, least of all Firan's, strayed long from the balcony, where it was rumored Darcalus would make his appearance—if indeed he honored the assemblage with his presence.

New arrivals still streamed in, each in gaudier finery than the last. Like those before them, they each gazed about in awe, then nervously fastened their eyes on the balcony.

Abruptly, almost crushing the final entering celebrant, the massive door to the courtyard crashed shut, the sound echoing in the huge chamber. A collective gasp went up, and one of the last arrivals—a gray, paunchy man who could have been Karawinn's father—turned and lunged at the door.

Not surprisingly, it would not open.

"Welcome, my friends, to Avernus."

In the moment everyone's attention had been on the closing door, a figure had appeared on the balcony. For just an instant, it was the ruined face of Azalin, its eye sockets glowing a fiery red, its tattered flesh hanging in shreds, that presented itself to Firan, appearing as it had at the moment of Irik's death.

But then it was gone, vanishing as if it had never been, leaving Firan to wonder if it had been nothing more than the product of his own desperate wish for this to be truly the one for whom he searched. In its place was a handsome, smiling face, topped with the golden curls of an adored child. Instead of kingly robes, he wore garments similar to those of the visiting barons, but of a material so black as to suck the light from the air around him.

"The feast is laid out," Darcalus said, and as he spoke, an archway reaching almost to the balcony appeared in the wall, revealing a second room nearly as large as the one they were in. A banquet table, heaped high with steaming platters and bowls, ran nearly the full length of the newly revealed room. The sight and scent of the mounded platters tugged at Firan almost irresistibly.

"Those with whom I have matters to discuss, enjoy the repast," Darcalus continued. "I will speak with you individually when you have had your fill."

A nervous silence greeted the words, and then the crowd was surging toward the banquet table. There were, Firan noted with some relief, only enough places set to accommodate the barons themselves. Had there been a place for him, he was not sure he could have resisted the temptation, even though the eating would have seriously jeopardized his mission. From Karawinn's scowl, Firan suspected that he had noticed the lack as well and was far less pleased than Firan.

"Master Firan," Oldar's soft voice came again, this time with an edge of fear, "someone is calling to me."

Firan turned on the boy with a scowl. "Then answer. You don't need my permission."

The boy shook his head, the fear showing in his eyes. "It is not here," he said, touching his ears. "It is in *here!*" His fingers pressed bruisingly against his forehead.

Firan's eyes went instantly to the balcony where Darcalus—the *image* of Darcalus—had stood only moments before. But the balcony—a promenade, really, easily a dozen feet deep—was empty.

Firan turned abruptly back to Oldar, all irritation gone from his face, all thoughts of the feast he was missing banished from his mind. Had Darcalus seen the boy? Picked his face out of the hundreds that milled about in the huge room? Was it Darcalus who called to him?

He reached out and touched the boy gently with his hand, probing with his mind for the creature's presence. Surely something of such incomparable evil could not hide its presence here any more than it could in the undead it controlled.

But there was nothing, not a hint of the corruption he knew possessed not only the creature's body but its soul. There was only Oldar himself, whose soul was as far removed from that creature's as day is from night.

And yet . . .

"Who is it?" Firan asked gently. "What does it want?"

The boy seemed somewhat comforted by Firan's touch, but the fear was still in his eyes. "I don't *know*," he said plaintively. "Perhaps it is my imagination, here in this spell-bound place. But I felt nothing like this the night you saved us at the poison spring." He shook his head as if to dislodge whatever clung there.

"Does it speak?" Firan asked.

Again the boy shook his head. "There are no words. It is simply *there*, a part of me! It wants—*I* want—" He struggled for words. "It is like when I awaken in the morning, and I realize my stomach is empty and that I must fill it. But this—this is as if my stomach were full and yet the feelings are there." He looked around, the fear deepening. "It wants to leave this hall. *I* want to leave this hall, to return to my home, and yet I also want to go deeper into the castle."

Possession! Firan realized. That is how it worked when practiced by someone superbly skilled. The one possessed was often not even aware of the intruder, so delicately did it hold the reins. Do this, it would say, and the one possessed would comply, never suspecting the action was prompted by anything other than his own whim or desire.

But who . . . ?

Surely not Azalin, who now called himself Darcalus! Skilled he might be, but the horror of his nature could not be so completely hidden. Of that Firan was certain beyond doubt.

But then he thought, I insisted on bringing Oldar with me to Avernus. I could not produce a plausible reason, even to myself, and yet I insisted. Another's deft hands on the reins of his own mind?

He shuddered and yet did not feel terror. Instead, a flash of hope was ignited within him.

A guide? Had his emergence from the mists at precisely that time and in precisely that place been not a coincidence but something that was preordained? Something that would lead, finally, to his goal of vengeance on the slayer of his son?

Somehow he didn't realize that these very thoughts could themselves be the result of those same hands gently shepherding him toward some goal not his own.

"Then let us go, young Oldar," Firan said finally. "Let us see what Avernus has in store for us this night."

 **SIX**

579, Barovian Calendar (continued)

Firan climbed the narrow, grime-encrusted stairs
uneasily, Oldar a hesitant step behind. Whatever spells
Darcalus used to guard the secrets of Avernus had thus far
proven shockingly weak and easily overcome, as if all the
creature's strength had been diverted to the massively powerful protective spells that Firan had felt as he entered the
castle under the protection of Aldewaine's amulet. The
only one that had presented Firan with even a moment's
difficulty was the one that shimmered darkly over the splin-
tery surface of the dwarven-sized door Oldar—or whoever
spoke through Oldar—had directed him to behind a night-
black drape in a far corner of the ballroom. Even as the
spell gave way before his murmured incantations and he
led the way through the flesh-tingling remnants, he had
realized they were likely walking into a trap, serving themselves up to Lord Darcalus.

Each hallway they crept through, each musty stair they
climbed, each deserted, darkened chamber they passed, the
more certain he became. Surely Aldewaine's protective
amulet did not have power this great, to allow them to wan-

der unchallenged throughout Avernus. Surely they were being led to some nether reach of the castle where even Firan's sorceries would be useless to save them.

And yet he continued, prepared for each moment to be his last moment of freedom, his last moment of life. What other choice did he have? He had long since abandoned, or decided to ignore, the twisted logic that had led him to suspect his own mind was being secretly influenced. If it were true, there was nothing he could do to counter it, so skillfully was it being done. If it were false, there was nothing to counter; he needed only to remain as alert and as prepared as he could possibly be for whatever lay ahead.

"Father?"

Firan froze at the word, uncertain if it had appeared whole in his mind or if it had emerged from Oldar's trembling lips. They had been climbing the cramped stairs for hundreds of steps, lit only by faint moonlight filtering in through archers' slits in the foot-thick walls, and Firan was beginning to wonder if this was the trap he had been anticipating, a spell-induced fold in space that kept one climbing the same steps again and again in an endless cycle. Except for his labored breathing, Oldar had been silent since they had found the beginnings of these tower stairs behind a concealed but otherwise unprotected door.

"Did you speak?" Firan asked softly.

The boy lurched to a stop. "I said nothing."

"And you heard nothing?"

The boy shook his head, but even as he did, his lips began to move, his eyes to widen in surprise. "Have you come to avenge my death, Father?"

Irik's spirit? Here? Firan braced himself against the grimy stone of the tower wall.

"Irik?" His voice was barely a whisper.

"Have you come to avenge my death, Father?" The repeated words emerging from lips so like Irik's were a knife to Firan's heart. Oldar's eyes remained frozen in shocked surprise.

"It is my only purpose in life," Firan said. "But I must be certain. Is Darcalus the one who slew you? The one who called himself Azalin then?"

"The one who slew me is in Avernus, but can you not find it in your heart to forgive him?"

Firan almost laughed, so startling were the words. "Forgive? Forgive the creature that slaughtered my son?"

"I have forgiven him. Surely you can as—"

"No!" A different anger welled up in Firan, an anger he realized he had felt countless times before. An anger at his son. "No! It is weakness, *inexcusable weakness*, to forgive your enemies! It is insanity to forgive your own slayer!"

"And yet I have. Can you not do the same?"

"Never!"

"But what will the killing gain you?"

"Vengeance!"

"Will it also gain you peace of mind?"

"Peace of mind? What spineless nonsense is that? Can you imagine I can ever have this 'peace of mind' you speak of while this creature still exists? His very existence is an open, festering wound to me!"

"Is there nothing I can say that—"

"The creature is controlling you! Or you are an illusion he has created to save himself!"

"I am your son, and I speak only the truth."

"Then tell me, how came you here? This is not your world."

"Nor is it yours, Father. Yet you are here."

"I followed the one who slew you, through the portal he

himself opened. But you——"

"My spirit was brought here to torment him!" Pain suddenly filled the surrogate voice.

Firan snorted in disbelief. "To torment an undead creature with a soul that thrives on cruelty and horror? A creature who can feel no remorse?"

"Perhaps he feels none yet, but he soon will——more than he imagines could be borne."

"But how——*how* did you come here?"

"I know little more than you, Father, though I have learned there are powers greater than the one who slew me. Have you not heard their voices?"

For a moment, a shadowy image flittered at the corners of Firan's mind, but he forced it away.

"The gods brought you here?"

"Whatever you name them, it is likely they who brought us all here. For their own purposes, I suspect. The only purpose I have found for my presence is to torment the one who slew me." Oldar's lips emitted a mournful sigh, though his features remained frozen in fear. "It may be my only purpose for existing."

Firan's mind was spinning. Could this truly be his son? For Irik to have been slain by this creature was horror enough, but for his spirit to be shackled to his slayer for eternity was unendurable!

But if it was *not* his son, if this were only another cog in whatever strange machinations had drawn him here . . .

Abruptly he cut short the dizzying spiral of pointless speculations. There was no way to prove or disprove their validity other than to forge ahead. He had come——been brought?——to this place to destroy this creature or die in the effort, and now, with Irik's own words to show that not only was Darcalus the slayer but that the soul of the slain was bound to that of the slayer, his mission was all the more urgent.

As if the spirit had divined his thoughts, it spoke through Oldar once again. "I will guide you to that which you seek, but I beg you again to end your vendetta before it destroys you!"

"Enough! I will end it tonight! With the creature's destruction or my own! Now guide me as you promised!"

For a long moment, Oldar was rigidly motionless, his eyes wide as he awaited the next words to emerge unbidden from his lips.

"As you wish, Father," the words finally came, the tone laden with resignation and regret.

Pressing his back against the rough stone wall, Firan made room for Oldar to climb past him. As the boy's face passed close by his on the narrow stairs, the diagonal scar on his forehead seemed to fade, the features to soften, and for a moment, it was Irik's face passing in the near darkness, not Oldar's.

But then the scar was back, the tendons in his neck standing out in clenched-jaw relief, the eyes those of the still-terrified Oldar. Again as if divining Firan's thoughts, the spirit said, "Do not worry about your friend, Father. He will be released unharmed as soon as my need for him passes."

Every nerve jangling, Firan followed as Oldar, his stocky, farm-boy legs moving almost as stiffly as a zombie's, continued up the steps. A massive timbered door appeared, but they continued upward. Firan faltered, struck by a sudden wave of pain as they neared a second door, this one a darkly glowing, bronzelike metal. At first he thought another of Darcalus's spells was gripping him, spilling out from the door it guarded, but he quickly realized it was more than that. There was no resistance to movement, only a growing pain that touched every part of his body, as if thousands of needles were pricking at every single nerve ending. Looking down at himself, he could hardly believe his body appeared untouched, that he was not oozing blood from every pore.

But then it began to fade, and within another dozen steps, it was gone.

Above him, Oldar had stopped on a landing facing another oaken door, this one stirring a deep unease unlike anything that had assailed Firan before, a dread that went far beyond the mixture of fear and anticipation that had accompanied him every moment since they had made their furtive exit from the ballroom.

There was a familiarity about the door, about the unblinking eye in its center, fashioned of beaten silver, the pupil a luminous ruby that seemed ready to suck him in as the eyes of that creature by the poison spring had almost done. It was, like the faces in the mists, as if he had seen it before but could not remember where or when.

Oldar slumped, almost falling. Firan caught him, holding him erect until the boy regained control of his body.

"This is the place you seek," Oldar said, his trembling voice once again his own.

"Is he gone? The one who said he was my son?"

Oldar swallowed noisily. "I know only that he is no longer commanding my movements or my words."

"Then go if you can. Perhaps you have been released as he promised. And hurry, if you are to escape Avernus under Aldewaine's protection. I imagine the ball is drawing to a close by now."

Oldar hesitated. "I would not leave you, Master Firan," he said, but it was obvious that duty, not desire, prompted the words.

Firan shook his head. "Go, young Oldar. Return to your own father as the Vistani counseled. Your role here is done, I imagine. There is nothing more for you to do but lose your life." As I well may lose my own.

Still Oldar hesitated, but only until Firan gestured back the way they had come. Then, as if a physical bond had been released, he darted past Firan and down the narrow stairs.

Firan watched until the curve of the stairs cut off his view, then listened for another hundred steps. Perhaps Irik—or whoever or whatever had spoken in his name— had spoken the truth, and Oldar would emerge whole and unharmed from this night.

Finally Firan turned back to the door, realizing as he did that his listening to Oldar's receding steps had been not out of concern for the boy but out of an unspoken desire to delay having to face what lay behind the damnably familiar door.

For a time, then, he stood silently, trying to force new memories to the surface of his mind. When he had emerged from the mists, his past had been a complete void, as featureless as the mists themselves. It was not until he had looked upon Oldar's face that the memories of Irik and the creature that had slain him came flooding back.

But those memories, he had gradually come to realize, were nothing more than a small island of light in a vast sea of darkness.

And the sight of this door with its beaten silver and ruby emblem seemed as familiar to him as Oldar's face had seemed, yet no new memories had emerged. Because he did not wish them to emerge? But what could he find beyond this door that could be more painful than the senseless slaughter of his only son?

Bracing himself, he touched the door, and found not even the slightest spell protecting it. It swung open almost before his touch, the ruby eye glinting in the darkness as if it were watching him.

As perhaps it was.

Gingerly he stepped through the door. There was no source of light but the moonlit slits sparsely scattered along the walls of the stairwell behind him, and yet he could see clearly.

The room was huge, large enough to occupy this entire level of the tower. And it was virtually empty, its rough stone floor bare except for a small pedestal in the exact center.

Firan's heart leaped as he saw what rested on the pedestal: a tiny golden sculpture in the form of a dragon's skull.

Azalin's phylactery!

The enchanted receptacle into which Azalin's black, corroded soul could retreat if his body was destroyed. The sanctuary in which it could bide its time and restore its strength. The haven from which it could then emerge to take up residence in yet another body and continue its depredations unhindered.

It had hung suspended from a gold chain about Azalin's neck as the creature plunged into the mists only seconds ahead of Firan. And now it was here, within his grasp, unguarded and vulnerable!

Firan hesitated in tense uncertainty. On the one hand, he was gripped by an overwhelming urge to charge across the intervening distance, surely less than a dozen steps, snatch up the skull, smash it to the hard stone floor and crush it under the heel of his boot again and again, and then intone the spells that would keep it from ever being restored, no matter how powerful the magic Azalin commanded.

But surely, all logic told him, this object, on which Azalin's continued existence depended, could not be this easily found and destroyed. Surely there were protections he simply couldn't sense. This was, his tortured mind screamed at him, the trap he had feared from the moment of his and Oldar's surreptitious departure from the ballroom.

So be it.

Every sense poised on a knife's edge, waiting for the first warning tingle of the protective spells that must certainly layer this room, Firan took a step forward, his boot scraping on the gritty, uneven floor.

But he felt nothing beyond the jangling of his own nerves. He felt not even the gentle tingle he had felt a dozen times on their circuitous route through the maze of halls and stairs and forlornly deserted rooms that had led him from the main floor of Avernus to this bleak and stony aerie.

Another step, and yet another, and still there was nothing.

Unless . . .

He stood stock-still. If he stretched out his hands, his fingers would be within inches of the tiny golden skull.

And he felt *something*. Not the tingle of a barrier, nor the inexplicable pain that had afflicted him during the last steps of his climb up the winding, narrow stairs.

Instead, it was the same aura of evil and degeneracy he had sensed when he had looked momentarily through the eyes of the undead creature into Azalin's. And as he had been drawn into those glowing eyes, he was being drawn now toward the miniature skull. Something was pressing him forward, like a cold wind at his back.

A spell? The phantom mind he had suspected of possessing Oldar?

Was *this* the trap, then? A force the like of which he had never encountered, a force that would grow inexorably more powerful until it sucked him in and then held him, helpless in a sorcerous web, until Azalin came like a giant spider to dispose of him in his own good time?

For a long time, Firan remained motionless, his mind racing uselessly, unable to grasp anything solid, anything that made sense. Nothing that had happened since his entry into Avernus had made sense, certainly not the finding of his slain son's spirit nor the misguided forgiveness and mercy it pleaded for on behalf of its slayer.

Pulling in a breath, he looked for the first time at the walls and smothered a roar of fury, all fears of a trap overwhelmed by what he saw.

The walls were covered with paintings, and the largest of the lot, directly in his field of vision, was an image that was ever beating at the doors of his consciousness: Irik, head bowed, a jeweled blade poised above his exposed neck for its downward stroke. And holding the blade in its flayed, dead hands, the hideous creature that . . .

Spasmodically Firan lunged the last few inches forward and grasped the skull. For an instant, the power that had been drawing him in became like the crushing hand of an invisible giant closing about him, pressing in on all sides, folding his limbs, curling his body, forcing his head down, until the tiny skull was pressed against his forehead as if it were trying to force its way into his own skull.

From somewhere, his own strength returned, redoubled.

Trembling like a poorly controlled marionette, he forced his body to begin to straighten, his arms to move, his fingers to release the horrid object, allowing it to crash to the stone floor.

To his amazement, the skull shattered into a thousand glittering fragments. And a terror-filled voice not his own screamed wordlessly in his mind, again and again.

At the same moment, the force that he had been struggling against vanished, and he staggered backward, coming up hard against the wall next to the door.

It was done. The creature's sanctuary was destroyed. All that remained . . .

All that remained was the creature itself, and his vengeance would be complete. And this world, this place called Darkon, would be rid of a monster.

Or it would be rid of a fool named Firan Zal'honan, whose powers were not nearly as great as he hoped or supposed.

He waited. The creature would come to see with its own eyes the destruction of its sanctuary . . . and to destroy the one who was responsible.

Firan's eyes went again to the walls, drawn inexorably to the depiction of Irik's death.

But it was changing!

Irik still knelt, his innocent face filled with stoic acceptance. The jeweled blade still hovered high above, ready to descend in its deadly arc.

But the hands that held it . . .

The hands that held it were no longer the rotting hands of a corpse, animated and held together only by some obscene wizardry.

They were whole and untouched by the corruption of death. And the face of the creature was itself beginning to change even as Firan watched. The patches of skull that had before showed plainly through were slowly being covered, first by decaying flesh, then by discolored skin that formed slowly and grew less hideous by the moment.

The eye sockets, once pits containing only a pair of hellish, glowing coals, now held writhing white slugs that slowly merged into the beginnings of eyeballs.

The hair, once only patches of stringy white strands that seemed ready to fall free, taking the underlying patches of scalp with them, was thickening and darkening, and—

The door burst open, and the creature whose image was being inexplicably altered in the painting lunged through, falling to its skeletal knees on the floor, its ragged hands scraping uselessly at the shattered fragments of the phylactery. Gone was the handsome, smiling, entirely illusory young man who had made a brief appearance, welcoming his guests to Avernus. Gone were the pitch-black, shimmering clothes the illusion had worn, replaced not with the kingly robes of Firan's nightmares but with the blood- and dirt-encrusted funeral shroud the body had worn when the creature had entered and possessed it.

This, Firan knew, was his true form.

And this was what he must destroy.

If he could.

The creature seemed unaware of Firan's presence as he lunged forward, his outstretched hands encountering no more resistance than they had when he had pitched the undead slave into the depths.

His hands closed about the creature's neck, his fingers biting into the rotting flesh that, a moment before, had been held firm by whatever obscene magic the monster commanded.

Abandoning its scrabbling for the scattered fragments of the golden skull, it turned in Firan's grip, the flesh shredding and oozing like some loathsome jelly. Even the bones were softening and writhing, like burrowing worms, under the corrupt flesh. The fiery eyes—the eyes, he suddenly realized, that were represented by the single blood-red eye imprinted on the door to this room—came around to bore into his.

To reach out, as they had earlier through the eyes of the slave.

The lipless mouth did not move, but a demonic mixture of screams and laughter rang in his ears. The same sadistic laughter that had filled his mind as he had been disgorged from the mists.

This was the trap, he realized, and he tried desperately to release his grip, to thrust the horror from him.

But he could not.

Its mutating flesh was holding *him!* He could feel a thousand tiny tendrils of putrefaction piercing his own skin and burrowing deep into the flesh beneath.

But even as his flesh was being desecrated by this abomination, his eyes were drawn forcibly back to the painting that now seemed to loom over him, as if it had been plucked from the wall and suspended in the air before him.

The transmogrification of the creature in the painting had continued. The flesh and skin had continued to regenerate, to replace one area of corruption after another. The things in the eye sockets had ceased their writhing and were coalescing into dead white orbs with tiny, central pinpricks that slowly expanded into glittering pupils.

It was, finally, a human face—the face the creature had possessed before it had taken its own life and, days or weeks later, returned from the dead to resume residence in its own reanimated but still rotting corpse.

A new scream ripped from Firan's throat, a wordless scream of horror and recognition and denial.

He remembered!

Everything!

It was not just this room that was a trap, not just this castle! This entire land, into which he had been disgorged by the mists, was a trap from which he could never escape!

His very *existence* was a trap!

And both were traps he had entered willingly, desperately, but which he would now give anything—*anything!*—to be free of.

With every ounce of strength in his body, with every scintilla of determination in his mind, Firan strained to pull back, but the creature's oozing, penetrating grip was unbreakable. Where it touched, its flesh was blending with Firan's, and its touch was inexorably spreading. His outstretched hands, originally clamped in fury about the creature's neck, were now engulfed by it. The putrefying flesh of what had been its torso was creeping up his arms, enveloping them like a foul-smelling, semiliquid fog, and he could feel it sinking its roots in his flesh as it moved.

And his legs—the lower part of the creature's body had slithered amorphously across the few inches that separated it from Firan's, and he could feel his legs being sucked in, as if he were sinking slowly, painfully, into a fetid, noxious swamp.

The only part of the creature that remained unchanged was the decomposing face, which moved slowly toward his own as his straining, trembling arms were absorbed ever more deeply, no matter how hard he struggled.

And the eyes . . .

The blood-red glow poured from the eye sockets with ever-increasing intensity. He could feel the flesh of his face being dragged forward even as he strained to hold his head back. Then it was as if his own flesh were being pulled loose from the bone to which it was attached, stretching out to meet and touch the approaching horror.

And then the face was touching his. The glow from the eye sockets blinded him, drowning every other sight, and he could feel the slimy flesh of the creature's face pressing against—and into—his own.

His nostrils were filled with the stench of corruption, his tongue smothered in its hideous taste as the moldering flesh enveloped him. He tried to scream, but his mouth and tongue and throat were filled by a suffocating putrescence that was . . .

. . . himself.

And the reunion was complete.

From out of the shadows, muffled laughter emerged. *Welcome to your domain, Firan Darcalus Zal' honan. Welcome to Darkon.*

From the countless portraits that lined the walls, his past selves seemed to join in the laughter as the sources of the images portrayed there began emerging from the dusty recesses of some newly discovered subterranean vault of memories nearly two centuries deep.

Behold, the shadows murmured. *These are the paths you freely chose.*

And he collapsed to the floor as the first and most terrible of the memories assaulted his mind.

PART II

OERTH

 **SEVEN**

246 CY (Common Year)

Two young brothers moved furtively through Knurl's twisting streets. It was the dark of the moon, and the city lay wrapped in cold, inky shadows. Had not the elder known the way by heart, the two would have been utterly lost.

Groping for corner markers and other guiding signs delayed them, as did the need to evade city patrols. Each time the brothers escaped a watch squad's notice, twelve-year-old Irik Zal'honan shivered and smothered a nervous giggle. Fifteen-year-old Firan, however, treated each near-miss as a triumph. Finally, no longer able to contain his elation, he laughed openly.

"Firan, shh!" the younger warned, his heart in his throat.

"Calm yourself, little brother," Firan said, his voice filled with elation. "There is nothing to worry about. No patrol can discover us. Consider: We were less than an arm's length from that last group of fools, and they walked right past us. How fortunate for Knurl's honest citizens that you and I are not evildoers. We could fill our pockets a hundred times over, and those simpletons would never find us."

Irik protested in a hoarse whisper. "You are unfair. This alley is as black as pitch. No one could have seen us in this hiding place. And we made no sound for them to hear."

"True, but that alone was not why they passed us by," Firan said smugly. Then, despite the tenseness of the moment and the urgency of the night's mission, he smiled. Such generosity, even toward witless patrolmen, was so typical of Irik, and but one of many reasons that the youngest son of Earl Turalitan Zal'honan was beloved by all. Firan's tone was gentler as he went on. "And *you*, little brother, soul of kindness that you are, always forgive the stupidities of others."

"I forgive them for being human, as I hope the gods will forgive *me* someday, when I go to their judgment."

Firan grimaced. "What pious nonsense is this? Neither of us will face death for long years to come. And with skill and cunning, we may avoid it entirely. Immortals can be bargained with or tricked outright, you know, and for both our sakes, I intend to outwit them and their grim judgments exactly as we have outwitted the patrols."

Irik gasped. "Great Istus protect you! Do not blaspheme and challenge fate!" However, no matter how earnest the prayer, there was an undercurrent of awed admiration for his brother's courage.

Firan spat on the cobbles. "Fah! I need no goddess's protection. I make my own, with potent and unbreakable spells."

The words reminded him of their appointment, and he tugged demandingly at Irik's arm, leading the way once more as they emerged from the darkened alley and hurried down the narrowing street.

Irik murmured anxiously, "What if Father or Ranald—"

"Do not worry about them! In Father's mind, we are safe

abed, and our elder brother's eyes are good only for finding the larder." There was both certainty and scorn in Firan's statement, and he chuckled as he imagined their father's reaction tomorrow. When the earl learned that Firan had disobeyed his commands yet again, and lured young Irik along with him on the night's escapade, Turalitan Zal'honan's wrath would be explosive—and futile. The prospect delighted Firan, adding spice to the night's adventure—as if it needed more!

The boys eluded more patrols—their father's own patrols!—with ever-increasing ease, and Firan's confidence became arrogance. They were in the clear now! Almost there!

He longed to shout defiance at the sky, warning the stars to beware. For tonight, Firan Zal'honan stood upon the threshold of greatness! A new master of the arcane arts would be born with the casting of the Grand Summoning spell! By tomorrow night, he would be powerful enough to rip those bright orbs from the heavens and wear the very stars as his crown!

How his father would rave and bellow when that happened! The old man's boringly familiar litany of warning rang in Firan's thoughts: "Sorcery is a curse on the land, Son! A *curse!* If only I were able, I would wipe that blight from Knurl forever! I would without hesitation or regret banish its foul practitioners, burn their obscene tomes and grimoires, and smash their wizards' paraphernalia, smash it to splinters beyond even their power to restore! Shun that curse as if your life depended on it, or most assuredly someday it will!"

Well, the old man would cease his ranting when the young Master Sorcerer took his place among the Great Initiates!

And if he refused to bow to the inevitable . . .

Firan pictured himself choking off his father's voice with a single gesture, needing to cast only the tiniest of spells from among the new wizard's vast arsenal to accomplish that insignificant yet monumentally satisfying deed.

And then, and *then* . . .

The old man would be forced to bow to his scorned second son, and to that son's formerly unappreciated—abhorred!—talents! Matters were going to change at Castle Zal'honan, and change drastically.

Soon, soon . . .

Irik's soft voice broke into Firan's vindictive fantasies. "Are you sure your friend will not resent my joining your secret rituals tonight?"

"Secret rituals? Ah! You mean the magic, the summoning." The older boy savored the words as he might a delicious viand. "Why do you ask? Surely you have not decided that you are, after all, afraid."

"Oh, no," Irik said, almost too quickly, betraying the unspoken dread of being thought childish or, worse, a coward. "After all," he went on, in what he hoped was a devil-may-care tone, " 'if we never take a risk, we are never truly alive.' Or so it is written by a most prominent philosopher. Tutor has shown me those very words more than once in his favorite scroll." The boy chuckled self-consciously. "Of course, philosophers are said to spend most of *their* lives in libraries, and the only risks they take are those of catching cold when they venture down drafty castle corridors in search of ever-more-ancient tomes." Sobering, Irik returned to his original concern. "I only feared that I might be intruding on something . . . private, something that you and Corsalus alone should share."

Amused, Firan reassured him. "Corsalus *insists* you join

us. So do I. In fact, it is imperative you do so. I explained the reasons earlier. I thought you had agreed."

"I did! I do! It all sounds so—so exciting. But I would not want to be merely 'little brother' one more time, hanging at your heels and bothering you with my presence, assigned a task that has neither meaning nor import."

The statement was a poignant echo of patterns shaped throughout Irik's twelve short years, patterns shaped living in a clever older sibling's enormous shadow. The boy was pathetically eager to share in Firan's forbidden adventures in exotic locales.

"You will not be a bother, I promise. And your task has both meaning and import. You will be an essential participant, no less so than I!" Firan glanced affectionately at the slender, shadow-cloaked form by his side. Even in this dark, stench-filled alley, Irik's sunny good nature seemed to hold the night at bay. Firan tousled his brother's mop of golden curls and said, "Just remember to obey my commands without question. Stay strictly within the lines I will draw. And once things truly begin, stand fast, no matter what you may behold. . . ."

" 'Whether it be minions of light or evil's worst demons,' " Irik recited, repeating part of a terrible oath Firan had made him swear before they left the castle. "I *will* obey."

"Good! Place your trust in me. My magic and Corsalus's are powerful enough to bind securely anything we summon."

"Anything?"

"You doubt my word?" Firan asked sternly, then relented as the boy tried to stammer an apology. "No more chatter, little brother. The time grows short. We must hurry!"

Their destination lay in the heart of Knurl's most disreputable section, crisscrossed with streets so narrow and filthy that elsewhere they would have barely been accorded the name. On previous visits to this sordid area, it had struck Firan that Corsalus's ramshackle hut was ill-suited to house a sorcerer's sanctum. But then Corsalus was not yet a true sorcerer, nor, in Firan's sour opinion, would the older youth *ever* achieve that exalted status. Admittedly Corsalus possessed some useful gifts and, far more important, access to several invaluable magical tomes. However, he lacked the skills and prestige of a genuine Master like Quantarius, Knurl Township's most highly respected practitioner of arcane arts. It seemed very significant to Firan that Quantarius had not accepted Corsalus as his apprentice.

But after tonight, the great Quantarius might consider taking *another* heretofore self-taught apprentice, one nearly five years younger than Corsalus but far more talented.

The brothers halted before a squat abode, little more than a hut, huddled under the city wall. Firan traced the three requisite symbols on the scarred wooden door and whispered the kindred phrases. He repeated gestures and words twice more, and the portal creaked slowly open.

Hastily Firan drew his wide-eyed sibling within, and the door swung shut behind them, though no hand was upon it.

Corsalus was huddled over a large, age-worn book, frowning with concentration, his lips moving silently as he read. At the brothers' entry, he glanced up and said curtly, "You are late. I had begun to think your nerve had failed."

"Never doubt me, Corsalus," Firan said, bristling slightly. "My word is my honor and bond. I told you we would be here before midnight, and I have not yet heard the watch call that hour."

He and Irik shrugged off their cloaks as the older boy continued. "Our father's scrutiny was more strict than usual this night, and his patrols seemed overly numerous in the streets, so we were slowed a bit. It takes some small time to produce even such minor illusions as were required."

Irik looked at him in startled surmise. "So *that* is how— I wondered why father failed to note our leaving, even when those gate hinges squeaked like a hundred hungry rats!"

Firan smiled in acknowledgment of his brother's tribute of amazement but said nothing.

Corsalus carefully closed and locked the ancient tome he had been reading and placed it atop a precarious pile of similar volumes.

Firan eyed the stack greedily. "When will you permit me to study those works? Surely you cannot question my ability to comprehend their contents, not after all the successful experiments we have conducted together."

"Oh, no, nothing of the sort, Firan." Corsalus's sharp Nyrondese features lit up in a charming smile, and he spread his hands in seeming apology. "But, alas! A blood oath binds me. I have sworn to keep the sacred books sealed against all eyes save those of my clan."

It was a dubious explanation in a well-worn argument, and the outcome of that debate never varied. The would-be sorcerers had begun as friends, meeting in secret to hone and polish their art. As time passed and moons waxed and waned, Firan's curiosity about the books had intensified, becoming frustrations, driving a wedge into the relationship.

If Corsalus would only let him examine the books! Just for a single night!

Such precious volumes were coveted repositories of magic from lost eras, and so far Corsalus had tapped but a fraction of their vast potential. Worse, he hoarded them like a miser, sharing only tantalizing tidbits with Firan.

Perhaps, Firan mused, allowing an edge of contempt to color his thoughts, those tidbits were all that Corsalus himself was capable of understanding. Who could know what marvels lay hidden within those musty pages, so long as they were watched over so jealously by one as dim as Corsalus? The tomes undoubtedly contained spells of immense power, spells far too complex for Corsalus to ever master, far too dangerous for him to ever attempt. Firan Zal'honan, on the other hand, whose abilities already far outstripped those of his friend, knew that *he* was capable of understanding—and applying!—anything and everything that lay between those ancient spellbound covers.

With ill grace, Firan put aside his annoyance for the present. There was work to be done, and he and Corsalus needed to work closely together. There could be no friction between them for this Grand Summoning.

And their spellcasting must begin immediately if the summoning was to be completed by daybreak.

For summonings were not like other spells. By their very nature, they were far more complex and time-consuming than any normal spell, but the rewards were similarly greater.

Summonings were, in a very real sense, the fertile soil from which other spells and powers were harvested. When creatures were summoned up from their own dark planes of existence, they brought with them the powers and knowledge of those dark planes, and it was up to the sorcerers who summoned them to control the creatures and to gather from them those powers, that knowledge, using whatever means were required.

And once that harvest was complete, it was the sorcerer's responsibility to banish the creatures back to the darkness from which they had been called.

Firan had earlier explained to Irik the role he would play. Childishly enthusiastic, the boy now helped them prepare, moving furnishings to clear an open space in the hut's center.

Chin up and eyes glittering with excitement, Irik let the young sorcerers anoint his forehead, eyes, lips, and breast. Then he aided them in applying the same magical ointment to themselves. Throughout this procedure, Firan and Corsalus chanted words from the ancient tomes, spells unspoken for centuries.

As the long-forgotten enchantments were uttered, thick shadows began to gather in the hut's rafters and corners. The would-be wizards exchanged glances, a silent conference of still-eager conspirators, and Corsalus picked up a small, ornately carved black box. Within it lay a small mummified corpse, a creature dead for untold years

Irik shuddered. "A *shasheek!* Where did you—"

"Its mummy," Corsalus corrected, eying the stiff little animal with morbid fascination, "obtained especially for this occasion."

Its shriveled lips had retracted in its long-ago death, revealing yellowed teeth still needle-sharp. Its desiccated skin was ridged and cracked like a map of forbidding mountainous terrain.

"This is a mirror for the species we seek to summon and bind," Firan explained. "Now hush, little brother. No more talking."

With that, he drew a knife—an arcane weapon acquired through illegal and unholy means, the seller had assured him. Seeing the blade and its strangely decorative inscriptions, Corsalus nodded approvingly and placed the mummified *shasheek* in the exact center of the floor.

Firan bared his forearm and drew the knife's tip along his

flesh, then handed the weapon to Corsalus, who did the same. "Irik?" Firan said, indicating that the youngest boy must participate in this part of the ritual. "The blade is sharp; the cutting can hardly be felt," he went on reassuringly.

Taking a deep breath, Irik followed their example. He followed them, too, as they used drops of their blood to trace out a diagram on the rough wooden floor. When they were done, the *shasheek* had been symbolically encircled by the red droplets.

Firan and Corsalus set lighted candles and grotesquely formed incense burners at six places around the diagram's circumference. Three marked-off spots remained.

"Stand there," Firan instructed, pointing to one of the marks. Irik gulped, but, faithful to his promise, obeyed without question. The older youths moved onto the other two marks.

The self-taught wizards chanted while clouds of incense and shadows gathered over the circle. Soon Irik blinked back tears and swallowed coughs amid dense smoke. His companions seemed oblivious to its irritations, for they were now totally immersed in their spellcasting.

Occasionally Firan fell silent, and Corsalus alone pronounced key phrases learned from the ancient books. At such times, the younger sorcerer endured deep frustration, fearful his colleague might not have memorized the words correctly. And if Corsalus misspoke during a crucial stage of the summoning . . . !

At long last, when the boys were nearly exhausted by the ritual and the intense concentration it required, when the final invocation itself had been pronounced at least a dozen times, the tiny mummy seemed to move.

But it was not the *shasheek*, they realized a moment later.

It was the air *around* the *shasheek*.

A shadow, not opaque like the ones that still hovered in the rafters above them but gray and translucent, had formed, giving the air a distorting thickness. The two sorcerers, despite their exhaustion, redoubled the intensity with which they proclaimed their invocation, visualized with even more clarity the creature they were now certain was approaching and the opening through which it would come—the opening that was forming even now, obscuring and distorting the image of the *shasheek* until they felt as if their eyes were being physically twisted in their sockets.

Then, in the space of a single heartbeat, icy cold filled the hut.

The *shasheek*'s mummified corpse vanished, and for a yard in all directions from where it had been there was nothing.

An opening!

And all around that opening, where the rough wooden flooring now came to an end, the translucent, distorting shadows blossomed, like a wall of flickering gray flames: the shield, without which they would be at the mercy of whatever emerged. It would hold the creature at bay until their words would—

A primitive part of Firan's brain convulsed with fear, but another part, that of the self-taught sorcerer, exulted.

The ritual had been successful! They had proven that the ancient tomes were genuine and their spells still effective! And they themselves were capable of wielding them!

Firan leaned forward, teetering upon the magic point of safety where he stood. Enthralled, he tried to peer into that pit of seeming nothingness, knowing that it was, in truth, an opening into a totally alien world, an opening the like of which had not been seen in centuries.

Corsalus was equally rapt, his lips forming the words, "*It worked!*" though he did not shatter the moment by speaking them aloud. Both sorcerers inhaled deeply, readying themselves for the next stage of the Grand Summoning.

They chanted afresh, more loudly and even more insistently, unafraid that any of Corsalus's neighbors might be disturbed and interfere. Magic guarded the circle and the three using it. Without the gestures and words Firan had employed, no one could enter or exit until the final words of the spell had been pronounced.

By now, Corsalus was sweating profusely, despite the unnatural chill that still filled the room. Firan watched his co-conspirator with sudden unease. With Firan not allowed to study certain of the spells, they were dependent entirely upon Corsalus!

What if Corsalus's nerve broke? What if his memory failed at a critical moment? At the moment when he must utter the key words, the only words that would both bind the creature to them and protect them from its wrath? The shield they had erected could not stand for long.

The icy cold dominating the room seemed to form a lump in Firan's belly. Then his inner nature seized control, steeling his nerve. He had never had access to the books stacked on the table, but he had studied others long and diligently. And he had his inborn gifts for sorcery, and an ability to concentrate on an object or a thought to the exclusion of all else. That was enough, surely, to overcome any catastrophe, should Corsalus falter.

And then it was time.

They could *feel* the creature approaching.

Corsalus, rigid with tension, spoke the final incantations. For minutes, the shadows that had hovered in the rafters had thickened and swirled, and now they were descending, cloaking the light from the flickering candles, half obscuring the opening. And the chill had grown more intense, with Corsalus's breath now giving visible body to the words that flowed from his lips.

Firan stiffened as a great ripping sound filled the room, as if earth and sky were rent by monstrous, cataclysmic talons. The hut shook, almost throwing the three youths to the blood-smeared floor.

Across the circle, Irik, his eyes bright with terror, bravely stood fast, somehow maintaining his balance against the upheaval.

And then . . .

It appeared.

Writhing like the shadowy smoke that surrounded it, it formed above the opening into nothingness, hovering. There was no solid form, only a shimmering dark aura, an overwhelming stench of pure malevolence.

Corsalus shouted frantically, spitting magical words like the arrows of a master archer in full-battle, rapid-fire stance.

The alien thing probed, thrusting against the translucent wall of distortion they had woven to contain it. Even through that wall, Firan felt its awesome power pulsing as it pushed hard against his breast, as strong as a physical touch, leaden with the bite of killing cold.

Abruptly someone was screaming.

No, *three* someones. The voices of three boys, united in helpless fear.

"Too strong, too strong!" Corsalus was shrieking. "I cannot hold it! The words are not right; they are not enough!"

The nightmare Firan had dreaded had come true. They had pierced the veil, summoning an abomination they had, in their arrogance, thought they could control, and now the only one of them who had studied the words of power that could hold and bind this monster that pressed against them through the weakening protective shell, this monster that burned with an unquenchable hunger for living flesh . . .

Searching his memory for any protective spell to buttress the one that was failing, Firan, in his desperation, managed to dredge up what seemed like a miracle. Screaming the words, flinging his hands high, he gestured wildly.

The pressure against his chest eased fractionally, then withdrew a man's pace. The movement within the seething thing became violent, resembling the mindless rage of a maddened beast.

It lunged, striking.

And was gone.

Smoke vanished, as did the ominous shadows. The candle flames fluttered wildly, dancing in a blast of unnatural wind, though no air stirred within the hut.

Slowly the flames steadied, and the world once again came into focus. Corsalus stood where he had at the start, as did Firan. He could scarcely believe they were alive.

Limp with relief, Firan turned to Irik.

For a moment, it seemed that all was well. Irik had stood his ground, as he had promised he would. The boy smiled through his lingering terror, a question in his eyes.

But even as Firan welcomed the sight of the boy, he saw something else. Irik had been enveloped by the protective wall of gray distortion! Somehow he had been pulled inside!

And something not of their world, something that sent an icy jolt of terror through Firan's entire body, had appeared! A shadow, thicker and more malignant than the ones that had hovered in the rafters from the start of their efforts, was forming around the boy, cloaking him from head to foot.

And as it formed, tendrils of even deeper shadow formed and swirled inward to touch the boy.

And the shadow, for just a moment, took on a face, a demonic face of pure evil.

And then it began to fade, but not because it was departing. Instead, Firan realized with new horror, it was seeping, slowly but inexorably, into the boy.

"Firan?" Irik's voice trembled. The terror that had begun to fade was returning, and the sound of his voice was as distorted as the light that emerged from within the protective shell.

"It's all right, little brother," Firan managed to say, knowing that he lied.

Without warning, the boy's muscles spasmed, and he dropped into a bestial crouch, a startled cry erupting from his throat at the sudden, involuntary movement. Firan gasped as the boy's skin, once as pure as the youngest child's, took on the grayish hue of ashes. His hair, a tousled golden blond, coarsened and stiffened but retained the tousled form. His fingers remained fingers but crooked unnaturally, as if whatever was trying to control them were more accustomed to talons.

And the eyes . . .

Firan's stomach seemed to congeal into cold lead. The eyes, once the softest blue, were bloodshot red, and yet . . .

And yet, it was Irik who peered out of them, terrified, his whimper becoming more guttural with each passing moment. The boy tried to straighten his crouching body, tried to reach out to Firan, but the creature within was already too powerful.

"No!" Firan roared, rushing toward Irik, but Corsalus was suddenly between them, seizing Firan and holding him fast.

As he had *not* held the summoned one back!

Cursing, Firan lunged for Corsalus's throat. "This is your doing! *Your* doing! If you had not failed—"

"*Firan! Help me!*"

A hoarse parody of the child's voice penetrated Firan's rage, and the rage shattered into grief and horror, almost driving Corsalus out of his mind.

The Nyrondese, taller and heavier, pinned Firan's arms and shook him bodily, shouting directly into his face. "It was not my fault alone, Zal'honan! *Both* of us failed. Do you not yet understand your own error?" He shook Firan harder, emphasizing the accusations with brute strength.

Stunned by the physical onslaught, Firan protested, "I made no error! Every syllable I uttered was precise and true!"

Corsalus's expression was cold with contempt. "More than *words* are required! Have you not realized that simple truth? Your thoughts must be even more rigorously controlled than your tongue, for they are the key! The spoken words are no more than a means of focusing those thoughts, those images that release the powers we summon up."

"But my thoughts were—"

"Your thoughts were muddled and imprecise! I heard it in the words you spoke! The syllables may all have been as precise and true as you claim, but their *feel*, their intonations were terribly wrong. I may have failed to restrain the creature, but it is you who turned it away from yourself and directed it to your brother. It is you who condemned him to a living hell."

Corsalus released his steely grip on Firan and stepped back a pace. "The mighty sorcerer, vaunted middle son of Earl Zal'honan," the Nyrondese said, sneering angrily. "Arrogant fool! Instead of banishing the creature, your thoughts were only of saving yourself, and with those thoughts, you bade it possess not you but someone—*any-one*—else!"

Firan blanched, while behind him the thing that had been Irik whimpered piteously, gutturally.

"So you see," Corsalus pressed on mercilessly, "*you* are at least as much to blame for what happened here as I."

EIGHT

246 CY (continued)

Firan moaned and sank to his knees as the truth settled over him. Corsalus was right. He knew—had realized almost from the moment he had first dabbled in spells—that the external aspects were only that: aspects.

Words and gestures and paraphernalia were not the whole. To control such forces effectively, one's total being had to act in concert. No matter what the tongue spewed out, if the mind spoke differently, the result could only be disaster.

And that was, Firan realized with a wave of self-loathing, precisely what he had done! His tongue had shouted imperiously, "Begone! Return to the netherworld from which we summoned you!"

But his mind had been screaming even more loudly, *Save me! Send this horror to prey on another!* His terror-filled thoughts had been only of saving himself, no matter the cost!

That cost now crouched, whimpering and terrified, on the floor behind him.

Coward! his mind screamed at him.

"Help me!" Firan cried, grasping at Corsalus's arms. "Help my brother!"

And Corsalus tried.

First, together with a trembling Firan, the Nyrondese strengthened the shimmering wall of distortion, the barrier that would contain the creature.

For now.

The barrier would hold until the creature fully adapted to this alien world it found itself in and regained the strength it had temporarily lost.

By which time its grip on Irik would be total and irreversible.

But neither of them possessed either the knowledge or the power to break the creature's hold on the boy. Nor did their frantic search through Corsalus's jealously guarded tomes yield hope.

And all the while Irik's whimpers, growing more guttural by the minute, were like daggers to Firan's heart. His intermittent pleas to the boy to resist, to fight the creature's inexorably strengthening grasp, only exacerbated the self-loathing that had held him in its grip since he had realized his own weakness was responsible for his brother's plight.

"Quantarius!" Firan exclaimed suddenly, wondering why the name was only now entering his mind. "We must fetch Quantarius! If any person can save Irik, it is he!"

The name was a talisman, imbuing him with sudden hope.

But Corsalus's reaction was very different. Eyes wide, the Nyrondese blurted, "No!"

"Why not?" Firan demanded, scowling. "Did you not seek to become his apprentice?"

The Nyrondese shook his head. "That is long past. If you wish to fetch him, fetch him yourself!"

"I would, gladly, if I were able! But you have told me often enough that he surrounds his estate with spells when he does not wish to be disturbed, as I suspect he will not in the middle of the night! And you have boasted often enough that you are able to bypass those spells and gain his attention at any hour!"

"That is all it was—boasting!" Corsalus said, backing away. "There are no spells. . . ." He broke off, shaking his head again. "There is no time! If anything is to be done to save your brother, we must do it ourselves! Now!"

"And further compound our mistakes? No! You will come with me to Quantarius! Now!"

"I cannot! I *will* not!"

Firan stared at him in disbelief, but then he realized the truth. "You still have hopes of becoming his apprentice!" he said, his fury giving him strength. "But if he learns how you bungled this affair, even those ill-founded hopes will be gone! You would sacrifice my brother for your own feeble—"

"No!" Corsalus blurted, but his expression showed he lied. "It is just that if we take time to fetch Quantarius, that thing may become strong enough to break free in our absence. It may break free even if—"

He broke off as the thing that had been Irik lunged at the wall of distortion but fell back, panting. It was not yet strong enough to break free, Firan realized, but soon . . .

He decided.

If Corsalus's earlier boasts were true—and he dared not take the chance they were not—he needed Corsalus with him! And he had no time to try to convince Corsalus by normal means, even if that were possible.

He had no choice.

A *geas*.

Firan had practiced this powerful enchantment but had never before had the courage to use it on another human. He had been tempted many times when his father was being even more obstinate than usual, but he had always held back, for even if it worked, it was not permanent. And unlike the minor illusions he had often created, the victim would be fully aware of the spell and what was being done to him.

And he would remember.

But now such considerations were trivial in the face of his brother's plight. It mattered not what Corsalus knew nor, once Firan's objective was achieved, what he remembered or did not.

Speaking rapidly, Firan focused his thoughts on Corsalus and Corsalus alone.

Hearing the words, the Nyrondese spun to face the boy, but in midstep he froze, his eyes widening in disbelief and shock.

"What—" he began, but his words were cut off as the spell-induced paralysis reached its peak. The Nyrondese could have been a statue save for his eyes, which apprehensively followed Firan's every movement.

"Please! Release me!" Corsalus managed to grate out between clenched teeth. "I did not mean what I said earlier!"

With a sharp wave, Firan created an invisible gag, choking off the lying babble. Unable to speak at all now, Corsalus grunted like an animal. Once the two had been friends, colleagues in their pursuit of magic, but now . . .

"Put the books in that bag and hand it to me," Firan commanded his one-time tutor.

Moving like a loosely strung puppet, Corsalus obeyed.

"Very good. We will take these to Quantarius. He may

find them useful in this night's work. Now, come!"

Firan loosened the unseen gag. "Release the shield from your door and we will be on our way."

"We cannot go to Quantarius!" Corsalus pleaded. "His estate is within a bowshot of your father's! And I—*we*— have to be out of your father's reach before he discovers—"

"Fool!" Firan snapped, tightening the gag viciously, leaving the older boy gasping for breath.

Releasing the shield himself, he propelled Corsalus before him into the filthy, narrow street. The shield restored a moment later, he paused to complete the geas, embedding the instructions—the compulsions—deep in his companion's mind.

Corsalus's eyes pleaded with Firan in the near darkness, but Firan only gestured him into motion.

"You would do well to cease your foolish resistance and move as quickly as possible, my Nyrondese friend," Firan said as Corsalus lurched forward. "Whether Irik is saved or not, your fate, if you are caught within Knurl, is a foregone conclusion. I will see to that! The only uncertainty is in how long my father's torturer will be able to keep you alive."

Corsalus paled, but after a moment, the lurching disappeared from his stride and he began to run, racing through the narrow streets and shadowy lanes at a reckless pace. Firan's shorter legs were hard pressed to keep up, but urgency lent them strength. It also seemed to enhance his unpolished skills as he cast concealing illusions with a speed and precision he had never before possessed, giving passing patrols not so much as a glimpse of them. Even the mage-lights he conjured up to guide their racing feet over treacherous pavements and stairways were as true and steady as if they had been called up in leisure from the safety of his own room.

They reached the city's more wholesome regions and went on into those inhabited by Knurl's prominent gentry. Despite their headlong pace, it seemed that half the night must have passed by the time Corsalus lurched to a halt in front of the plain oaken gates of the Master Sorcerer's estate.

Firan loosened the gag. "Do what you must to penetrate the spells!" he demanded harshly.

"There are no spells!" the Nyrondese wailed.

Scowling, Firan yanked hard on the porter's bell.

And the gate swung open, untended.

With a sharp glance at Corsalus, Firan stepped through. There was no resistance, and the sorcerer's home, three stories of whiteness that glimmered in the moonlight, stood before him. He gestured Corsalus to precede him along the wide walkway to the sorcerer's front door.

They were barely a dozen feet within the gate when the door swung wide and a pale light spilled out across a symbol-laden terrace. Despite the urgency that gripped him, Firan stopped short. Corsalus lurched to a stop as well.

A moment later, Quantarius himself, accompanied by a pair of bleary-eyed servants, appeared in the doorway and strode out to meet them. Firan was momentarily taken back by the appearance of the squat, muscular, red-bearded sorcerer, clad in a plain brown robe cinched loosely at the waist. The youth knew the master by reputation, but had seen him few times previously, and then only from a distance. On such occasions, in more formal dress, he had seemed taller and more regal. Approaching across the terrace, he looked like a stocky middle-aged craftsman, and not remotely regal except perhaps in his fully erect bearing and direct gaze. A tired smile crossed his face as his eyes fell upon Corsalus.

"Well, my young supplicant," the master said with a sigh as he stopped barely a yard from the older boy, "what trouble brings you to my doorstep *this* time?"

Abruptly Corsalus wheeled and fled through the gate and into the darkness, running like a frightened deer. Firan raised his arms to hurl an arresting spell, but rough, powerful hands caught his wrists. "Let him go," Quantarius said. "The geas that brought him here with you at his side is at an end, is it not?"

Startled that the nature of that spell had been instantly apparent to the man, Firan stammered, "Y-Yes. Once your door was opened to me, he was free to go."

"And you are . . . ?"

"Firan Zal'honan, Master," he said quickly, suppressing the twinge of disappointment that he had not been recognized as easily as the spell he had cast. "And I am in desperate need of your skills."

The tired smile returned to the wizard's rough-hewn face. "Ah. The middle son of the one who would, if he had the power, eradicate my kind from all the world. I gather from your performance with the unfortunate Corsalus that you differ in that respect from your father."

"My father is a fool!" Firan flared, but the wizard raised a calming hand.

"Be that as it may, what is it that you require? And is it connected with the volumes you carry?" Quantarius indicated the bag Firan still clutched at his side.

The boy's eyes widened. Quantarius can smell magic the way others can smell a newly baked pastry, he thought. He had heard it often but was still startled to see it demonstrated so plainly, first with the waning geas and now this.

"It is," he said. "They belong to Corsalus, and we used certain spells therein to perform a Grand Summoning, but—"

"I suspected as much," Quantarius interrupted, all traces of the smile gone from his features. "It was doubtless performed ineptly, for I felt the reverberations that accompanied the opening of the way even here and wondered at their source. And now you find you can neither control nor banish that which you summoned? Is that the basis of your need?"

Firan gaped, then flushed in shame. "It is," he admitted, "and worse. The thing we summoned has taken possession of Irik, my younger brother. It is hideous, what he is becoming, and we must—"

A scowl like a thundercloud silenced him.

"You involved a child in your foolishness?" The wizard shook his head sharply, as if erasing the thought, and turned to the servants who accompanied him. "We have no time to waste! Put my best team in harness and bring the carriage here immediately!"

All sleep gone from their eyes, the two servants raced away. Quantarius turned back to Firan and held out his hand wordlessly. Swallowing, Firan proffered the bag he had been clutching.

The wizard did not look inside. "I will study these as we go," he said. "Where does your brother await us?"

"In Corsalus's home. I can direct you."

"There is no need. I know the way," Quantarius said, shaking his head, then turning and striding back across the symbol-laden terrace. The door closed behind him, silent and untended, and Firan was alone.

As he waited, pacing nervously, his stomach churned. If they were not in time, if Quantarius, despite his obvious powers, could not save Irik, if their father . . .

No! He could not succumb to his fears! If his brother were to have a chance to live out the night, he must retain his wits, must do everything in his power to assist Quantarius, even if that were limited to keeping out of the sorcerer's way as he worked his saving magic.

Somewhere beyond the house, a horse whinnied, and moments later a second, wider gate opened in the stone fence at the foot of a carriage path. The carriage itself appeared then, so quickly that Firan wondered if even the harnessing and other preparations were handled here by other than normal physical means. Firan raced across the grass to the drive as the carriage door, embossed in gold with the wizard's crest, opened even before the polished conveyance came to a stop.

"In here," Quantarius said sharply. The plain brown monk's robe had been replaced by a robe of gray, a few discreet symbols of power on the chest and back, boots visible below its hem.

As Firan clambered into the mage-lit interior, he saw that most of Corsalus's ancient texts were stacked on the seat opposite the wizard, while one lay open in his hands.

"The summoning spell—" Firan began, but Quantarius cut him off, gesturing for him to sit next to the stack of texts.

"—is of no interest to me at the moment, Zal'honan. The creature is, after all, already here. Only your silence will be of use to me now."

Chastened once again, Firan half fell into the seat as the driver snapped the reins and urged the animals forward into the darkened street.

After only a few seconds, the carriage rocking as it rounded a corner, Quantarius closed the volume he had seemed to be engrossed in and laid it aside, scowling. Quickly he picked another from the middle of the stack on the seat next to Firan, but instead of opening it, he held its cracked leather cover close to his face, his eyes closed. The mage-light that filled the carriage interior dimmed as, after a moment, Quantarius inhaled deeply, and the murmured words of an incantation eased from his lips.

Firan sat transfixed as he realized what the sorcerer was doing. He was breathing in the very essence of the spells the ancient volume contained, searching out those that would be of value. Even now, Firan, with his brother's very life at stake, burned with envy at this display. He had heard that such abilities existed, but he had never truly believed it.

Finally the scowl that had hardened the sorcerer's rugged features softened, and he nodded minutely, the faintest of satisfied smiles touching his lips. Opening his eyes, he opened the volume, his touch as familiar as if he had handled the ancient pages a thousand times. The mage-light brightened and illuminated the carriage interior as if it were daylight. For several minutes, his eyes devoured the ancient crabbed print.

Finally he nodded minutely once more, closed the volume, and laid it on top of the first. His eyes turned to Firan, whose heart was suddenly racing.

"So, lad, you want to learn?" He paused, his gaze becoming intense. "I correct myself: You *must* learn. Thirst for magical knowledge is an aura surrounding you. I foresee that unquenchable desire as a cornerstone of all your future skills. It will guide your destiny, for good or ill."

"Would you teach me, Master?" Firan blurted and then, when Quantarius's features did not immediately wrinkle in scorn, stumbled on. "If I learned naught else from all of this, it is how much I do *not* know, and not knowing is agony almost as great as knowing that I may have been responsible for my brother's death this night!"

Instead of hardening in scorn, the sorcerer's expression softened once again. "Yes, I imagine it is," he said quietly, "for one of your gifts. But before we can discuss an apprenticeship, there are the current problems to surmount. How much time do we have before your father is upon us?"

"Until well after daybreak, certainly," Firan said, sudden pride filling his chest. "He will not even see that Irik and I are not in our beds until then."

"Another geas, lad?"

"No! I would not dare, not on my father!"

"Lesser enchantments, then, to avert his eyes from your bed? To see from the corner of his eye what you wish him to see? To believe that the sounds of your leaving were but the products of a dream? And what of the servants? Did you enchant them as well?"

Firan nodded. "All that might venture into our rooms."

"Let us hope you cast those minor enchantments with greater care than you and Corsalus exercised in attempting a major one. Tell me, what will the earl do when he finds you absent? Will he simply await your return and administer punishment? Or will he send his patrols to search you out?"

Firan swallowed, nervous under the sorcerer's gaze. "I fear he will send out his patrols when he finds Irik missing as well."

"And does he know where to send them? Does he know of your liking for Corsalus?"

"He knew of it in the past, but he forbade me to see him again—forbade me to consort with *any* Nyrondese. He has no reason to suspect I would do so this night."

Quantarius shook his head tiredly. "No reason other than your willful disobedience in other matters. And what will he do if he finds your brother and sees what your ill-considered actions have done to him? Will he allow me to attempt to save the child?"

"Not if he is able to prevent it! He will insist that priests, and only priests, treat my brother!"

The sorcerer's face clouded. "Priests have their rightful sphere, but they know nothing of this obscenity you have called up! If they lay hands upon your brother, he is of a certainty doomed!"

Reaching up, he rapped sharply on the roof of the carriage. An instant later, there was a snapping of the reins, and the already breakneck speed of the carriage as it careened over the cobblestones became even greater.

Firan fell silent, his eyes riveted on the shadowy buildings as they flashed by. Now and then a startled patrol hastily cleared the way.

And then, almost before it seemed possible, the carriage was lurching to a stop in the rutted dirt street before Corsalus's hovel.

Without a word, Quantarius leaped to the ground and brushed aside the spell sealing the door as though it were cobwebs, then marched inside, Firan anxiously on his heels. The sorcerer took in the scene at a glance and grimaced, murmuring an incantation that thickened the failing gray wall of distortion that still surrounded the creature that had once been Irik Zal'honan. It looked up and snarled, clawing at the shield, and Quantarius calmed it with a gesture.

As Quantarius circled the grotesque form, studying it from all sides, Firan knelt on the floor just beyond the safety of the shifting gray, resisting the impulse to reach through and stroke the forehead, already marked with a pattern of emerging scales. "Be brave, little brother," he said softly. "I have brought Master Quantarius. He can surely remove this dreadful curse."

The only response was a bubbling noise, the sound a drowning reptile might make. The eyes, though, were still those of a terrified twelve-year-old. As those eyes met Firan's, the younger boy's lips parted, revealing the beginnings of yellowing fangs, and sounds emerged.

Not a snarl this time, nor a reptilian bubbling, but a guttural attempt at words. "I did not mean to fail you," they said, at least to Firan's guilt-ridden mind.

"It was not your failure but mine!" Firan cried through a suddenly constricted throat. "I brought this upon you! You stood your ground as you were commanded."

"Silence!" Quantarius snapped. "Such utterances are of no aid to your brother or to anyone! Our only hope is to transport your brother to my sanctum, where my spells have greater power. And where your father will not immediately come to search and interfere."

"But if you take him from within the shield—"

"With your help, the thing can be contained for the brief time the transport will take. But you must guarantee that you will obey my every command without hesitation and with all your heart. If you fail, it could mean not only your brother's life but ours as well."

"I will do anything to undo what I have done!"

"Very well." The sorcerer pointed. "Stand there, just touching the shield. And stand silently! Make not a sound while I—"

Without warning, the door of the hut smashed open, almost knocked from its hinges. An instant later, a horde of uniformed guardsmen poured into the cramped room,

Firan's father at their head.

Quantarius had been right, Firan realized in horor! The enchantments to conceal their absence must have failed the moment he and Irik had departed!

"Blasphemer! Stealer of my sons!" Turalitan Zal'honan thundered, crashing into Quantarius, dealing the master a blow that sent the sorcerer sprawling. To Firan's horror, Quantarius's head struck the edge of the rough wooden table that had been shoved against the wall to make room for the summoning. With a muted cry, the wizard collapsed to the floor and lay as if dead, a trickle of blood spreading across the floor from his head.

"Father!" Firan screamed. "You must not interfere!"

"Where is Irik?" the earl demanded, his voice stentorian in the confines of the tiny room. "Where have you and your blaspheming friends taken your brother?"

"He is there!" Firan shouted back, pointing at the thing that still crouched beyond the shifting wall of gray. Its face was barely a face, covered with scales shading now from ash to black. Its bulging torso had already ripped the boy's tunic, which now hung in unrecognizable rags. "And Quantarius is the only one in this land who can save him!"

"Do not play me for a fool!" the earl shouted, barely glancing at the creature his son had become. "Whatever it is, my men will make short work of it. Now, before I burn this hovel to the ground, tell me where—"

With a guttural snarl, the thing plunged against the shield and fell back.

But as it did, Firan noted with horror that the gray was lighter, closer to transparency than it had been when they had entered and Quantarius had strengthened it. And Irik . . .

The change was accelerating! Already the creature was Firan's size, and the scales that now fully covered its snouted, bestial face were glistening black. The fingers, merely bent to the shape of talons before, now were tipped with needle-sharp claws.

Firan's eyes darted to Quantarius, who moaned but did not awaken. With the sorcerer unconscious, the spells he had renewed were failing!

The earl gestured to his men, and they reluctantly ringed the still-snarling creature.

"No, Father!" Firan pleaded, then turned and dropped to his knees next to Quantarius. Grasping the sorcerer's shoulders, he shook him violently. "Awake!" he shouted. "Awake!"

The sorcerer stirred, but even as he did, the shield seemed to vanish completely.

Swords drawn, the earl's men advanced on the creature, but a moment later, as if caught in a sudden maelstrom, their bodies were whirled and twisted and sent crashing against the walls, bleeding and broken, one impaled on his own sword.

And still the change accelerated! The size of a grown man when the earl's guards had drawn their swords, it was now nearly twice that, the remnants of Irik's clothes falling from its blackened, scaly body in shreds! And the face—it held now the demonic features Firan had glimpsed when the way had first been opened.

Only in the eyes . . . only in the depths of the eyes did a trace of Irik remain.

And now it advanced on the earl, who backed away slowly, his blade held before him.

"What *is* this abomination?" he asked, his voice shaking.

A crimson-robed priest appeared in the door but could only gape and stagger backward out of view.

The earl jabbed with his sword, but it was easily turned

aside.

"Irik!" Firan cried. "You cannot slay our father! You must resist! Until Quantarius awakens, you must resist!"

The creature's eyes shifted to Firan and the fallen sorcerer, and it hesitated. It snarled, its fangs now inches long. It slashed the air with its talons.

And the earl lunged, swinging his blade with desperate strength.

For an instant, it was as if time had wound to a sudden stop, the blade only inches from the creature's neck. For another instant, the eyes were not bloodshot red but shimmering blue as they turned back toward the earl.

And the blade continued on its way, even more rapidly.

It bit into the scaly flesh, almost without slowing, as if in the grip of some magical power, not the grip of a mortal.

The creature's head, its eyes still a shimmering blue, spun and crashed to the floor, spewing reddish black blood in the air. The body stood for a full second before toppling.

The earl staggered backward against the wall amidst his fallen guards, his bloody sword dropping to his side.

Quantarius lurched to his feet, his eyes still dazed but clearing. Too late, too late!

The ripping sound that had nearly deafened Firan bare hours before came again, and the room was once more icy cold. Shadows swirled in the air, obscuring Firan's vision. The floor beneath the creature rippled and faded. For a moment, the opening was once again before him.

And the creature vanished.

And the shadows.

And the icy cold.

The rough wooden floor was once again whole.

And Irik had returned.

In numb disbelief, Firan beheld a sea of blood, now

turned red, and the final spasms of his brother's true body, abandoned by the creature that had sought to possess it.

The head, once again blond and tousle-haired, lay where the creature's had fallen. Its lips quivered, and a spark of awareness filled the boy's fast-dimming eyes.

Awareness . . .

And forgiveness?

Firan's throat constricted so tightly he could not breathe. Darkness clutched at his senses, and the room began to spin around him.

The last sound he heard as darkness and silence closed in was his father's scream of rage shaking the walls.

NINE

246 CY (continued)

Obeying the earl's strict orders, servants had been miserly with firewood, and the room's hearth cast barely enough heat to keep the frost from the walls. But the callous punishment failed its purpose. Though Firan had risen from sickbed only yesterday, he barely felt the chill; resolve warmed his blood. Moving briskly, he crammed his small collection of books into traveling cases, cushioning volumes with wadded-up garments.

"As poor a job of packing as I have ever seen." The words, forced past a mouthful of food, were badly distorted. Ranald Zal'honan's bulky shape overflowed a chair. Juice dripped from his lips and plump fingers as the earl's firstborn devoured a meat pie.

"Advice on tidiness from *you?*" Firan said, disgusted.

His older brother ignored the gibe, continuing to eat noisily. "I cannot fathom why you are in such a hurry to leave Knurl. And you just recovered from . . . what did Father's chirurgeon call it?"

"The fool called it a punishment of the gods!" the young sorcerer said, slamming case lids and fastening them securely. "As you well know!"

"Ah, yes, I remember now. Your punishment for causing the death of our beloved brother Irik. A most merciful judgment, would you not agree? Three days of fevered unconsciousness in payment for a life cut so tragically short?" Mock sadness dripped from the words as juices from the meat pie dripped from his lips. "You and your sorcerer friend—Quantarius, I believe he is called?—appear to me to have been treated with remarkable forbearance, both by the gods and by Father."

"I would not count Quantarius's sentence of exile, with less than a day to prepare, as forbearant!"

"It was not death, and the time allowed was more than our brother was allowed," Ranald said blandly, licking his fingers.

Firan could barely restrain himself from slamming his fist into his brother's porcine face. "It was not Quantarius who was responsible for Irik's death!" he said, his voice tight with the effort to keep from shouting. "*It was Father himself!* It was *his* action, *his* refusal to allow Quantarius to practice his craft that was responsible for Irik's death! *And* for the deaths of six of Father's personal guards!"

Ranald smiled, obviously pleased at the success of his quiet goading. "Even if that were true, it was still your misguided attempts at magic that put the poor child in danger in the first place. Even your sorcerer friend agreed to that before he departed."

Firan bit his lip, unable to argue with this one bit of truth, as Ranald, the heir to all Zal'honan lands and titles, heaved himself out of the chair and waddled to a nearby table. "You have not touched this nice luncheon the servitors left," he chided.

"Eat it yourself. I do not want it." The older boy needed

no further invitation. Watching the gluttonous display that ensued, Firan grimaced and said, "It seems eating is what you do best, that and toadying to Father."

Again talking through a food-stuffed mouth, Ranald said, "I simply do what Father tells me. It is much easier than arguing with him, a thing you never learned." He gulped down chunks of butter-drenched bread. "Are you certain you want none of this? It is quite delicious! Cook has outdone herself."

Firan waved as though shooing away insects. Ranald shrugged. "Suit yourself. But you ought to eat something if you mean to depart from Knurl today, and you still so weak." He did not notice his brother's angry glare at the use of that last word. Ranald wolfed down more bread and said, "They tell me it is some distance to . . . where did you say you were going?"

"Eastfair, far out of Father's jurisdiction."

"But why . . . ? Oh. That is where your miscreant wizard has found refuge?"

"He is no miscreant!"

Ranald laughed, his belly shaking. "Do not be so quick to take offense, my dear brother. It is not good for one's constitution. In any event, why are you so wed to the idea of following him into exile? You need only to renounce your heretical beliefs and blasphemous practices and Father will welcome you back into our family with open arms."

"You would not understand!" Firan grated. "It is a matter of honor! One does not renounce one's beliefs and principles for the convenience of a warm bed. Or a well-laden table," he added, grimacing at his brother's continuing gluttony.

"I understand quite well," Ranald said, shrugging. "Better than a stripling like you, I suspect. I understand who has power and who does not. I understand that principles are no match for power. And I govern myself accordingly, as I shall someday govern this land. You would be wise to do the same."

"So speaks the wisdom of the overflowing larder!" Firan jeered.

Ranald smiled again, a morsel of meat visible between two teeth. "The wisdom of a full stomach . . . yes, indeed. But tell me, since you are so set on this fool's journey, do you expect this Quantarius to welcome you with open arms?"

"He has agreed to take me as his apprentice," Firan said, a touch of pride overcoming his anger momentarily.

"Has he indeed? And was this agreement made before or after the recent unpleasantness between himself and Father?"

"Before, but—"

"But he is a man of principle and honor, like yourself," Ranald said, "and would never go back on his word over anything as trivial as having his life and work uprooted and being cast out in a single day."

"He *is* a man of honor and he *will* honor his word," Firan said, though a doubt had suddenly blossomed in his mind. He had not seen the sorcerer since that night, and the promise, he realized belatedly, had been a promise to *discuss* an apprenticeship, not a promise to bestow one on him without question.

"Do I detect a note of uncertainty in your eyes?" Ranald asked after a moment, then nodded understandingly. "Perhaps you would like to reconsider your principles before you take this action. Remember, though you could regain Father's favor by renouncing your blasphemies now, I doubt that he would be so generous once you actually take this journey and shame him before his subjects. If your sorcerer friend rejects you and you return here, I doubt that a thousand renunciations and pleas for forgiveness would soften Father's heart."

"Even then I would not return here!"

"Then you will likely starve. Unless . . ." Ranald eyed Firan's bags suspiciously. "Have you been into the family coffers?"

"I am taking my mother-right inheritance," Firan snapped, "nothing more! I will survive."

Firan flung open the door of his suite and picked up his cases. "Stuff yourself to your belly's content, Brother, on feasts and banquets and houses and lands. I want nothing from Father. Nothing!"

For the first time, a genuine emotion crossed Ranald's face: surprise. "Will you not even bid him farewell?"

"Farewell?" Firan shook his head violently. "I would rather bid him fare to the blackest pits of the farthest netherworld and spend eternity there!" As he stormed down the stairs and out of the mansion, Firan's anger continued to spill forth in a litany that cursed his father with every breath.

At the stables, he was careful to saddle and pack only the animals due him from his mother's will. He had already paid and released his few servants from any obligation to him, wanting no companionship. Well mounted, though minimally supplied, he rode out of Knurl.

The ebbing sun's bitter winds swept eastward across the Flinty Hills, making Firan glad he had worn his best fur-lined cape. Despite his discomfort, the icy weather seemed a good omen, for it was hurrying him toward the city where Quantarius now resided.

That night he camped in a village several leagues from the Teesar Valley. He ate peasant fare and slept in a drafty barn and was more than satisfied. Such food and lodging were humble, but they symbolized freedom.

Freedom! He now had the freedom to study whatever he wished, to delve into all the knowledge his father so foolishly tried to ban.

The knowledge that could have saved Irik!

As he traveled onward, snow blanketed the land, and ice filmed ponds and streams. The wind never stopped blowing. And yet Firan was merry. Like a child with a new toy—and the newfound freedom to enjoy it!—he practiced his spells as he rode along. At times, he experimented with weather shields, giving himself and his animals a bit of respite from the wintry blasts. Though he was not skilled enough to make such spells last long, the brief successes heartened him all the same. They proved that the shock of Irik's death had not ruined his ability to perform effective magic.

The month of Fireseek had begun before he reached his destination. Firan drew rein and let his horses take a breather before descending the final hill. He stood in his stirrups, eagerly peering down at Quantarius's new home.

Eastfair lay at the head of the Flanmi River. Loaded barges were leaving the piers, breaking shore ice and heading for open water, then heading downriver to Rauxes. Dockmen readied more boats for departure. The busy scene bespoke the center of rich and growing trade.

And such commerce and riches in turn bespoke a need for many services, magical as well as mundane. There were surely noblemen and merchants by the hundreds in need of spells, love charms, and enchantments—aid in removing foes and obstacles from their paths, help in climbing the ladder to power. He could find no better place in which to learn his trade.

If Quantarius did not reject him.

When Firan arrived at the wizard's new establishment, smaller by far than what he had so hurriedly vacated but still spacious, his knock was answered by one of the same servants who had greeted him that night in Knurl. But this time his eyes were sharp and unforgiving, not bleary with interrupted sleep.

"I am Firan Zal—"

"I know you well," the man said, studying the youth expressionlessly, coldly. Finally he nodded and motioned Firan inside.

"The master is resting," he said, his tone stiffly accusatory. "His injury has not yet fully healed, and sufficient rest is essential."

"I would not disturb—" Firan began in apology, but the other cut him off.

"Nor will you. I will bring word when he desires to speak with you."

"Then he *is* willing to—"

"I will bring word *if* he desires to see you," the servant said, and Firan found himself alone in a dimly lit front hall.

Seating himself on a hard oak bench, the only accommodation in sight other than the floor, he waited.

And waited.

He heard sounds of furniture being moved and trunks set down in other parts of the dwelling. Even so many days after the great sorcerer's arrival from Knurl, much unpacking must remain before the new residence was fully habitable. To Firan, it was a reminder—as if one were needed!—of who was responsible for the wizard's injury and all the disruption of the sudden move to another home, another city: his own father.

Had Ranald been right? Would he be turned away? It would not be fair, blaming him for his father's sins, but he could understand how Quantarius might be inclined to do so.

And as the minutes passed, and then the hours, the more likely that inclination seemed. Firan's hopes eroded, dejection settling around him like a cloak.

Full dark had long since fallen and his stomach had long rumbled in hunger when the cold-eyed servant returned. Firan stood up abruptly, wondering if he was about to be ordered out.

"Follow me," the servant said curtly.

Sudden relief made him almost weak-kneed as the servant led him not to the outer door but in the direction from which the sounds of unpacking had come until recently. The corridors were now emptied of servants, however. Asleep in their beds, no doubt, he thought, a flash of irritation at his long wait momentarily ameliorating the nervous churning in his stomach.

After more turns and corridors than he would have expected possible in this dwelling, Firan was shown into the master's suite. The main room, a library, obviously had been among the first occupied by the new lord of the residence; there were no unpacked trunks here, and the shelves were in good order, lined with neatly arranged books, which Firan eyed greedily even in the midst of his uneasiness.

Quantarius sat in a thronelike chair. He steepled his forefingers and stared across them as though he were sighting a weapon. "Firan Zal'honan," he said, making the name a flat statement of identity, holding neither warmth nor enmity. "Why are you here? Has your father exiled you from Knurl as well? He had cause, certain enough."

The comment cut the boy to the quick. But keenly conscious of what he had to gain—or lose—he bit his tongue and thought carefully before he replied. "I was not exiled, Master. I left of my own accord to follow you."

"To bring more disaster upon my head? Will your father follow you even here?"

Firan shook his head vigorously. "He could not! Eastfair is far beyond his jurisdiction."

"But not beyond his reach, I would venture. If a child such as yourself can find his way here, so can assassins."

"That is not his way!" he said, bristling at being called a child.

"Ah! So you would defend his honor! Was it honorable that he slew his son?"

"He did not know!"

"Was it honorable to attack the only one who could save his son?"

"He did not know! I tried to tell him, but—"

"He is ignorant, then, but honorable?"

"Yes, but—"

"And you . . . do you consider yourself honorable?"

"Of course!"

"And therefore truthful?"

"Always!"

"Was it honorable and truthful what you did that night? Attempting to deceive your father with enchantments? Letting him think you were abed when you were abroad in the night, consorting with one your father had forbidden you to see?"

"I had no choice! It was the only way I—"

"The only way you could participate in that which your father forbade?"

"Yes! You of all men must understand my reasons!"

"I understand your disobedience, your lies."

Firan slumped, suddenly realizing he had lost. "Is there nothing I can say?"

"Only the truth will serve you, as it serves us all."

"But I have told the truth!"

"The only truth I see is that you will do *anything* to practice the magical arts."

"*I will!*"

"Will you then do the one thing that is needed if you are to become my apprentice? Will you henceforth honor the truth and your word in all things, not just when it is convenient but when it is inconvenient as well, even intolerable?"

"Yes! But how can I prove to you . . ."

To Firan's surprise, Quantarius suddenly smiled. "You have already begun by doing what you have done today: You have departed your father's house not by stealth but openly, knowing full well the consequences."

Firan's stomach seemed to turn over in his body. Could he have heard aright? "What more must I do?"

"Naught for now. On that unfortunate night, you readily displayed your raw talent, the like of which I have rarely encountered, and you displayed as well your many failings, impatience being high among them. Today, however, you have shown yourself to have at least developed a modicum of patience." The wizard smiled again. "I suspect you noticed that the bench in the entry hall was not selected for its comfort."

"That was a test?"

Quantarius chuckled momentarily, then sobered. "All life is a test, Apprentice. Do you have the stomach for it?"

Firan's heart leaped at the word: Apprentice.

But then it fell, as if suddenly turned leaden.

Irik!

If not for that night, the night of his brother's death, this time would not have come. Firan's good fortune was structured on his brother's terrible death. The two events were inextricably linked!

"You do well to realize the debt you owe your brother," Quantarius said softly, and Firan did not question how the wizard knew his thoughts. "And you would do well to keep that debt fresh in your memory, for the temptations will be many on the path you have chosen, the pitfalls deadly to both body and soul."

"I will!" the boy vowed, not knowing the depths to which that vow would lead him.

TEN

255 CY

Dawn's first faint glow revealed a cloudless sky, presaging a hot, clear day. Firan sighed and applied himself to the conjury necessary to conceal his employer's troops. In perfect weather like this, the process was tedious; it was much easier to confuse the eye when the weather was overcast or thick with rain and fog. But no matter. Quantarius had taught him to work with whatever lay at hand.

Soon the preparations were complete, and all that remained to remove the guardsmen from human sight was the turning of the final key, the utterance of the words that would bring the waiting forces into full play. He would have preferred not to wait but to turn that key now, for there were other matters that would demand his attention when the battle was about to begin. Quantarius, however, insisted that if such spells were left in place overlong, those who were under them would themselves become disoriented and lose much of their effectiveness. Firan had seen no evidence of such things, but he was not in a position, yet, to contradict the master.

Pushing the errant thought of disobedience from his

mind, he turned to more urgent matters. His mortal eyes closed, he anchored his earthbound body safely to the soil and set free his Sight. As swift as thought, and as free, it soared above the forested hills north of Eastfair. His lips curled in a self-satisfied smile as the target of Merchant Glodreddi's expedition came into view.

Almost as clearly as if he were physically present, Firan saw the raiders from Bone March, a well-armed band of mercenaries, squatting around a dying campfire. Only their sentries were fully alert. Obviously their leaders believed their camp secure. They had, after all, engaged a conjurer of their own. Firan regarded the lowly hedge wizard scornfully. The man was his elder by decades yet had set no traps to foil the Sight of prying enemies. He had laid on a few spells that would raise an alarm if physical intruders approached, but that was all. Such ineptness begged for defeat.

"Sorcerer?" The tentative call brought Firan back to his physical body in an instant. Merchant Glodreddi's chief of security stood before him, asking anxiously, "Have you news for us? Should I rouse my men?"

"No need yet, Chief. Those overconfident thieves out there will not be astir for at least another candlemark. Let your men break their fast at leisure."

"Do the foes have no conjurer to warn them of what we intend?" the officer asked, still worried.

"Only an incompetent whom Master Quantarius would not accept even as a raw apprentice. He is certainly no threat to us." Firan smiled broadly and nodded, aping the reassuring mannerisms he had seen Quantarius use hundreds of times during these past nine years. The master used the technique to win his client's trust, and Firan found it worked equally well for an apprentice. He could not occasionally help but think, however, that trust could be had in other, surer ways, even though Quantarius firmly eschewed such uses of even minor enchantments.

Over the next candlemark, his Sight once again roaming free, he diligently observed virtually everything that transpired in the mercenary camp. As the raiders began final preparations, he began his own, summoning Glodreddi's officer. "It is time to ready your men. The bandits are mounted and riding in this direction. They plan to set up their ambush below us there, directly above the road."

A ferocious grin split the soldier's scarred face. "What a surprise awaits those murdering dogs! When they attack our decoy caravan, the outriders will engage them forward whilst we pounce on the gang's flanks and rear."

"Just as planned. And I will meanwhile blind the mercenaries to your presence until you are all but upon them."

The man sighed wistfully. "How I wish you had been with our army during our campaigns against the barbarians last year, Sorcerer. We sorely needed someone so marvelously skilled in magic. But our general was a miser and begrudged your master's price."

"Unfortunate. But practitioners of these arts must eat, too, and thus we must insist upon a fair fee for our services." Diplomacy and tact were among the many things Quantarius had taught Firan, though the apprentice did not always choose to use them. This time, his answer was exactly the right touch, and the man agreed, saying that a good craftsman was worth any price.

Firan barely heard the man. A warning tingle had raced up the wizard's spine, telling him the prey was near. A moment's Sight showed him the approaching gang and allowed him to gauge their speed and course.

"The enemy is just around the bend of that stream,

Chief," he announced, pointing, then busied himself with the words that would spread the waiting cloak of invisibility over the main detachment of troops.

The officer and his men readied their horses and weapons and waited as the ambushers rode into position downhill. Stealthily Glodreddi's troops closed the gap while Firan kept close watch, ready in an instant if their cloak of invisibility faltered in the slightest. Pridefully he noted that, even in the full morning light, there was not so much as a shimmer in the air to betray them. And that fool of a hedge wizard was oblivious to the forces that, to one of Firan's abilities, fairly crackled as they approached.

A clatter of wheels alerted him to his next task. As the decoy caravan entered the valley, Firan delicately cloaked the well-armed outriders. leaving visible only the seemingly defenseless wagons, laden with cargo and ripe for the plucking.

The hook was baited. The mercenaries snapped at it greedily, sweeping down the hill, waving their weapons and howling like the savages they were.

Firan raised his arms and, in a single grand gesture, brought all illusions to an end. As if a great curtain had been torn aside, Glodreddi's troops suddenly appeared to the enemy's view. One moment the foe was unopposed. In the next, they were beset on all sides by trained defenders. Instead of unprotected wagons full of rich goods, there was a caravan bristling with armed soldiers. And behind the attackers rode mounted guards, weapons leveled and grim determination in their manner.

In a heartbeat, the invaders' threatening howls had turned to bleats of alarm. And then they were fighting for their lives.

Firan watched, alternating between his Sight and his

mortal eyes, ready to provide whatever assistance might be needed. He was fascinated by the fury and excitement of the battle, but never more so than when mortal wounds were delivered. His darker gifts were aroused by each such incident, regardless of the side on which the dying men had fought, for with his Sight he could observe the spirit energy that rose from them, each and every one. From some emerged a wispy halo that faded from existence in an instant. From others came a cloud like the morning mists that hovered for minutes, swirling with the frantic energy of a whirlwind, before finally thinning and dissipating. There must be a way, he thought whenever he witnessed the phenomenon, to capture those energies before they scattered and were lost. If he could only find that way, a way of snaring and storing that energy, as the power from a summoning was snared and held . . .

Tearing his attention from the clouds of death that rose from every part of the battlefield, Firan saw that, amid the confusion, the hedge wizard had fallen prey to desperation and was creating shabby, soundless illusions of befanged beasts, hoping to distract Glodreddi's troops and make an escape. Barely exerting himself, Firan quashed the illusions, turning the sham monsters into the insubstantial puffs of smoke they were.

Except for one: a horned dragon whose saberlike teeth and claws could, were they only real, rip a man apart in seconds. Smiling coldly, Firan took that one under his control.

Slowly he turned the illusion toward its now terrified creator and bared its fangs in a stentorian snarl.

Firan could feel the hedge wizard's heart almost bursting from his chest as what had been his own poor creation advanced on him. Gone were the indistinct scales, the faded eyes, and all the other washed-out images. In their place was a vibrant, living creature out of his worst nightmares, the very ground shaking with each approaching step.

Finally the hedge wizard regained his voice and screamed out the words that would end the illusion.

But the illusion was no longer his to end.

Nor, he began to fear, was it entirely illusion.

The hedge wizard could feel its hot breath, smell the foul odor of its last meal, hear its rumbling snarl.

You do well to cower in terror, Firan's voice said into the hedge wizard's mind.

"No, please!" The man fell to his knees, hands clasped in supplication. "I will do whatever you want, give you anything you wish!"

The voice laughed in his mind. *You have nothing I would accept other than your life, though I have no use even for that. Your continued existence, however, is an insult to those who practice the sorcerous arts.*

"I will practice no more! I will begone from this land and never return!"

The voice laughed again with an arctic coldness. *You speak the truth*, it said, *though perhaps not precisely the truth you intended.*

The jaws of the illusion that was no longer entirely an illusion opened wide and then closed, and the land was soon burdened by one less weak and incompetent fool.

And Firan Zal'honan was content with his accomplishments, at least for this day.

ELEVEN

270 CY

Firan's escort dodged noisy groups of merrymakers as his litter was borne through the gaily decorated streets of Eastfair. The sorcerer had wanted to avoid the worst of the festival's revelry, but that had proved a vain hope. Only after many delays and detours did he finally reach his destination.

As he stepped out into a well-paved lane, his lantern bearer pointed to an ornate gate door fronting a palatial estate. Other equally rich mansions lay nearby, for this area was reserved for the homes of the city's nobility.

"Hold!" an armed guard challenged. "Be you Master Quantarius?"

"Firan Zal'honan, Master Quantarius's apprentice."

The guard scowled. "My master will not be pleased. One of his stature does not wish to be—"

"He will be even less pleased if you detain me at his doorstep," Firan said sternly. "His message indicated that his need was urgent."

The guard's scowl took on a tinge of fear, as Firan had expected it would. "As you wish," the guard said, but added defiantly, "Do not be surprised if he sends you packing."

Firan only smiled thinly as the man threw the door wide for him and stood out of the way.

Within the residence, an obsequious majordomo caused no further delays but led Firan straight to Lord Nerof's suite.

"At last!" the nobleman cried, sitting up in his canopied bed and reaching a scrawny arm out for the thickly brocaded dressing gown a second servant held ready, but then his face fell.

"You are not Quantarius," he pouted as he climbed from the bed and seated himself in a richly hued, downy-soft chair in front of a ceiling-high fireplace. Firan carefully refrained from noting aloud that the man, bony and unattractive under any circumstances, looked like a badly treated stork drowning in a sea of pillows.

"My master begs your forgiveness, my lord," Firan said, bowing. "He is unable to attend you tonight, being sorely indisposed. He sends me in his stead with assurances that you may place your complete confidence in my skills. I am Firan Zal'honan, at your service."

Nerof harumphed and hawed unhappily but eventually acquiesced, sending his servants out of the room and out of earshot. "I must have the aid of your kind, so if Quantarius cannot come, I suppose I have no choice in the matter," he finished, and gnawed his fingernails.

Firan was torn between annoyance and disdain. This fool believed his problems were unique. Most of Quantarius's clients did. But Lord Nerof's difficulty was something the sorcerers had dealt with hundreds of times previously. The master's apprentice knew he would find little challenge here, more in the soothing of a frightened and spineless client than in dealing with the problem itself.

Abandoning his abused nails, Nerof said, "This situation must be handled with the utmost delicacy."

"My lord, I am the epitome of discretion."

The nobleman glanced over his shoulder, as if fearful a servant had returned unseen and lurked behind the velvet drapes. In a shaking voice, he stammered, "M-My *life* has been threatened. Can you imagine such a thing?"

Firan smothered a laugh. Such "imagining" was virtually unavoidable. Nerof's correspondence with Quantarius had dropped hints like autumn leaves. Master and apprentice had had little trouble divining his true meaning from the letters themselves, nor had it been difficult to confirm it through the Guild of Sorcerers' spies. Nerof thought his "situation" a secret, but by now Firan understood it far better than Nerof himself and had come well prepared to deal with all its aspects.

"Poison is a cowardly weapon, my lord," he said, feigning outrage. "Fortunately I am expert at countering all manner of venoms and toxins."

The nobleman's eyes widened in amazement. "But how did you know? Yes, it *is* poison. She told me I am as good as dead."

"Calm yourself, sir, and give me the details, please." Firan had no need of details, but if this excitable lordling was not allowed to talk, his feelings would be hurt. He also might become stingy when the time came to pay, particularly since he was probably still not completely recovered from his disappointment at Quantarius's absence.

"Yes, yes, I will reveal all," he said, heaving a dramatic sigh.

But still he had to be coaxed. Smothering his impatience, Firan pretended to pry the full story from the embarrassed man. To help him bear his shame, the sorcerer used several subtle enchantments, overcoming Nerof's chagrin and loss of face.

His problem was a woman, of course, as the guild's spies had confirmed to the sorcerers earlier. Nerof's cast-off mistress wanted vengeance, and she had engaged a wizard notorious for employing poison and other pedestrian means.

When the scandal was finally fully revealed, Firan concealed his prior knowledge and his scorn. "An intriguing dilemma, my lord, but not insoluble," he said, though he inwardly longed to say, "Your problem is minuscule, hardly worth Quantarius's time or mine. It barely constitutes an exercise fit for our school's youngest pageboy."

But the client was wealthy, his position lofty, and he was, as most ugly men are, extremely vain. Wounding that vanity was not politic. Nerof would pay handsomely for peace of mind and his illusions. "Satisfy the client," ran one of Quantarius's cardinal rules. "No matter that his problem be petty, satisfy his need."

Firan said soothingly, "I know what must be done, my lord. I will need your full cooperation if the spells are to succeed." Nerof nodded, hanging on the sorcerer's every word. "Please stand before me, just there. Look straight into my eyes and concentrate. Think upon the person who would commit this awful deed."

"Will . . . will this hurt?" the nobleman asked warily.

Less than being poisoned might, Firan thought, then said aloud, "Only a tiny bit, my lord . . . a mere prickling of your skin, as though a limb had gone to sleep for a short time." He adopted a stern tone and went on. "You must remain absolutely silent, and we must not be interrupted. The magic I am about to perform is intricate and danger-

ous. A wrong word might bring disaster upon us all."
Though the warning was in this case arrant nonsense, the
memory of an occasion when a similar warning had been
literal truth was still a lingering scar on Firan's heart, even
after nearly a quarter of a century.

Nerof listened, wide-eyed, and did exactly as Firan bade
him. Then Firan himself recited a lengthy series of strange
words, punctuating these with loud, startling cries that
made his client jump in fright.

All the time that Firan engaged in the noisy charade, he
worked genuine sorcery with his inner senses, searching
the surrounding mansion for deadly substances. He located
dozens of poisoned objects: wine, perfume, gloves, under-
garments, and a box of cosmetic patches. He found the last
item an amusing touch. The castoff woman definitely knew
her former lover's every foible, including his affectation of
those facial decorations. He could not help but think, however, that the only such patch that would help Nerof would
of necessity be vastly larger than any of these.

Firan clapped his hands, and the envenomed objects suddenly appeared in a heap at his feet. "All that was tainted
by her wizard's magic lies before you, my lord. None of
these would kill you at a single stroke. But an accumulation
of doses would eventually rob you of strength, appetite,
and finally of your life."

Nerof shuddered, horrified by how close he had come to
a slow and gruesome death. The sorcerer raised his hands
again and gestured, saying, "I now render these banes
harmless."

The poisoned objects burst into incandescent flames.
Chanting, Firan passed his hands rapidly above the fire,
and the tainted pyre vanished. Not even ashes were left to
show where they had lain.

Nerof gaped in awe, looking from the empty carpet to Firan and back again. Bowing, the sorcerer explained, "Your enemies will trouble you no more, my lord. I have returned the poisons and their cleansing fire to their source: the woman who wished you dead and the wizard who supplied her with the means."

Lord Nerof's jaw dropped. Then he smiled. It was not a pleasant expression. "Oh, excellent! I like you, Sir Apprentice. You shall find me very grateful, very grateful indeed. Quantarius, the times he has tended to my problems, struck me as a wonderful sorcerer, but rather too . . . lenient. You, I see, are not."

Firan acknowledged the compliment with a knowing smile. For another candlemark, he danced attendance on his client. Playing the flatterer, he endured seemingly endless inane babble before he discreetly brought a yawn to Nerof's face. Explaining that enchantments such as had been employed often made the subject tired and in need of sleep, he urged Nerof to rest and took his leave.

Though false dawn was in the sky, many of the festival's revelers still clogged the streets. Scowling at the annoyance, Firan hurled a spell over the noisiest mob, and they staggered out of his way, all of them reeling under a sudden attack of nausea. Some were so affected it was doubtful they would be on their feet again before the end of the festival. Firan nodded in satisfaction and waved his litter bearers onward.

The delays meant that it was nearly full day before he at last arrived at the Master Sorcerer's establishment. Suppressing a yawn of his own, Firan walked through the long halls. Around him, staffers were replacing burned-out clock candles with fresh ones. Despite the late hour, the apprentice went to his teacher's rooms, knowing Quantarius would be awake and awaiting his report, even of this routine matter. Once, the master would have wanted to hear only of the most unusual of cases, but of late, as Quantarius ventured forth less and less, even the most mundane case seemed to take his interest.

But the master's face, its once-red beard long since become grizzled and now white, was not this morning alight with expectation. Rather, his square features were solemn to the point of being somber. For a moment, Firan wondered if Nerof had become displeased with some aspect of the night's performance and had somehow gotten word of his displeasure back to Quantarius.

"Is something troubling you, Master?" Firan asked softly.

The old sorcerer drew in a preparatory breath, an inward sigh. "I have received news, lad, of your family."

"I have no family but you, Master, who took me in." The words came automatically, almost a litany, but this time Quantarius did not respond in his usual manner of gentle reproach and pleased acquiescence.

"Your father may be dead," Quantarius said.

For an instant, Firan's stomach lurched, but his features remained untouched. The inner reaction, however, was puzzling to him. He had not consciously thought of the man in years, and then only with flickers of unalloyed hatred.

"He *may* be dead? Is this court rumor that has come to your ears?"

Quantarius shook his head gently. "There has been a formal notification to the city's authorities that Knurl has a new ruler: your elder brother, Ranald. There was no mention of the fate of your father."

"Then he is surely dead," Firan said tonelessly, "almost certainly of natural causes. Ranald would have neither the courage nor the inclination to take power in any other way."

The old sorcerer looked uncomfortable at Firan's words but said only, "The announcement said only that Ranald had become earl three weeks past. It was not concerned with the late ruler's fate but stressed mostly the new lord's titles and honors."

"My brother has no honor worth speaking of." Firan laughed harshly, humorlessly. "As for a title, they can call him 'Ranald the Glutton.' But such matters are of interest only to the unfortunate residents of Knurl."

"You have no wish, then, to send greetings of any kind? I am told, unofficially, that a query as to your well-being was received in conjunction with the announcement."

"No doubt in hopes of learning of my demise, so as to assure himself of a peaceful, unchallenged reign."

Quantarius seemed to consider his remark for a time, then said, "As you wish. We will discuss the matter no further unless, at some future date, you wish assistance in laying your personal demons to rest."

"They have never been more at rest than now," Firan began with unexpected heat, but the old sorcerer waved him to silence.

"Now tell me of the night's work, lad. It went smoothly, I trust?"

Firan brought himself up short, taking a moment to submerge the anger he had thought long since subdued and to restore the mood that would allow him to speak with lightness of the night's work with that fool Nerof.

"It was as we expected," he said, and went on to describe what had happened, chuckling over Lord Nerof's silliness more than once. Again and again during the conversation Quantarius called him "lad." Firan was used to this and did not protest, though such restraint was less easy this day. If nothing else, the death of the earl had brought home to him his own age, almost forty, not far from the age his father had been at that last fateful meeting, and the term seemed singularly inappropriate. Still, he owed much to the master, and it was little enough to ask that he bear with the old man's harmless idiosyncracies. In Quantarius's eyes, Firan would always be the talented youth who decades ago had sought the master's tutelage in sorcery.

"Nerof was most generous," Firan concluded, offering to Quantarius the rich purse he had been given.

The older man waved it away. "Keep it, lad. You earned it, if for naught else than suffering through his foolish chatter. However," he added with a gentle frown, "I wish you had foregone the harsh punishments you meted out."

"To the woman and that outlaw wizard she hired?"

"Them, and the harmless, if irritating, revelers."

Firan shrugged. "The latter will be the better for a few hours of nursing their aching heads and roiling guts. Festival is almost over, anyway. As for Nerof's paramour and her ally, I merely made small repayment for a crime they tried to commit, a crime difficult to prove to the authorities. Their burn scars should make that pair think twice before attempting a similar act elsewhere. And they *are* alive. I did not poison them as they would have poisoned Nerof, and I could have."

"I know," Quantarius murmured, obviously troubled, as he had been in the past when his star pupil had dealt out such sentences to other malefactors. "We are not gods, lad. Sorcery is a tool to be used with great care and not abused." He paused, staring into nothing, then added, "I, too, have known that terrible temptation to judge and punish. I felt it that night we first met, when your father struck me down.

But we must resist it, lad . . . we must."

Before Firan could reply, the older man broke into a paroxysm of coughing, clutching his chest, and Firan bent toward him, deeply concerned.

"No, no, lad. Do not fret over me," the older man wheezed. "This is just a touch of my old menace, pleurisy. Comes upon me every fall, every fall. . . ."

"Then let me ease your work this autumn," Firan said. "I will tend to your clients and supervise the other apprentices until you are recovered."

Quantarius smiled and nodded, his rebuke of moments before seemingly forgotten. "Now *that* is a temptation I shall not resist. You have my leave, and thank you, lad. 'Tis time you stretched your wings to their fullest, eh?"

Firan's heart leapt at the unexpected words. He had made the same offer before, but it had always fallen on seemingly deaf ears. "It is I who thank you, Master, for the opportunity to prove myself," he said, genuinely grateful.

"As I am sure you shall, lad. Now, take yourself to your bed for a time before you assume your new duties. Even sorcerers must sleep."

"As you wish, Master."

Returning to his well-appointed apartment, however, Firan felt far less like sleep than when he had first returned from his night's work. Some of the more mundane implications of Ranald's announcement had begun to percolate in his mind.

An informal query as to his well-being, indeed!

Better they had sent formal notification of his father's death and funeral, not to the faceless governors of Eastfair but to himself, a close blood relative of Knurl's ruling family. He would not have gone, of course, unless to dance on the old tyrant's grave, but it would have given him great pleasure to refuse.

Or perhaps he *would* have attended, he thought with a smile as he remembered the green-faced revelers who had staggered, retching, from his path. What better way for Ranald the Gluttonous to be introduced to his subjects than by becoming victim to his own gluttony and depositing the half-digested remains of his most recent gorging on their father's bier in full view of clergy and mourners?

The image pleased him, even though it had not come to pass. At some future event of equal solemnity, however, if his Sight could ever be extended to such distances . . .

Smiling at the possibility, Firan drifted toward sleep.

 **TWELVE**

275 CY

Quantarius was lost in a dream of youth.

His mother, dead these fifty years, was calling him in from the field where he had been helping his father gather in the crops.

"Take this to your father," she said, handing him a sack of fruit and bread and meat. "With this late a harvest, he hasn't the time for a proper meal."

And he ran.

His step was sure and swift, and there was not a trace of the aching stiffness the elder dreamer knew so well, nor the shortness of breath and fits of coughing that sometimes seemed ready to tear his lungs from his chest.

His father was young and vigorous, his hair and beard a flaming red, his brow beaded with sweat as he set the scythe aside for a moment and took the offered food.

"You must eat as well, lad," his father said, returning the sack as he took a piece of meat and another of bread into his mouth and took up the scythe as he chewed.

The boy took an apple and bit into it, the tart flavor bathing his tongue.

And Quantarius awakened, blinking at the intensity, the seeming reality of the dream, at the taste of the apple that persisted until his mouth watered.

And he saw his apprentice standing over him.

Smiling.

"Firan? What is it?" He tried to push the dream from his mind, but the tart taste of the apple remained on his tongue, the deceptive feeling of strength and vigor in his limbs.

"Surely you have not forgotten, Master. This is the day I have worked toward all my life."

"Ah, yes, lad, I remember well," he said, ignoring the fragments of the dream he could not banish. "Today you set aside your apprenticeship and go out into the world on your own. You begin the journey to Rauxes."

Firan nodded, still smiling. "My caravan is readying itself even now," he said, and the muted sounds of wagons being loaded, teams of horses chafing in harness, filtered lightly into the room. "But I would not leave without a parting gift for the one who has had the patience to make this possible."

"There is no need."

"Perhaps not, but there is a desire, a gratitude that you cannot deny."

Quantarius sighed. "As you wish, lad. Now, what is this gift that brings such a smile to your face?"

"Sit up and you will know."

"Give me your hand, then. I have been dreaming of my youth, but I fear the reality is still—"

"Do not be so quick to judge what is reality, Master," Firan said, standing back rather than offering the helping hand that Quantarius had requested, the helping hand that he had needed to rise for many days past. His pleurisy had returned this year with unprecedented vigor, and while it ravaged his lungs, his joints had fared little better.

Firan beckoned, a touch of smugness entering his smile. "Sit up, Master. Reality may no longer be as harsh as you think."

Quantarius frowned. The taste of the apple had faded from his tongue at long last, but the feelings of vigor and strength remained. It was as if . . .

In a single motion, almost effortlessly, he sat upright.

Firan laughed delightedly. "You see, Master! Do not be so quick to judge reality!"

"Firan!" The old man's voice was filled with alarm. "What have you done?"

"I have given you a gift of years! Not as many as you have given me, perhaps, but as many as I was able to deliver."

And Quantarius remembered, years ago, his apprentice speaking of deaths on the battlefield and the escape of the life energies and his wish to capture them and make use of them.

And Firan was nodding, grinning, as if reading his thoughts.

"No, lad, this is not a gift I can accept!"

The broad smile fell from Firan's face. "Surely you are jesting, Master."

"In such matters I do not jest, lad. I cannot accept life stolen from the dying."

"Whose deaths would otherwise have been utterly wasted, Master! Instead, I harvested their energy to do good. Surely that cannot be wrong!"

"I will not sit in judgment on your actions, lad. I say only that I cannot accept—"

"You must! You deserve it, as that band of assassins I drained dry did not! And you yourself accepted the commission to root out and crush their murderous guild!"

"But not to do *this!*" The old man, no longer quite as old, shook his head vigorously as he threw the covers aside and stood. "Not only is it wrong, it is dangerous!"

"Dangerous?" Firan frowned. "How so?"

"These were assassins you drained! And now their energy, their essence, resides within me!"

"It is their life energy I took, not their souls! It is no different than the flesh of animals you consume every day. Their flesh becomes yours. You are still Master Quantarius—as you will be, now, for many years to come."

"Nonetheless, I will not—I *cannot* accept this gift!"

"Nonetheless, you *will*," Firan said, unable to keep the anger out of his voice. "The spell is irreversible, but I would not undo it even if I could! In time, you will come to your senses."

This was to have been the happiest day of his life: the end of his apprenticeship, the beginning of a new life—the beginning of *two* new lives, his own in Rauxes and the master's renewed life here. But now . . .

"Those who prepare my caravan for departure require my attention," he said abruptly. "I imagine we will speak again before I depart."

His heart heavy, Firan made his way through the maze of rooms and corridors to where a steady stream of his servants still carried cases and trunks to the wagons waiting in the morning sun. The men chattered enthusiastically, anticipating the upcoming journey as Firan himself had anticipated it until only moments ago. He and his people and property would ride in a comfortable private caravan, as well guarded as a prince's entourage, but there was little joy in the prospect now.

Why was the old man so obstinate? Was he so wedded to

the belief that death was inevitable that he could not see reason? Surely he could not truly be concerned about the vermin Firan had drained! Surely even he could not be that tenderhearted, that foolish!

For much of the morning, Firan hovered around the slowly filling wagons, directing where no directions were needed, chastising where praise would have been more appropriate, and chastising again for the resultant grumbling.

Finally, when the last trunk had been firmly anchored, Quantarius appeared. The servants gaped at the transformation, the vigorous stride, the beard already returning to a shade they had not seen in more than a decade. Ignoring their stares, he went directly to Firan.

"I would speak with you elsewhere," he said.

Firan's heart leapt. Had the old man come to his senses so quickly? "Gladly, Master."

In the estate's spacious rear courtyard, Quantarius stopped under an apple tree a dozen yards from the nearest outbuilding and turned to Firan.

"There is something I must tell you," the old man said, his somber tone robbing Firan of the hope that had momentarily resurrected his spirits.

"If it is only to further emphasize your refusal of—"

"It is not, but your 'gift' *is* the reason for my deciding to speak. What I have to say now is in regard to what I have seen in your future, not mine."

"Clairvoyance?" Firan asked, suddenly very interested. To see into the future was one of the few talents he possessed to only a negligible degree. "What have you foreseen?"

"I have not spoken of it before because it had no meaning, and I feared it was simply a result of my own failing abilities."

"And your renewed life has restored your faith in your talent?"

The old man shook his head. "What you have done has lent possible meaning, dire meaning, to what I have seen."

"And what is that?" Firan asked impatiently.

"I have seen honor, of course, and great power, both magical and political," Quantarius said, temporizing, "far greater than I have ever achieved . . . but greater sorrows as well."

"Lowly gypsies have foretold more than this," Firan snapped.

The old wizard pulled in a breath. "It is after your greatest triumph and your greatest sorrow that . . . *something* happens, something that removes all trace of you from my ken."

Firan frowned. "My death? Is that what you speak of so indirectly?"

"Not death as I know it, nor as I have ever foretold it. Death is an end of the mortal body, a juncture of the spirit. What I have seen in your future is neither, and that is why your actions today have driven me to speak, to warn you."

"Warn me of what?" Firan demanded when the old man fell briefly silent.

"That there are worse things than death. Do not try to cheat death by doing to yourself what you have done to me. Death doubtless has its own peculiar ways of collecting such debts a hundred times over."

"That is what you see? Death's revenge for my having cheated it of a few paltry years?"

"I do not know what I have seen. I know only that it makes me uneasy, both for you and for myself."

Despite his efforts, Firan could not rid himself of the icy

shiver that traced its way along the base of his skull and down his spine at Quantarius's words. Hiding the shudder, he tried to turn it into a careless shrug.

"Whatever awaits, I will meet it squarely," he said. "You can be assured of that." He glanced toward the waiting caravan. "For now, I go to Rauxes. Fare you well, Master."

"And you, lad, and you, even though you do not heed my warning."

With no more ceremony than that, Firan departed from the establishment where he had spent so many of his adolescent and adult years. Quantarius, his limbs still vigorous, his eyes still clear, climbed to the top floor of the mansion and watched from a high window until the caravan disappeared over the southern horizon.

Firan, however, did not look back.

# THIRTEEN

283 CY

Firan looked down at his dying enemy with grim satisfaction.

It was rare that two sorcerers on opposite sides in a conflict even saw each other, let alone faced each other in battle. Such was normally the job of the soldiers and generals, but this campaign, particularly in its last stages, had been far from normal.

For months, a murderous band of rebels had fought against the ruling house, not through open warfare but through tangled plots and counterplots that had eventually ensnared all the complex political factions of Rauxes. A few days past, it had all come to a violent head, in no small part due to Firan's unheralded aid to the royal family. Many had died and many a traitor and assassin had been unmasked, some among the richest and most nobly born families of Rauxes.

Then, in a desperate attempt to salvage their tottering conspiracy, the rebels had struck at the ruler's very heart, again not with open and honorable battle but with the weapons of cowards. Under the twin cloaks of night and sorcerous spells, they had kidnapped Prince Edron. If not for Firan's remarkable Sight, guided by clippings of the prince's hair, taken fresh every new moon for just such an eventuality, they might have succeeded. Almost certainly the prince would have died.

As it was, he had still almost died.

With General Darst's raiding party grouped in the valley, well beyond the range of the enemy wizard's more limited Sight, Firan had cloaked himself in the most powerful spell in his grimoire and had set out for the mountain tower where his Sight had located the prince.

All had gone well until the general's raiding party was discovered, not by the rebel wizard's Sight or any other sorcerous means but by one of the far-flung patrols the remaining rebels had spread throughout the countryside. Signals had reached the wizard at the very moment Firan was cautiously penetrating the spells that enveloped the tower.

And the enemy wizard, alerted, had sensed Firan's presence despite the cloaking spell.

But in the end, it had not saved him. On the contrary, the wizard's fate would likely have been less severe had he been taken unaware, the prince safely and quickly rescued. As it was, his consternation at finding Firan almost upon him led him to unleash every power at his disposal willy-nilly, like a man who wakes in the darkest time of the night to find a scorpion within his bedclothes.

Firan, with some relish, had responded with power and precision.

And now the battle was ended, the rebellion over, its ringleader lying charred and dead, his wizard accomplice dying.

Outside the tower, General Darst and his men were

approaching through the sleety remnants of the demon gale that had raged for nearly an hour.

Inside, the air still reeked from the energies that had been loosed, and the prince lay bound and mortally wounded next to the dying wizard.

Firan leaned close over the limp form of his enemy on the stone floor before him. A small sign of life still flickered in his eyes. There was time to claim the spoils of victory, but little more.

He pressed his fingers tightly against the sweat-drenched brow, living eyes locking with those of the dying.

The body convulsed as knowledge was ripped from a fast-fading consciousness. Firan smiled as he finished, wondering what old Quantarius would think of this use of his teachings. For the principle Firan used was the same principle that Quantarius had used so innocuously to absorb the essence of a magical volume without opening the cover, but Firan had refined it to near perfection and enhanced it and applied it to a living mind.

And the dying wizard's knowledge was his, though most would doubtless prove useless.

Firan trained his Sight upon the other and saw death was indeed fast approaching.

The energy Firan had seen depart a thousand times on a hundred battlefields had already begun to sift lightly from the wizard's body. Hovering close, he took the energy into himself, as he had taken the knowledge.

Smiling at the irony, he directed a portion of the life energy into the prince's body and watched, satisfied, as the worst of the wounds so recently inflicted healed and the prince stirred in his bonds, which Firan then quickly loosed.

From a hundred feet below came the sound of a battering

ram smashing at a door.

"Come up, General," Firan called when he heard the huge oaken door at the base of the tower crash to the floor. "His Grace requires your aid."

With no sorcerous power to maintain it, the storm's fury had spent itself rapidly. By the time the general, winded, entered the room, moonlight streamed through its shattered windows.

"The prince?" General Darst said anxiously. "Is he . . . ?"

"Injured, but I have ministered to his worst hurts." Firan forbore to explain the principle of stealing life from a dying victim to aid one still alive. He doubted that Darst would have the same misguided scruples that Quantarius had possessed, but there were other reasons for keeping such an ability secret. "Nevertheless, I think it best if a professional healer attend him."

"Fetch the chirurgeon!" the general bellowed, sending a soldier galloping back down the stairs at a reckless pace. "A physician should see to your hurts as well, my lord sorcerer."

Firan fastidiously straightened his torn and bloodied robe. "Wizardry dealt my wounds, and wizardry shall mend them. These are already half healed," he said. Soldiers eyed his barely visible abrasions and cuts and shook their heads in awe.

"Lord sorcerer . . . ?" Prince Edron's voice trembled, showing the aftereffects of captivity and much rough treatment, but the young man insisted on thanking his rescuer personally. Though the strain told upon him, he would not lie down again until his honor was satisfied.

As the chirurgeon rushed into the tower and knelt beside Edron, Firan turned to the general. "I will leave the prince in your charge. I shall be on my way, with your leave."

"Of course. I will assign you an escort. And may I say it is not only the prince who thanks you." Firan nodded absently, accepting praise as his due.

As he moved toward the stairs, an officer trotted at his heels, whispering tactfully, "I will make certain that proper recompense is sent to your establishment, my lord. . . ."

"It is of no moment," Firan said, brushing the suggestion aside. "My actions were those of a loyal citizen coming forth when news of the prince's kidnapping reached me."

Hours later, bathed and clad in fresh raiment and dining upon the latest delicacies his kitchen had concocted, Firan was in a reflective mood. The offer of recompense, though he would certainly not turn it away, was truly of little moment. What *did* matter, at this point in his career, was that news of his feat would spread throughout Rauxes and the lands surrounding. His clientele, already vast, would increase still further, but more importantly, so would his power and influence. Money had long since ceased to be a real concern, but power . . . ah, that was another matter, particularly here and now.

Prince Edron was free. The rebellion in all its underhanded intricacies was dead. Order, once on knife edge, was restored to all of Rauxes.

For now.

But the ruling house of Rauxes was not known for its firmness of hand. Often they seemed as unduly merciful as Firan's old teacher. True, they had executed a number of the conspirators, but others had been simply jailed. And even greater leniency would probably be the rule for many of the lesser lights. There had already been talk of how some had been "misled" by the true conspirators and deserved nothing worse than loss of title or land.

Firan sighed, as he often had when confronted by Quantarius's misguided forgiveness of people who deserved the sternest of discipline, not benign absolution for their sins, repented or unrepented. Like the old wizard, the ruling house of Rauxes simply did not understand that ruthless punishment insured a chastened populace and greater order in the long run.

Such firmness was the only sane policy. Steady guidance by a strong hand. And if some malcontents called it tyranny, they should be dealt with, swiftly and justly and publicly. When enough examples were made . . .

"A distinguished messenger to see you, my lord."

The words of Firan's steward broke into his reverie. He smiled. "I imagine it is a courier bearing a gratitude payment from the general and the royal council."

"No, my lord, a rider bringing a letter from Knurl's warden. He offers these credentials." In the servant's hands was a sheaf of papers bearing an official seal Firan had not seen in years.

Concealing his embarrassed annoyance over his mistaken assumption, wishing for the thousandth time that his gifts in the area of clairvoyance matched his gifts in other areas, the sorcerer skimmed the document.

Neither the stranger's name nor his credentials meant anything to Firan. He certainly could put no face to it. But that should not be surprising. He had departed Knurl nearly forty years past. It was likely that the warden's messenger had been a mere babe in those days, not someone Earl Turalitan's second son ever would have met.

"Show him in," he said brusquely, speaking more loudly than he had intended. "I shall learn nothing while the man waits out in the hall."

The steward admitted the envoy and his three attendants, who carried small, costly boxes, the sort which usually contained gifts. The strangers' faces were lined with fatigue, as though they had ridden many hours without rest. Yet, significantly, they had taken time to wash away the travel dust and dress in courtiers' attire before presenting themselves to the wizard. The four bowed low and removed their caps. Then their leader advanced and knelt before Firan's chair.

Puzzled by this obsequious behavior, the sorcerer gestured impatiently. "Well? What has the warden to say to me?"

"My lord, he earnestly prays that you will return to Knurl."

"And what does Ranald have to say regarding this invitation? I would not have thought myself welcome in his township."

"He is dead, my lord. He died upon third Waterday last."

"Of a burst belly, no doubt!" Firan said with a dry laugh. "When he finally expired, he must have required a grave large enough to hold an ox, eh?"

"I know not, my lord," the messenger said in obvious discomfort. "Warden Rehajo bade me only inform your lordship that you are the sole surviving Zal'honan heir. He begs you to claim your inheritances—livings, lands, and all rights of dominion over us."

"Sole heir?" The wizard lifted a questioning eyebrow. "What of my brother's offspring?"

"Regrettably, my lord, none of his children survived him," the envoy said, signaling his attendants to come forward. Hurriedly they knelt beside him and opened the richly adorned caskets they carried. Each chest held jewels, gold, and silver.

Gesturing to these treasures, the messenger said, "The warden also bade me deliver your lordship's taxes for this season. We brought further rich goods, which we have left in the keeping of your steward. And we stabled ten pure-bred horses, the finest in Knurl, with the most reputable local hostler. The steeds await your lordship's inspection when it shall please you. The warden hopes you will find this tribute satisfactory."

The messenger paused to clear his throat, then went on with obvious unease but with equally obvious sincerity, "It is not only the warden who beseeches you thus, Lord Zal'honan. All honest folk of Knurl hope for your return. Please! Assume your rightful place as our ruler!"

Firan eyed the envoy warily. Considering his recent musings about Rauxes, this was a most timely and a most tempting offer, but also most unusual. A son who had been disowned four decades past was not a common choice to inherit a crown.

Mentally pronouncing an incantation of truth, Firan asked, "Why does the warden address me through an emissary? Why did he not come himself on a matter of such import?"

Unable to speak falsely, the man said, "My lord, the warden fears to leave Knurl lest disorder utterly destroy city and township in his absence."

"Destroy them? How?"

"The earl your brother never really governed us," the messenger said, a slight expressionlessness the only evidence of the effects of the incantation. "Thus, of necessity, Warden Rehajo was forced to take many of the burdens of state upon himself, to the serious neglect of his own estate's affairs. But with each passing year, the malefactors he fought grew ever bolder, like wolves scenting weakened and vulnerable prey. These evildoers knew that the law limited the warden's powers, and they took advantage of that fact."

Unconsciously Firan had clenched his fists, infuriated by what he was hearing. What a cruel, ironic joke fate had played on Knurl and the House of Zal'honan! Irik, as conscientious as he had been handsome, would have ruled city and township superbly, Firan was sure, but he had never had the chance. Their father had seen to that! Instead, Ranald the Glutton had become earl—and had wallowed in feastmaking, indulging the appetite that had eventually killed him, while his city and township fell victim to predators! The faithful warden had struggled to stave off disaster, sacrificing his own interests in the effort while Ranald ate his way into an oversized grave, and his resources and strength were almost at an end.

"These malefactors who threaten Knurl . . . who are they? What manner of evil do they commit?" There was dark menace in the sorcerer's tone, and his piercing gaze seemed to impale the messenger.

The attendants eyed their companion fearfully as he continued his recitation of troubles they had doubtless expected would remain unspoken until the warden himself could reveal them. "Bandits attack almost every caravan using our roads, my lord. Trade has all but come to a standstill. Thieves who lurk within our city walls harass and rob our merchants and common folk at will. Cutpurses, brawlers, and other human carrion infest every street, making life cheap. And Knurl's ancient clan feuds have flared into open warfare; many innocents have been killed in the crossfire of their murderous clashes. Worst of all, there are . . ." Even under the incantation of truth, the envoy hesitated, but finally succumbed. "There are those of . . . of your profession, my lord."

"Sorcerers, you mean?" Firan inquired evenly.

"Yes," the envoy blurted, "but not of your stature or honor, my lord. They . . . they are certainly the dregs of the profession, as those others who prey on us are the dregs of their own."

"Go on," Firan said quietly. "I will not be offended. On the contrary, I have just dealt with one of my profession who is doubtless of the type you describe. Even kidnapping was not beneath him. Unfortunately, there are many who disgrace the honest and honorable practitioners of the arcane arts."

The envoy nodded in gratitude. "They have flooded in upon us, my lord," he went on, less hesitantly now. "As it became known in neighboring lands that the earl your brother had small concern for our woes, workers of sorcery joined the other evildoers in terrorizing our citizens and filling their coffers."

While the envoy spoke, Firan's mood gradually shifted. At first there was only rage at what his father and brother had done, what they had allowed to happen to Knurl, but that was soon overwhelmed by the delectable irony of the situation. His father would be spinning in his grave if he knew that the disowned son and his despised magical arts were being called upon to save what the other son had let slip through his grease-stained fingers.

"The warden did right to send you to me," Firan said. "It is unfortunate that the law forbade him to do so before my brother's death."

Freed from the trance he had not known lay upon him, the messenger said hopefully, "My lord? You will come to Knurl, then?"

"And at once!" Firan exclaimed, suddenly caught up in the excitement of the challenge. "Plainly, order must be restored to Knurl as quickly as possible, before even more damage is done. The warden cannot continue to fight so many enemies alone, particularly not when some are practitioners of the same arts as myself. I will deal with *those* personally, and I will help the warden smash all the other two-legged wolves ravaging my people and my lands," he finished, smiling in a manner that made his listeners grateful that his vengeance was not to be aimed at them.

* * * * *

Early the next morning, while his servants were beginning the packing that would doubtless occupy them for several days, Firan presented himself at the palace in Rauxes and, after many an attempt to dissuade him and a few tedious ceremonials, he was free to depart. The envoy and his attendants, who were to be Firan's main escort, were waiting when he emerged into the late morning sun, the ten steeds they had so presciently brought him from Knurl saddled and ready.

His Sight ranging far ahead, Firan was easily able to avoid the first covey of assassins who had set up an elaborate ambush only a few miles from Rauxes. He smiled as he sent word back to Prince Edron, who would be eager to repay a small part of his debt for his rescue by leading a detachment of his best troops to overrun the would-be ambushers.

The second group was hidden, so they vainly believed, in the thickets of the Adri Forest not far beyond Edgefield, where the only road skirted the forest well within arrow range. Here one of the rogue wizards thought to use his own sorcerous powers in the engagement, but he was no more effective than the pathetic hedge wizard who had foolishly stood against Firan in Eastfair.

"See to the traitors' identities," Firan ordered when all attackers lay dead or mortally wounded, their own arrows turned back upon them. "I would know the name of whoever wished me dead." As his followers obeyed, dealing merciful death to the few survivors, Firan tended to the rogue wizard, frozen and near death in the backlash of his own feeble spells. There was, however, nothing in his thoughts or knowledge worth salvaging. Even his life energy was oddly tainted, so that Firan let it dissipate, unhindered, into the death-laden air.

The envoy returned from his grim task to report, "These assassins were in the hire of Baron Sennefort, my lord."

"He is one of the largest thorns in the warden's side, is he not?" Firan said with an almost indiscernible smile. "Well, I would say Sennefort's power is due for a downturn. Doubtless it has already been greatly diminished by this little encounter. Let us proceed on our way and discover who else has interest in stopping me from claiming my inheritance."

The group that awaited them in the tiny village of Stulwick, however, greeted Firan not with arrows and spells but with cheers and shouts of joy. The same rumors that had led to the ambushes had spread to the general populace as well, and the peasants had watched with trepidation as Sennefort's men had marched through only days earlier, arrogant in their confidence that they could deal with Ranald Zal'honan's long-lost brother with ease. The villagers' joy upon learning how wrong Sennefort's surly and abusive troops had been was unbounded, and many joined the new earl's escort, some on horses more used to plow harness than saddle, others on their own sturdy legs.

And so it was in the next village, and the next, and the next, as word of the new earl's coming—and the exaggerated defeats dealt to the forces of Baron Sennefort and the other villainous usurpers—ran before him. By the time Firan reached the city of Knurl, his escort had grown fifty-fold, enhanced by an enthusiastic civilian army not only of peasants and farmers but also of honest noblemen, young and old, who had been terrorized and ousted from their ancestral lands as Knurl had been driven ever further into chaos.

A beleaguered Warden Rehajo and a delegation of prominent loyal citizens met Firan at the gates of Knurl. The aged soldier doffed his helmet and spoke for all. "Welcome, Lord Zal'honan! How this township has prayed for your strong hands to guide us!"

"It was *your* strong hands that protected Knurl during her long travail, Warden," Firan responded generously, his voice carrying to the farthest reaches of the gathering throng, "yours and the hands of these other good citizens. Such unflinching loyalty and courage shall not go unrewarded."

"My lord, the only rewards we seek are peace and order for our land."

"And you shall have it," Firan promised, his expression intent. "Until today, you have been most unevenly matched in this struggle, Warden. The bravest soldier or civilian is rarely capable of defeating wizards unaided. But henceforth we shall strike them hard on both fronts, with sorcery and with force of arms so great that—"

A sudden scream cut across his words as dozens of eyes leapt in terror from Firan and the warden to the battlements above the city gates. Turning, Firan saw the source of their terror: A cloud that could have come from the heart of the darkest thunderstorm boiled out from those fortifications and was descending rapidly, not toward the crowd but toward the warden and the new earl.

Without hesitation, Firan sent his Sight plunging into the roiling miasma while his mortal eyes, no longer blinded while his Sight was abroad, spied a tiny figure peering down from the farthest reaches of the battlements, far from the city gates. Spear points and billhooks raised, Firan's self-appointed protectors drew close about him, but he waved them away as, within the deadly cloud, his Sight traced the tangled threads of power that drove it, traced them back through flimsy barrier after flimsy barrier to those who had created and launched it.

For a moment, he felt their fear as they sensed his immaterial presence. For another moment, he savored that fear and let it build.

Then, as the roiling blackness was about to envelop him, Firan seized those threads of power and sent the deadly cloud flowing back toward its now terrified creators. Vainly they tried to wrest power back from him, then to throw up shields to block or divert it, but when it descended upon them, their only thoughts were of escape.

Muffled screams came from somewhere beyond the battlements, then silence.

And the figure on the far reaches of the city wall turned to flee, though he surely knew it was useless.

Firan reached out as if with an invisible arm and plucked the figure from the battlements and brought it to hang, helpless, above the crowd.

"Baron Sennefort!" the envoy, still at Firan's side, cried.

A murmur arose from the crowd, then a deafening roar as a rock erupted from the shouting mass. Sennefort screamed as it struck, followed by another. And another. The barrage continued until Firan raised a hand.

"We do not wish his death . . . yet," Firan said.

"Please, my Lord Zal'honan!" Sennefort cried through bloody lips. "I swear upon my honor, I did not—"

"You have no honor to swear by, Sennefort!" Firan said, his ringing voice carrying to the edges of the crowd and beyond. "Now be silent. You will not speak further until you lie in my dungeons. Then I shall bid you reveal the names of all your conspirators in crime. When that time comes, you will tell me everything, even as you beg for death."

With that, Firan let the baron fall to the ground, his mouth sealed until Firan chose to release it. He gestured to the warden's men. "Take him!"

As this grim scene had been acted out, the crowd had been rapt. Now a single aged voice spoke loudly into the silence.

"Azal'Lan," it said, and again, "Azal'Lan . . ."

Then a second voice took it up, and another.

For a moment, its meaning eluded Firan. He had not heard the term since childhood, and then only from one or another of his tutors.

But then it came back to him. It was a term in old Oeridian, a term not used in his lifetime nor in the lifetime of anyone now living.

For there had been no Azal'Lan in his lifetime, nor for a century before.

There had been no wizard king, for that was the ancient word's meaning.

But now . . .

A slow smile spread across Firan's hawklike features.

Now, once again, there was.

Firan Zal'honan, *Azal'Lan.*

He raised his arms high in acknowledgment.

Slowly the word came to more and more lips, as if

emerging from a thousand memories, one by one, until it was a thunderous chant, a paean to what he had, in his long absence, become.

Firan Zal'honan had come home.

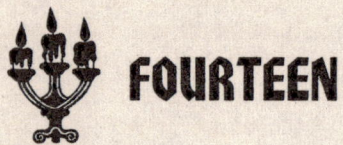

FOURTEEN

283–308 CY

In the years that followed, Firan swore fealty to the distant Malachite Throne, more as a matter of convenience than conviction. A small percentage of the taxes that were gathered and an even smaller levy of troops was small price to pay to avoid the occasional scrutiny of the leaders of what amounted to a loosely held empire, leaving him essentially free to rule as he pleased.

And what pleased him was to govern Knurl with a hand that was undeniably heavy. Equally undeniably, his rule was fair and equitable, for all knew that his wizardry was such that the truth could not be hidden from him. Only those who feared the truth had reason to fear his punishment. Many, however, were not at first ready to subjugate their will to his, no matter that the results of such subjugation would have been in their own best interests. The clans were the worst offenders in this regard, resenting as they did those laws which suppressed their age-old feuds, forcing them to coexist peacefully. Their resentments, however, were largely kept hidden after the chieftains of two of the most resentful and unruly clans were executed, slowly and publicly.

Priests were also troublesome at first in their close-minded opposition to all things magical, but once it was clear to their followers that priestly mumbo jumbo was just that, meaningless nonsense that, unlike the Azal'Lan's spells, had no effect on the real world, their number dwindled precipitately until the few priests who remained within Knurl were reduced to begging in the streets.

Even the few remaining malcontents, however, could not deny that Knurl prospered under the rule of the Azal'Lan. There was peace. Trade thrived. Law-abiding citizens were safe in their houses and when traveling the highways. Criminals all but vanished from the realm. The few who survived—who were *allowed* to survive as needed examples, it was said by some—hid in sewers and out-of-the-way dens and constantly feared for their lives. They knew that the gallows or the block or fates even worse awaited anyone foolish enough to arouse the Azal'Lan's wrath.

In the eighth year of his reign, Firan turned to matters of dynasty.

Of late, he had begun to note that, despite the repeated infusions of life energy, signs of aging were coming upon him. His outward appearance was still that of a man twenty years his junior and showed no signs of deterioration, but his physical vigor was declining year by year. He thought often of Quantarius's cryptic warning about not using his powers to cheat death and was forced finally to admit to himself that someday, despite his powers, his life would come to an end, perhaps not in ten years or even a hundred, but sometime.

And when that time came, the thought of leaving his people in the same situation his father and gluttonous brother had left them in was anathema to him. Their loyalty deserved better of him.

An heir was required, a son whose growth and development he could guide and shape until he was capable of ruling in the Azal'Lan's stead.

But selecting a mate presented certain difficulties. If he chose from among the prominent local families, inevitably rival clans would cry "favoritism!" To avoid the risk of renewed civil war and the resultant annoyance of having to put it down, he decided to seek a wife elsewhere.

There was no lack of candidates, for many prominent leaders of neighboring realms aspired to become Azal'Lan's father-in-law, whether the daughters relished the prospect or not. He was by now feared and respected throughout the Flanaess, though certainly not loved by all. Nonetheless, a parade of courtiers came to Castle Galdliesh, each boasting of his candidate's beauty and virtue, of her large dowry, and of a valuable trade or military alliance that would accompany the woman to her marriage bed. Most, however, departed in hasty embarrassment when simple incantations of truth revealed their gross exaggerations and outright lies.

But a few of the envoys, perhaps more aware than the others of the Azal'Lan's abilities, spoke the same truth before and after the incantations.

And of these few speakers of the truth, the most truthful was the ambassador from one Count Delaric. He also represented one of the most attractive candidates, as evidenced by the miniature he carried with him of the would-be bride, a pretty, slender, blue-eyed young woman, her sharp features framed by golden hair.

"Her name is Olessa, you say?" Firan asked after a moment's study of the tiny portrait.

Delaric's ambassador bowed low and said, "Yes, my lord. Lovely, is she not? And her dowry is *very* generous: five thousand crowns and numerous birthright lands and livings. The count her father also is prepared to sign a treaty of mutual defense, drawing upon his close bloodlinks with ruling houses from Kaport Bay to Rauxes."

"Later. I am more interested in his daughter's fruitfulness."

The envoy smiled confidently. "The Lady Olessa is descended from a most honorable and fertile race. Its females always bear healthy sons."

"And she is anxious to bear mine?"

The envoy hesitated. "She will obey her father in all things," he said uneasily.

"But not with eagerness? Is that what your words suggest?" Never one to step back from a potential challenge, Firan was intrigued. Here was a challenge the like of which he had never experienced: the challenge of winning the heart of a reluctant woman. It would, he imagined, be more difficult than the defeat of a rival wizard or any other operation on the battlefield, yet certainly achievable.

The envoy swallowed nervously, then nodded. "It is true," he said, "as you would no doubt soon learn elsewhere. The Lady Olessa is enamored of another, but the count will not let that stand in the way of this union. Indeed, he has opposed that other and welcomes your attentions."

"I see," Firan said softly, and then, after a moment's consideration, "Very well, give me the lock of her hair you were told to bring."

Still uneasy, the ambassador placed the golden strands in Firan's hands, and Firan waved him from the room.

Since Firan had located Prince Edron, nearly a decade

had passed, and the sorcerer had refined his ability in such matters even further. Pressing the golden hair closely against his forehead, he loosed his Sight.

Within moments, while his mortal eyes continued to keep close watch on the door through which the envoy had retreated, his Sight was soaring through the cloudless sky, unseen and unhindered by distance.

Even as he heard the envoy begin pacing nervously beyond the door, his Sight swooped soundlessly into an apartment in Delaric Castle, many leagues distant from Knurl.

Olessa was even younger and fresher than her portrait implied. But her beauty was temporarily marred by tears of anger as her maid tried to calm and comfort her. "There, there, Precious," the old nurse said. "It is no good reddening your eyes that way, my dear. If your father commands it—"

"I will not obey!" Olessa wiped away her tears with a clenched fist. "I *refuse* to be sold to an aged charlatan as though I were nothing but a—a brood mare!"

She shook her head violently, her blonde tresses flying. "And I will *not* be!" she said, her voice lowering in volume but not in intensity. "Tomorrow night, Eritai, I escape from this horrid place! Parras has everything planned. At full dark, I will slip out of the castle through the secret gate in the garden. Parras shall have fast horses waiting just beyond the walls, and we will ride like the wind to the north country, where Father's patrols cannot reach us! Oh, promise you will help us, Eritai! And that you will keep our secret! If Father learns of our plans—"

"He will not, Precious, not from my lips! But consider what you are doing. . . ."

Olessa's naive romanticism amused Firan. It would

indeed be a challenge to not only win her heart but also to mold that starry-eyed girl into a wife worthy of the Azal'Lan. He would tutor her patiently, as long as needed, guiding her to a mature understanding of him and the world. He would begin with the easiest task, that of disabusing her of the false belief that he was a "charlatan." Once his true nature was made clear to her, her tractability in other areas should increase markedly.

But even before that, there was a purely practical matter to be dealt with.

Letting his Sight fade from his consciousness, he called loudly for the envoy to return.

"Do you know a Parras of Delaric?" he asked as the envoy reentered the room.

The ambassador blinked, obviously startled. "How—" he began, but cut himself off. "He is Baron Venturian's fourth son," he said warily.

"Of great import?"

The ambassador shook his head. "His family has some modest country holdings and an adequate pedigree, but they lack any true significance in our affairs of state."

"Then I imagine your master will have few regrets when this insignificant fourth son ceases to appear at court—particularly when you reveal to the count that the young villain was planning to spirit the Lady Olessa away as his bride."

The envoy's jaw dropped. "My lord, it is indeed Parras of whom the Lady Olessa is foolishly enamored, but how did you know?"

Firan smiled thinly. "Few things are beyond my ken, Ambassador."

The envoy swallowed audibly. "When is this—this elopement to be?"

"They have laid plans for tomorrow night."

"Then we are lost! My swiftest courier could not reach Delaric in less than two days, my lord! I cannot warn the count in time to—"

"Calm yourself," Firan said dryly. "With your able assistance, I will deal with the matter myself. You may inform the count of what we have done here when you return."

"But I do not understand!" the ambassador protested.

"Nor need you."

Without warning, the sorcerer splayed out his spidery fingers across the startled envoy's forehead.

"Concentrate," he told the man. "You have visited the Venturian estates, have you not? Then concentrate on them. Think of nothing else."

The envoy, heart pounding, tried to do as he was instructed, and eventually the sorcerer said, "Good . . . that is good. I shall have no difficulty in locating the young man." He released the shaken ambassador and stood back.

"Now, go! Be on your way to inform your master of Parras's treachery. Inform him also that Olessa is my chosen bride."

Firan smiled in satisfaction as the ambassador scurried from the room. Then, after a leisurely sating of his palate with the finest vintages and an assortment of costly dainties, he sent forth his Sight to locate the upstart Parras Venturian.

* * * * *

When the fourth son of Baron Venturian died in a mysterious hunting accident, Olessa, as Firan had foreseen, was shattered by grief. As he had not foreseen, however, she flatly refused her father's orders when the count, ignoring her screams and tears, ordered her to prepare for travel.

When she refused, the count proceeded to have his daughter beaten into obedience, but her punishment was cut short when Firan's Sight came upon it. In a moment, the effects of the beatings were lifted from Olessa's body and heaped upon the one who had administered them.

This action did convince her that Firan was no charlatan, but it did little to win her heart. "If you truly desire my gratitude, my Lord Azal'Lan," she said coldly to the ghostly image he had projected into her room, "resurrect Parras and reunite me with him."

"Some things are beyond even my powers," he told her, withdrawing to allow her to grieve alone, neglecting to tell her that, regardless of his powers and her pleas, her would-be lover would remain forever beyond her reach.

A month he waited, showering her with gifts, hoping still that she would come to her senses, but it was not to be. In the end, only the count's threats of torture and death, not against her but against Eritai, the old nurse and her only true confidante, were sufficient to send her forth to Knurl, dowered and closely guarded by a picked army of retainers whose loyalty to her father and to the Azal'Lan was unquestioned.

Azal'Lan's township of Knurl, all unknowing, greeted his betrothed with joyous festivals that lasted for weeks. Oddly, though she refused to warm to her soon-to-be groom, her smiles when she was in the company of the festival-goers were genuine, and they in turn came quickly to adore her.

The formal ceremonies, however, were far from joyous. Conducted with considerably more decorum, they were held in the privacy of Castle Galdliesh, witnessed only by the richest and most influential, with whom Olessa, though she always maintained a civil demeanor, was obviously less enamored than she was with the peasants in the streets.

She even seemed indifferent to the priceless cloth of gold in which she was attired and to the fortune in gems that Firan had bestowed upon her.

The true hollowness of his triumph, however, was made clear to him on the wedding night and many nights to follow. Though he veiled himself and their private rooms in a magical glamour calculated to arouse any woman to the heights of passion, his bride lay in his arms like a marble statue. It was only for the sake of Eritai's continued well-being that she submitted to him, and not even his spells could coax any show of genuine affection from her. Even bestowing gallows-gathered life energy upon the old nurse had no effect, and he soon began to suspect that winning her heart was one challenge he would never be able to meet.

Even more disturbing was the fact that she did not conceive. Even her adamantine unresponsiveness could be tolerated if only she gave him a son. To that end, he consulted endless chirurgeons and witches adept in women's mysteries, but to no avail. Even his own vast arsenal of sorcery produced no discernible results.

Still, he was not one to surrender easily or quickly once he had accepted a challenge. Additionally, in sharp contrast to her private demeanor, her public face was faultless, particularly when dealing with the peasantry. Among that fickle-minded group, she was equally as popular as he, perhaps even more so, and he knew that to discard her and choose another would not be accepted. He could, of course, proceed in the face of their anger and that of her father and his allies, citing her barrenness as good and sufficient reason, but he preferred otherwise.

As the weeks became months and the months gathered into years, his bafflement and irritation turned into frustrated anger, but that anger only increased his determination, particularly on those occasions when Olessa would say disingenuously, "Perhaps it is the will of the gods that I am barren."

"You have seen the esteem in which I hold them and their priestly representatives," he said, his voice laden with sarcasm as he recalled with long-held rage the death of his brother.

Essentially the same exchange was made a hundred times, until one day something he had not seen before glittered in the depths of her blue eyes. "If the fault lies not with the gods," she added with the faintest trace of a smile, "then perhaps, since your physicians and witches have found no fault with me, my failure to conceive is the fault of another."

For a moment, her words were a meaningless puzzle to him, but when their meaning became clear, his mind reeled.

Was it possible? Fear was a sudden ache in his belly. *Could* the blame be his? His physicians had not investigated that possibility, nor could they. Neither was there a spell to determine such things, at least none that he had discovered.

"May I go, my lord?" she asked quietly. "I have a consort's duties to perform—a gathering this afternoon of the Honored Matrons of Knurl."

Smothering a curse, he waved his assent and watched her descend the tower stairs. She moved at a leisurely pace, regal, cool, and untouchable, caring not that she had shaken him to his core.

And he remembered, without ever having forgotten, that Quantarius had been childless. "My life was not one that could be well shared with a wife," the old sorcerer had said dismissively, and Firan had thought nothing of it.

But now . . .
Now he could think of nothing else.

* * * * *

Slowly the months and years crept by.

A decade passed, one of fairly steady progress for Knurl, occasionally punctuated by internal feuding and brief, violent external upsets. None of these events seriously troubled Firan's rule, for his arts were equal to such petty challenges. His people were proud of their Azal'Lan, the first to rule in the land for more than a century. The law was scrupulously obeyed, particularly in the aftermath of one of Firan's notoriously harsh public punishments of condemned criminals. The Malachite Throne, more than content with the taxes he rendered and the levies he sent to serve in the overlord's forces, never interfered. Neighboring rulers both envied and feared him.

And yet he knew no pleasure in life, knowing that, unless he succeeded in producing and properly raising an heir, he would be no better than his father or his unlamented, gluttonous brother.

Outwardly uncomplaining, Olessa accompanied him on numerous secret hunts through the depths of herb lore and darker magics. She willingly drank foul potions and endured grotesque experiments, as did he, in their futile efforts to engender an heir. So-called experts boasting of mastery in these arts died by the dozens, often at Firan's own hands, for that was sometimes the only solace to his fury and anguish in the wake of yet another failure.

He imagined that his subjects were laughing behind his back and making crude jokes at his expense. The thought was a knife in his vitals, racking him with chagrin. The mighty Azal'Lan, who could destroy men with a crook of his finger, unable to sire a son to rule when he was gone!

In his desperation, he went so far as to bespell a hapless peasant woman already proven fertile and take his will of her. If he could beget a bastard from her, then he would know that the fault after all lay with Olessa and would know that he must discard her, no matter how much upset it would cause.

But the peasant woman did not conceive, not even after numerous attempts. Unlike the boastful experts, she was allowed to live, with only her memory of the incidents removed.

Firan filled his days and nights with matters of state and sorcery, studying, practicing, honing his arts, searching out new knowledge, ever in hopes of finding the one bit that would salvage his life and give it meaning. But acquiring knowledge gave satisfaction in and of itself, truly the only real satisfaction he could find now.

And then, in the twenty-fifth year of his reign and the seventeenth of his barren and loveless marriage, he stumbled upon a priceless bit of magic. Its origins were lost, but he suspected it had been created by a jealous man. With this spell, a wizard could trap his wife's entire past history in a mirror of polished obsidian. In that glistening black glass, he could then discover the one thing he most desired to know about that woman—the identities of paramours or whether or not she had betrayed him to his foes, for example. When he had pinpointed what he sought, the practitioner could either destroy his erring spouse or simply erase the event itself, making it as though it had never been except for a slowly fading memory.

A strange spell indeed, Firan reflected, though he did not expect it to be of any great use. Until he had found that the reason for Olessa's inability to conceive was not within herself but within him, he would have fallen on this bit of magic with glad cries, but no more. Still, his curiosity goaded him on, and he focused his will and spoke the words to initiate this odd magic.

What would the glass decide he most desired to know? Intrigued, he peered intently into the shining darkness and saw a younger Olessa huddled in furtive conference with a gypsy. Their voices sounded eerily insubstantial, like reflections of the tiny images themselves, and Firan strained to hear what they said.

"Once this is done, you cannot undo it," the gypsy warned. She glanced nervously over her shoulder and added, "I like not this meeting. If the wizard who would have you for his bride discovers us—"

"I care not," Olessa said, tossing a heavy purse onto the table. "There is more silver than you can earn elsewhere in a lifetime. Make me barren and resistant to all his loathsome enchantments, and to be doubly sure, make him unable to beget a child as well." She bowed her head and wept so softly the sound was lost in the obsidian. "My dearest wish was to bear Parras a son. But he is dead, and my father has betrayed me. My only wish now is that my womb remain empty until I join Parras in another life. It is the only way I can honor him now."

And the gypsy, after a discreet glance into the purse, began.

When the images faded, Firan was speechless with rage, his fists clenched so tightly blood trickled from his palms.

All those barren years! The torture he had undergone! All because of gypsy magic worked upon a foolish, grieving young woman!

But it was not too late, now that he knew the secret. . . .

With supreme effort, he mastered his anger and murmured the words that completed the mirror spell and erased from reality the events it had just displayed.

And Olessa was no longer barren.

A vengeful smile bloomed on Firan's sharp face. His wife, lovely still, had never denied him his conjugal rights, though he had almost abandoned that privilege during these last few years. Tonight he would demand them once again. She would probably be surprised, but not as surprised as she would be when the outcome became apparent.

And lest she then seek to undo his work as a magician and a man . . .

Firan focused anew, weaving an unbreakable charm, ensuring that once with child, Olessa *must* carry it to term and deliver it successfully. Seventeen years had been wasted, but his treacherous wife now was under an absolute compulsion to bear the son he would sire tonight.

For the first time in all those years, his heart was filled with a cold, controlled joy as visions of Olessa's payment for her crime danced in his mind.

* * * * *

The pregnancy was difficult, and Firan made it no easier. Knowing that the memory of her dealings with the gypsy would fade unless it were constantly renewed, he reminded her daily and gloated of his final victory. Each reminder only redoubled her desire to destroy the thing that grew within her womb, but the spell was too strong, even as her anger and frustration grew during those nine months to match what Firan had experienced for the last seventeen years. Even so, she maintained the same adamantine silence that she had maintained throughout all the years of their couplings.

The labor was long and even more difficult than the pregnancy, though Firan's spells could easily have eased her pain. In time, the midwives began to fear for her life, but he was unmoved.

"No matter," he said grimly, "so long as my son survives."

When it was clear that the moment was imminent, he leaned close to her sweat-streaked face, twisted in agony by the effort that his spells were forcing upon her.

"There is something else you should know," he whispered. "The death of young Parras was not an accident, nor was it the doing of your father. It was mine and mine alone, done with the same magic that now forces you to bear my son."

The stone and ice with which she had sheathed her spirit for seventeen years cracked with a terrible scream, and even the spells Firan held her under were not enough to keep her from thrashing wildly as she hurled curses at him. Only the combined strength of the midwives could pin her bodily until the fragile burden she bore could emerge.

With her last breath, she spat at his vulpine face, the saliva equally mixed with blood. As she fell back, her tangled golden hair further dampening the pillow already stained with her blood, there was a tiny wail, growing louder and stronger with each second.

The midwives sobbed, grieving, even as they swaddled a tiny red-faced lump of humanity—the son she had been forced to die to bring forth.

The chief midwife held out the long-sought child, and Firan gathered the baby into his arms. Adoringly he gazed at the wizened little face.

"Irik," he murmured, nuzzling the infant's delicately soft

face. "Your name shall be Irik, the same as my dear lost brother. Irik Zal'honan, son of Firan Zal'honan, Azal'Lan of Knurl."

His courtiers cleared a path to the adjacent balcony, and Firan stepped out to the railing. He cradled the newborn in his arms and presented Knurl's next ruler to a cheering populace.

FIFTEEN

308–327 CY

Irik's early childhood was a special time for Firan, a
haven amid the turmoil of steadily increasing political ten-
sions. As the years passed, the boy not only came to resem-
ble his namesake physically but also to exhibit the same
sunny good nature. Everyone loved the lad.

Though he did not inherit his father's gift for sorcery,
Irik was highly intelligent and quick to learn. However, to
his father's dismay, he could also be idealistically stubborn,
not unlike his late mother. He also seemed to have inherited
her preference for the company of peasants to that of the
more highborn, and no matter what lectures Firan delivered, no matter what punishment he meted out, the boy
would not yield in that preference.

The first time Firan became seriously concerned for the
boy, however, was shortly after his tenth birthday, on the
day an object lesson was to be delivered to certain increasingly fractious clans.

After only five years of peace among the clans, petty
fighting had once again broken out, and a young boy of
Irik's age, belonging to neither clan, had been killed by an

arrow meant for another. Within hours, Firan had summoned the leaders of the two clans whose members had been involved and given them a choice: offer up the one who loosed the errant arrow or offer up themselves. While one, though scowling, scurried off to locate the guilty party, the other, whose memory was obviously even shorter than his temper, was defiant.

The next day, Firan announced a double execution, to be held in the town square for all to see. Attendance by all clan leaders within a day's ride was mandatory, as was attendance by all members of the two clans whose arrows had claimed the innocent boy's life.

It was time, Firan decided, for his son's serious education to begin. It was particularly appropriate for him to bear witness to this execution, he thought, because Irik had, albeit against his father's wishes, been acquainted with the slain boy.

But to Firan's dismay, Irik was far from appreciative of the fact that justice was being done. Instead, despite his father's stern admonitions, he hid his face as the one who had loosed the fatal arrow—a headstrong young man of seventeen—was having his life snuffed out by an arrow driven into his heart by the father of the slain boy. Nor would he uncover his eyes when the short-tempered clan leader met his more conventional fate at the hands of the headsman.

"You cannot hide from the world," Firan lectured sternly as they returned to Castle Galdliesh. "Nor can you shirk your responsibility to that world and its people, as did my brother. Without a leader—a *strong* leader, and just—the ordinary folk are helpless. Open your eyes, boy! Border raiders plague us, and Bone March and Nyrond are constantly rattling their sabers, as they will doubtless continue to do. And even if those external threats were removed, even if the people were not victimized and preyed upon by villains, they would flounder and fall victim to their own weaknesses."

He regaled the boy with tales of the chaos that Ranald's neglect had led to, the chaos that only Firan's own firm hand had been able to quell.

But the boy seemed unmoved by his father's reasoning, not only in the aftermath of the execution he had refused to watch but also for three long years after. More than once, as his father tried to discuss upcoming decisions with the boy, Irik pleaded for leniency for one petty lawbreaker after another. He continued to refuse to observe the punishment, whether it be the headsman's block or a simple flogging, unless compelled by minor enchantments.

And the sunny disposition that had been the child's hallmark, and Firan's delight, for the first years of his life faded into unrelenting gloom.

Firan began to despair. He doubted that, even with the continuing infusions of life energy, there would ever be another heir to the Zal'honan name. He even considered enchantments, though he knew that such things could bring about only obedience, not a change in the boy's heart. And without such a change, Irik would never be capable of ruling. His soft heart—his *weakness*—would make even the day-to-day decisions impossible for him to make logically.

But then, a few days after the boy's thirteenth birthday, at the execution of a petty thief whose name Firan could not even remember, everything changed. As Firan was preparing the small enchantment that would keep his son's eyes open and trained on the block, Irik shook his head.

"Your compulsion will not be required, Father," he said quietly.

Firan's heart leaped. Had the boy finally come to his senses?

"You are willing to observe the punishment?" Firan asked, skeptical in the face of his hopes.

"I am," the boy said solemnly, his blue eyes harder than his father had ever seen them.

"Is there a reason for this change of heart?"

The boy swallowed and nodded. "The one to die is known to me, Father, as is the reason for his crimes. It is as you have so often said: He wished to prey upon those weaker than himself."

"And how did you reach this conclusion?"

"He told me so himself, not in words, perhaps, but in his actions."

"And you now feel he deserves his fate?"

The boy swallowed again. "I fear that he does, though I surely take no joy in that fact."

Firan nodded. "Nor should you. Death is a solemn business. The only joy one can take in today's display is that the example it sets keeps others from following the same path into thievery."

"I pray that it does," Irik said, his hard blue eyes returning now to the block and the waiting headsman.

In light of the sudden change, Firan considered an enchantment to verify the truth of his son's words, but he could not bring himself to pronounce the incantation, perhaps—though he could never admit it to himself—because he feared what that truth might prove to be.

He would watch closely, and if the boy wavered, gave any indication of weakness, there would be time aplenty for wringing the truth from him.

Gradually Firan's skepticism faded as the boy remained steadfast in his newfound common sense and began to take an interest in the affairs of government, something Firan had vainly tried to encourage for years. Gone for good, however, was the sunny disposition that had dominated the boy's early years, and while Firan often regretted its absence, he soon decided that it was more than a fair trade for what had been gained: a sense of responsibility, a feeling for justice, an ability to face and deal with the harsh realities of life. All were absolute essentials for the one who would one day rule Knurl, indeed for anyone who aspired to rule any country, no matter how large or small.

And Knurl, despite everything Firan had done, was becoming increasingly difficult to rule. His edicts no longer quelled unrest as they had in the earlier years of his reign. The severest punishment had less and less effect. Public executions, once his most effective tool, began to fail him. Instead of inspiring fear and caution in all, they inexplicably seemed to breed only increased resistance, even among the families of the executed. Rebellion seethed below the surface of Knurl's body politic like a festering wound, too deep and too inflamed for even his sorcery to fully control.

Despite the difficulties, however, Firan was at last content, knowing that his son was at his side in all things and would be, in spite of a lack of sorcerous talent, a worthy successor.

But then, days before Irik's nineteenth birthday, Firan's chief of security came to him, a look of unease on his weathered features as Firan looked up from the diplomatic letters he was reading.

"Well? What have you to report?"

"As you know, my lord, we have been investigating a conspiracy whose eventual aim was to smuggle a number of Nyrondese traitors of the clan Kirilarien across the border to their home."

Firan nodded impatiently. It was a matter of small import, whether half a dozen minor troublemakers were caught and executed or escaped to Nyrond, where they would make no more trouble. Dozens had already been dispatched, and their movement was dying.

"I take it you captured them?" Firan prompted irritably. "Else why are you here?"

The chief nodded, shifting his feet nervously. "One and all," he said. "The sorcerer we engaged was able to use the spell you provided with utmost effectiveness. Their sense of direction was completely addled, just as you said it would be, my lord. They wandered about aimlessly, like ants whose nest has been trodden upon. It was a simple matter to round them up."

"Very good," Firan said, turning his attention back to his papers in dismissal. "Deal with them as we have already dealt with their comrades."

"I fear there is more, my lord," the security chief said, an unsteadiness creeping into his voice.

"Well?" Firan snapped, looking up again. "If there is something you feel I must be told, then tell me!"

The chief cleared his throat, working up the courage to speak. "There were more than the half dozen we anticipated, my lord. There were nearly a score of Nyrondese, including the leader of the clan, and—and they were being escorted by nearly a dozen of our own, including members of the nobility, some of extreme rank and importance."

Firan scowled. "Do you have doubt of their guilt?"

"None, my lord, but—"

"Then your course is clear. They will be publicly executed, as have those before them."

The chief was almost trembling now. "I have brought one of them here, my lord. I—I did not feel it my place to—"

"It is not your place to continue testing my patience! Now, what is it you wish? I ask for the last time, before your name is added to the headsman's list!"

The chief froze for an instant, then drew himself to rigid attention. In a loud voice, he called, "Chetan, bring in the leader of the conspirators!"

The door the chief had entered through minutes before swung open, and Firan gasped, as if struck by a mighty blow.

His hands bound, his head held high, Irik Zal'honan stepped into the room before the quaking Chetan.

SIXTEEN

The castle gates swung open at daybreak, and the people of Knurl poured into the courtyard a thousand strong. The morning sun, barely clear of the eastern hills, gave the castle towers an ominously bloody tinge as, in the shadows below, the headsman, his craggy face bare of the usual leather mask, massive axe resting rigidly over his shoulder, stood waiting on the broad granite terrace that overlooked the courtyard. The anticipatory murmur of the crowd echoed from the parapets as the first in the human wave halted at the foot of the steps less than a dozen yards from the wooden chopping blocks that lined the edge of the terrace.

When the courtyard was filled and the last straggler edged in and stood pressed against the cold stone of the outer wall, a small wooden door opened at the base of the castle wall below and to the left of the terrace. One by one, their ankles shackled, the prisoners emerged and laboriously trudged up the narrow steps to the rear of the terrace and then across the broad expanse to where their assigned blocks waited. One by one, fettered by the chains, they lurched into a kneeling position behind the blocks.

Except for one.

Tall and beardless, his blond hair falling loose over his forehead, the final prisoner, his legs unshackled, crossed to the final block and stood erect, his eyes staring over the heads of the crowd.

A louder murmur spread through the crowd as first one, then another, recognized the Azal'Lan's son and hastily nudged his neighbor.

Slowly the sun crept higher, the shadow of the courtyard wall retreating down the front of the castle and then, even more slowly, across the terrace toward the kneeling, sometimes trembling prisoners.

Finally, when the first ray of the sun struck the headsman's axe, the crimson drapes at the rear of the royal balcony parted for an instant, then flowed together as if they had never been apart. The Azal'Lan, his jeweled crown glinting in the sunlight, thickly furred robe gathered about his shoulders, stood for a moment looking around the crowded courtyard. His eyes drifted across the line of prisoners, pausing only momentarily on the one who remained standing.

He nodded at the headsman.

The murmur of the crowd became a muffled roar.

And it began.

Each time the axe fell and a body went limp, the head smacking onto the granite terrace, the sounds of the crowd became louder and more exuberant, building to a screaming chant of approval.

When finally the headsman, his boots slick with blood, came to the last block, a hush fell over the crowd. Irik stood straight, his eyes still staring, unseeing, out over the masses, waiting for the order to kneel. The headsman looked nervously to where his king still stood on the balcony, alone before the drawn crimson drapes.

For a full minute, the tableau held, the only sound the anticipatory shifting of a thousand pairs of feet.

Abruptly Azal'Lan's robe parted and a raised right hand emerged, palm out, an unmistakable gesture to stay the axe. A disappointed murmur rose from the crowd while the headsman, unable to repress a sigh of relief, slumped momentarily, then stiffened to await dismissal.

But it did not come.

Instead, Azal'Lan turned sharply, thrust aside the drapes, and strode from the balcony. Puzzled and nervous, the headsman waited. The murmur from the crowd grew to a rumble. Near the far end of the line of blocks, one of the bodies spasmed inexplicably, its hand slapping against its fallen head, sending it bounding bloodily down the steps. Screams, not of approval this time, rose from the crowd, and the wall of people in the front surged backward in movements as spasmodic as those of the body, forcing those at the rear hard against the wall, gasping for breath.

The head came to rest in a shallow depression, where the closest had stood watching the axe fall. Its eyes, jarred open by the tumble, stared blindly up at the retreating spectators.

The huge oak and iron castle door creaked and stirred. All eyes, even those of watchers still pressing backward from the errant head, shot to the door. Ponderously it began to grate open.

It was barely ajar when Azal'Lan strode out. His furred cape was swung back over his shoulders, freeing his arms. In the same hand that had halted the headsman's axe was held a broad-bladed, curved sword, its ornate grip nearly as jewel-heavy as his crown.

As he strode forward, he waved the headsman aside.

He halted where the headsman had stood. He motioned for his son to kneel.

For a long moment, Irik remained standing. He turned his face toward his father. "I forgive you," he said softly, his voice carrying only to the nearest in the crowd.

"But I cannot forgive what you did," Firan said, "the deceit you practiced, nor what you have become."

Irik bowed his head, eyes closed. "Nonetheless, I still forgive you."

Gracefully, regretfully, he dropped to his knees and laid his head on the block.

Firan moved into position next to the block. He raised the massive, razor-sharp blade.

"Let all who witness my action today," he said, his voice suddenly stentorian, driving all else to silence, "take forth the word that justice and the law apply equally to all!"

With the final word, he brought the blade down in a glittering, deadly arc. Blood spurted, spraying his boots as the body twitched and the head pitched, faceup, to the granite of the terrace.

Its eyes, in Firan's mind, focused on his face as the lips once again offered the unattainable forgiveness.

The crowd, utterly silent during the act, erupted into a frenzy of cheering, then fell silent again as their Azal'Lan abruptly turned his face from them and strode back across the terrace, his footprints recorded in his son's blood.

Minutes later, when all the bodies but one had been removed, a shimmering gray haze rose up out of the blood-stained granite, drifting and thickening until the entire terrace was hidden from all prying eyes. When finally it lifted in five days' time, all the blocks but one were gone. Behind the one remaining, a pedestal of solid marble rose from the gray granite of the terrace. Atop the pedestal lay a sarcophagus, elaborately and intricately carved of the very stone on which the block had stood.

There was no name carved on pedestal or sarcophagus, but no one doubted what lay within, nor for whom the brief and anonymous service, unattended by the king, was performed that night at sunset.

* * * * *

For four eon-long nights, Firan longed for sleep, yet feared mightily that it would come.

On the fifth night, when the few mourners brave enough to reveal themselves at the service had long since departed, shadows formed in the upper reaches of his sleeping chamber, shadows much like those he himself had summoned as a child, but shadows that had, this time, come unsummoned.

And a voice spoke out of the shadows.

"Do you have no doubts, Father? No doubts at all?" it asked.

And when, knowing it was not his son, he did not reply, a second voice emerged. "You worked your hateful magic on my womb to create him, and yet now you have slain him."

And a third, high-pitched and childlike: "You could have saved him with even greater ease than you could have saved me, my brother, had you so chosen. And yet you did not. Were we both so evil in your eyes that we deserved such deaths?"

"Perhaps it is behind your eyes that evil exists," the voices said in Quantarius's kindly tones, "rather than in the world before them."

"My son was not evil!" Firan shouted, finally goaded into

responding. "He was weak! And for one in his position, that is even worse! Evil can be rooted out and defeated, but weakness is insidious! Until it is tested, it cowers undetected. But when the time comes and evil confronts it, it fails, and evil flowers!"

"Is his weakness not your own?" his long-forgotten father's voice asked. "Did you not sire him? Did you not raise him? Did you not instill in him your deepest values?"

"No more than you were capable of instilling yours in me!" Firan shouted.

The voices laughed, as none had ever laughed in life. "You were as great a failure, then, as I," his father's voice taunted. "Is that a sign of your strength?"

"Who *are* you?" Firan screamed. "What do you want of me? Have I not suffered enough?"

"Only you can say, Father. Only you can know how much you have suffered and whether it is sufficient for your crimes."

"I have committed no crimes! I have upheld the law! I have meted out justice!"

"Then you have no regrets, Father?"

"Of course I have regrets! Your betrayal—my *son's* betrayal—was a source of greatest anguish, as was his death—his *necessary* death!"

"But your own actions, Father, your own actions. Is there nothing you would have done differently?"

"I would have controlled him more closely. I would have somehow taught him more thoroughly! If I had known of his weakness, I would have burned it out of him!"

"And if you were given a second chance?"

"There will be no more chances! I have seen ninety-six winters, and even my magic will not provide another Zal'honan heir!"

"You doubt your powers, Firan?" The voice of Quantarius, tinged with a sarcasm he had never employed in life, took up the questioning. "I do not remember a time in all our years together that you expressed the slightest doubt in your abilities."

"I was younger then and did not know the cruelty of life."

The Quantarius voice laughed, as if at a secret joke. "We speak not of a new life but of a second chance with the one you sired and slew."

Firan shook his head angrily. "My magic will not raise the dead, any more than it will produce another heir."

"Perhaps not. But there is more magic in the world than you yet possess."

"But little! I have spent my life searching, and there is little I do not possess!"

The voices laughed again in chorus. "You have spent your life searching, and yet you have never come to *us*," the Quantarius voice said.

"You are my own delusions! Soon you will be gone!"

"And if we are real? If we can give you your heart's desire? Would you spurn us?"

Hope flared within Firan. Was it possible?

"Ah!" the Quantarius voice chuckled. "You doubt our unreality despite your words."

"*Prove* that you are real!"

"You think you can command us, Father?" Irik's voice was filled with an iron defiance it had never held in life.

"Then tell me what it is you offer."

"Your heart's desire," the voices chorused against a background of muffled laughter.

"And what is that, if you know me so well?"

"To gain new powers. To never know the grave."

"The power to restore my son to life?"

"If you wish it. But it will not be easy or simple. You will need to use to the utmost what powers you already possess. You will need to labor mightily. And you will need to *believe*, else you will fail."

"Then give me a reason to believe!"

Again there was the muffled laughter, this time chilling his spine. "For Irik's sake," his son's voice said, "we will. We will give you the first necessity, which ordinarily you would have to construct with your own hands."

In the far corner of the room, where the shadows were deepest, they deepened even more, and one of the shadows drew in upon itself and seemed to grow solid and detach itself from the others, forming a tiny cloud of blackness. It floated toward the bed where Firan sat upright.

It settled in his outstretched hand, and he felt its icy weight.

And he felt sleep coming, the first in five long days.

He struggled to keep his eyes from closing, but he could not. He could feel the thing in his hand shifting, squirming like the mummified *shasheek* more than eighty years ago. Through the shrinking slits between his eyelids, he saw the shadow in his hand begin to dissipate, swirling back to reveal what lay beneath. Something golden and horned and writhing was the last thing he saw before sleep overtook him.

* * * * *

When Firan awakened, night was again falling.

He shuddered at the startlingly vivid memory of the nightmare—the voices of the long dead and the newly dead, the taunting, the shadow solidifying in his hand. . . .

He gasped.

On the silken cover of the bed, next to his right hand, lay a tiny golden skull of a horned dragon.

Gingerly he touched it, and the muffled laughter of his nightmare filled the chamber.

It had been real.

Or he was still dreaming.

Or insane.

He grasped the skull tightly, the horns pressing painfully into his palm until blood trickled through his fingers.

It was real.

And as the laughter faded, he "remembered" a thousand things that had never happened. And he "remembered" a thousand things that he had never been told, and yet he knew they must be done if he were to obtain his heart's desire.

The golden skull was the gift of—of whatever power lurked behind the voices.

As was the "memory" of what he must do, the spells he must cast, the ingredients he must find.

Perhaps he *was* insane.

But it didn't matter.

He had, he realized now, slain the one living thing on Oerth that mattered to him, and if he was sane, this was his only chance for getting it back. If he was not, there was nothing more he could lose.

Conjuring up a parchment scroll and quill, he began to write before his "memories" could fade.

* * * * *

For more than a year, Firan worked, memorizing spells as he had never memorized a spell before. There could be no error, no lapse of memory, no loss of concentration at a vital moment. And in this complex task, every moment was vital, every moment of every spell.

Emissaries were sent to every corner of the Flanaess and returned with magical ingredients—herbs and powders and roots and bones and countless more objects of all descriptions. For less savory objects, the nature of which he dared not share with even his most trusted lieutenants, he ventured forth in a cloak of anonymity and secured them himself and locked them away in his chambers under the most powerful of protective and preservational spells.

Finally all was collected.

Everyone, from most trusted advisor to lowest scullery maid, was sent from the castle, all doors bolted behind them. The shadows and their damnable voices, if they returned, would be distraction enough.

But they did not return, though occasionally a ripple of muffled laughter echoed in the spell-choked air.

Finally the spells had all been cast and all actions taken save one.

The one from which there was no turning back.

Lingeringly he caressed the tiny golden skull, now suspended from a golden chain about his neck—the repository of his soul, or so said the voices. Soon he would know if the truth lay in their words or in their laughter.

With both hands, he lifted the carven metal chalice, filled with the nauseating, roiling yellow brew, from the bench on which he had spent the last dozen hours mixing it. Slowly he carried it through the deserted rooms and halls to the royal balcony.

For several minutes, he stood in the moonlight, looking out over the city in the valley spread out before him. And at the granite sarcophagus on the terrace barely a dozen yards below, the focus now of all things.

"If I never again see you in this life, I will surely see you in the next."

And he drank, fighting to keep the foul-smelling brew from being spewed out the moment it touched his tongue.

He swallowed, clamping his lips tightly together. His stomach churned, and sweat suddenly poured from his clammy skin, worse than the worst fever he had ever fallen victim to. His head felt as if it were about to explode.

He drank again.

And again.

As the last draft passed his lips and the now empty and corroded chalice clanged to the floor of the balcony, he had to clamp his hands on his jaw and throat to keep it down. His entire body was wracked with nausea, and as the heat of the fever left, it was replaced in an instant by a blanket of ice that enveloped him like the approaching death it was.

And the shadows formed in the air around him.

"Welcome, Firan Zal'honan," the voices chorused, and the laughter came again. "Welcome to immortality. . . ."

Finally, blessedly, unconsciousness claimed him.

* * * * *

When he awakened, Firan began to learn the truth of what he had become.

His true appearance, he realized when his senses had fully returned, was now as hideous as the brew he had forced himself to drink.

"But you can cloak yourself in illusion, even to your own eyes," the voices said.

And he did.

He had no need for food or drink. Nevermore could

either pass the grim remnants of his lips.

He had no need for sleep. His eyes, glowing coals deep within their sockets, could never close again.

He could approach no living creature without that creature—beast of the field or human—shivering in fear. Never more could he feel the touch of living flesh that did not struggle to be free.

But he could still rule the land—and with even greater strength than before.

And he could accomplish feats of sorcery he had only dreamt of in his mortal life.

On the fifth night of his increasingly unsatisfactory resurrection, he stood before the sarcophagus, the laughter of the shadows echoing through the empty castle behind him as he began intoning the words of life.

The moon had barely cleared the courtyard wall when he detected the first sign that the words and gestures, recorded on the same scrolls as those that had led to his own transformation, were anything more than a final, cruel joke: a faint rustling sound from within the sarcophagus.

In his mind's eye, he saw the detached head, its relentlessly forgiving face no different than in the moments before the blade had fallen, shifting on the silken pillow until the stub of neck pressed itself into place atop the shoulders and sealed with a faint crackling of power that whispered through the stone to Firan's ears.

Hope surged within him, but even as it did, he could not help but realize that the sensation was a pale imitation of what it would have been had his unbeating heart been set to racing, had the lifeless nerves that could experience neither pain nor pleasure been set to tingling.

But it would suffice. The bargain had been struck, no matter how deceptively the shadows had spoken, and he could not, would not, rescind it even if he could, not for such trivialities.

The rustling grew louder, as if the entire body were shifting and writhing as the life-force reentered and filled it like wine pouring into a flaccid wineskin.

Firan raised his hands until they almost touched the massive sarcophagus cover that no mortal hand had strength to raise.

Slowly, with the bleak grating of stone on stone, the cover began to creep aside.

As the first rays of moonlight filtered through the widening opening into the sarcophagus, an anguished scream shattered the night.

And the muffled laughter of the shadows surged through Firan's mind.

"Why?" The single word emerged from the sarcophagus like a curse, stabbing into Firan's ears and mind alike.

A hand appeared, its misshapen fingers scraping at the edge of the sarcophagus as the cover continued to grate, inch by inch, to the side.

A face erupted into view as the body of his son lurched into a sitting position.

But it was not the remembered forgiving face. It was a face ravaged by months of rot and decay.

Were he still within a mortal body, Firan would have gasped and screamed. As it was, a chill descended on him, the like of which he had never experienced even in the death that had preceded his transformation.

"Why did you call me back?" The lips moved like grave worms, not living flesh.

"To give us both a second chance!" Firan pleaded.

"I want no second chance! I want only to be released!"

"You have to understand! You have to persevere!"

Firan's plea was met only with a moan of renewed anguish, and the piteous creature grasped at its head as if to rip it free once more. "I do not have your strength, Father, nor do I desire it!"

Firan spun to face the castle and the shifting shadows that now half obscured the crimson drapes behind the royal balcony.

"What trickery is this?" he roared. "He is no more alive than I! For him to exist in a form even more hideous than my own was not my wish!"

"You wished him returned from death, Zal'honan," the voices murmured in chorus. "If you wish for more, then you must yourself search out the means. You have already been given more than most men would ever dream of." The tiny golden skull glowed warmly on his chest.

"If I had known—"

"If the future were known, Zal'honan, what then would be the value in your vaunted strength and courage?"

Firan stiffened into iron rigidity.

He turned back to the sarcophagus and looked upon the thing that was emerging like a decaying caricature of a butterfly from a granite cocoon.

A silent gesture, and the stony grating of the cover ceased as it teetered on the verge of crashing to the terrace floor.

"I will find the means, my son," he said, his words as hard as the stone itself. "I will find the means to restore you to true life, not this travesty I have brought upon you now."

"No! My only wish is to be released! Your newfound sorcery drew me back from rest, and it can release me as well! I beg of you—"

"Be strong and be patient, and all will be well, I promise. I failed you once but I will not fail again!"

At a gesture, the decaying body went limp and fell from sight, the tattered fingers of its hand losing their grip on the edge of the sarcophagus. The cover, grating more loudly than ever, began to retrace its path.

A mist appeared, flowing out through the narrowing opening and hovering as the shadows had hovered in Firan's chamber, then swirling and darting upward like a frightened bird, only to fall back, exhausted and powerless. Again and again, as the cover continued to grate toward closure, the mist fluttered upward and fell back.

When the opening finally vanished, the mist continued to hover and then, for just a moment, seemed to take on Irik's pleading features.

Then it was gone, as if absorbed by the stone itself.

"I will not fail again," Firan repeated, turning from the sarcophagus, the glowing coals that were his eyes glaring at the shadows as they slowly faded from view. "I will find the means to restore you to true life, though I search forever. . . ."

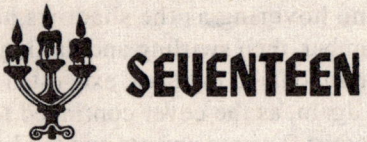

SEVENTEEN

329–391 CY

For threescore years, Firan Zal'honan searched.
And ruled.
And conquered.

Illusions cloaked his hideousness, but his undead aura still affected every living thing that came in contact with him. No animal could approach without descending into the spasms of primal fear, and even the bravest of his aides trembled in his presence. As time went by, he tired of the inevitable reaction to his very existence, the constant necessity of maintaining the illusion of humanity, and he withdrew from all but essential contact with others. Like a great spider, he lurked within his lair at Castle Galdliesh, manipulating Knurl's laws, trade, and wars through proxies and through sorcery.

Existing in an almost constant state of frustration and rage, he became feared as no previous leader of Knurl had ever been. Through conquest, he expanded his never-ending search for the spell that would restore his son to true life, not to the grotesque parody of life that he had accepted for himself. He seized the Teesar Valley, the Flinty and

Blemu Hills, the Adri Forest. When conquered peoples dared rebel, his Sight unerringly ferreted out the responsible parties and all their cohorts, and the resulting vengeance was so swift and savage it spawned legends. No one who survived these reprisals ever challenged him again. Even the Malachite Throne, which officially opposed such expansionism by any of its subject lands, did nothing more than send an occasional envoy with a scolding letter, and Firan continued to follow his own path and no other's.

Though he protected Knurl from barbarian incursions and other invasions, a few citizens still complained about harsh laws. These he punished, though not as severely as he did those who spread seditious rumors that he was not quite . . . human. *That* truth must be suppressed at all costs. If his true nature ever became known, his superstitious subjects might rise against him in such revulsion and outrage, in such overwhelming numbers that even the most accomplished wizard could not put them down. Therefore he personally hunted down the tellers of such tales and slew them without mercy, then secretly returned their mutilated corpses to Castle Galdliesh where, using the same spell he had misguidedly used in his attempt to restore his son to life, he added them to his ever-growing army of the undead.

There were, of course, attempts on his life, as there had always been. In his present condition, he found it delightfully ironic that dozens would lose their own lives in attempts to assassinate a man already dead and then be added to the ranks of the undead themselves.

In one instance, the irony was redoubled when, after twenty years, the son of an executed clan leader attempted to avenge his father's death, only to be slain by the father's shambling corpse as it rose up to defend its master. From that time on, Firan saw to it that the two were never parted, their undead bodies forever standing double watch over the vault where all confiscated clan wealth, including what had once been their own, was kept.

Still, the core of his existence was the search, though he never revealed to anyone, not even the searchers themselves, the true reason for that search, letting them believe what they wished, neither affirming nor denying. Nonetheless, two generations of his most trusted agents constantly ranged far and wide, seeking out all necromancers and practitioners of black arts who claimed to know the secrets of resurrection. The majority of these were proven charlatans, the remainder self-deluded. The latter died quickly, their bodies left for family or friends to mourn. The former perished slowly and in agony, and their bodies would never rest.

And then, in his one hundred and sixtieth year, the one hundred and eighth year of his reign, one of his searchers returned from the Nyrondese city of Innspa, which his armies had only recently taken. The searcher's name was Stakaster, and for ten years, despite his Nyrondese ancestry, he had been as close to a trusted confidant as the Azal'Lan could ever have.

He was also the only member of Firan's living staff who could approach Firan without trembling. The first time he had approached, it had been obvious that he had felt the effect of the aura, but he had controlled his reaction, thereby impressing Firan as much with his courage and strength as with his seeming intelligence and wisdom.

He was also virtually the only one in decades who had answered almost precisely the same way before and after Firan's incantation of truth.

And now, as he was ushered into Firan's private quarters, a mixture of excitement and unease showed plainly on his face.

"You have found something of interest, then," Firan said.

"Possibly of great interest, my lord," the officer said, presenting Firan with a black vision glass that reminded him of the obsidian mirror that had long ago revealed Olessa's treachery. "This cost more than a score of lives, including our best necromancer's."

"Those who take service with me know the risks," Firan said, examining the mirror.

A wolfish grin momentarily erased the unease from Stakaster's face. "Aye! And the rewards! And rewards are not without their price!" Then he sobered and said, "Before he was slain, the wizard had spied upon a gypsy ritual, capturing it in that very glass."

"Did he indeed?" Intrigued, Firan concentrated his will and desire upon the artifact. Images formed on its gleaming surface, just as the images had once formed on the obsidian mirror, but unlike those other images, these were wordless and silent.

But the images alone told him that here, for the first time, was perhaps what he sought.

A nobleman's body filled the glass. His had been a violent death, and not a recent one. His throat was cut, and decay had already eaten at his corpse. Despite that, several mourners clustered about the deceased and wept, no doubt imploring the gods for a miracle.

Then a small group of gypsies appeared. A brief, unheard conversation followed, and a great deal of money was exchanged, even more than Olessa had paid all those years ago. Pocketing this, the gypsies gathered about the corpse and began to chant soundlessly.

Slowly decay melted from the nobleman's limbs and face. The terrible wound at his throat closed, clean new

flesh sealing the nearly decapitating gash. The chest rose
and fell. The former corpse, once again a man, opened his
eyes, and a smile curved his lips, lips no longer gray with
death. Friends and kin helped the resurrected man to his
feet, where, after a moment of unsteadiness, he stood
unaided and embraced them.

Firan had long ago left behind the ability to shed tears of
happiness or to feel his pulse pound with excitement. Nevertheless, he shared the emotions he saw enacted in the
mirror.

And he said, "I would have that spell."

Stakaster bowed his head. "Would that I could deliver it,
my lord, but what you have seen was enacted before the
invasion. The gypsies fled Innspa under cover of the night
and their own numerous enchantments."

"Then find them! Use whatever men and means necessary, but find them!"

Stakaster's head remained bowed. "I fear that even your
entire army would not be sufficient to the task. I personally
put eight Nyrondese informants to the torture in an effort to
find where they had fled, but it was to no avail. And you
have seen in the glass only one small aspect of the powers
these gypsies possess. Only the most accomplished of sorcerers could trace them to whatever haven they have sought
refuge in."

"Then so it shall be. I will track them down myself!"

"No, my lord!" Stakaster's eyes shot up to meet Firan's.
"There are many who would take your life, but nowhere are
they more numerous than in Nyrond!"

"Do you take me for a coward?" Firan flared angrily.

"Never, my lord, but—"

"Then begin preparations! We leave for Innspa at dawn!"

And so they did, escorted by a cadre of the Azal'Lan's

most trusted guards, an uneasy Stakaster at Firan's side, a spellbound stallion beneath him. And this time, unlike on his triumphal journey from Rauxes more than a century before, there were no cheering crowds, no villagers eager to follow, but neither were there cowardly enemies lying in ambush. Instead, the roads they traversed were virtually deserted, peasants and nobles alike finding work that required doing behind drawn shutters even at high noon. Even when they crossed into Nyrond and drew near Innspa, it continued, as if word of their coming had gone before them and emptied the streets of all but occasional patrols of occupying forces.

"And where are these would-be assassins you fretted about, Stakaster?" Firan asked derisively as they approached the night-darkened mansion where the resurrection had reportedly taken place. Now, however, it was deserted, its owners apparently having fled like the gypsies when the invasion began.

But it was not the owners who interested Firan, although he would have liked to have spoken to the one resurrected in the glass, if only to see if his newfound health was still as good as when the images in the glass had faded.

The room was as it had been in the glass. The table on which the body had lain still stood in its center, and, though table and room had been thoroughly scrubbed, the psychic imprint of what had happened there could not be removed.

And it was enough.

For one as accomplished in wizardry as Firan Zal'honan, it was enough.

Loosing his Sight, honed now for well over a century, he saw the trail the gypsies had left, faint as the faintest dust mote in moonlight, but enough.

And it led to the depths of the Adri Forest.

"Guide us to them from afar," Stakaster said. "We will bring them to you."

"And risk that their magic will outwit you?" Firan asked scornfully.

"But we are a hundred strong, my lord. Surely—"

"Magic the like of theirs could likely defeat a thousand," Firan said. "Now come. We have no more business here."

Striding from the room and returning to where the horses waited, Firan renewed the spell that kept the animals from bolting at his approach. On his own stallion, he notched the control even tighter and thought for a moment of finding a replacement. Even the sturdiest animal could not stand up forever to the constant battering by its instinctive desire to flee and the ever more oppressive spells required to keep it functioning.

But there was no time. When dealing with any whose magic was as strong as that of this band of gypsies, even a moment's delay could be fatal to his purpose, and far too many moments had already passed.

With his Sight to guide them, with his enchantments to ease their fatigue, they rode without halt until, well into the following night, he called a halt.

"My lord?" Stakaster looked at him quizzically.

"We will hold here," Firan said. "The gypsies are encamped a half hour's ride ahead, but there is something I do not understand."

"I will go forward alone, my lord. If there is danger—"

"If there is danger ahead, I will deal with it!" Firan said, signaling for silence.

His Sight hovered over the gypsy encampment. There were concealment spells shielding it from prying eyes, but they were no barrier to his Sight. Nor would they be a barrier to even the rankest hedge wizard. They could be detected and penetrated—dispelled, even—by the most rudimentary of counterspells.

That was not right. It was incomprehensible to Firan that people with the powers these gypsies had demonstrated before would employ such ineffective magic now.

Unless . . .

Unless they were simply overconfident. To their minds, there was, after all, no possible way anyone could have traced them here, so thoroughly had they obscured their trail with other, far more effective magic. And here, deep in the Adri Forest, there was, they would think, no danger from anyone who might have been searching for them in Innspa. And their concealment spells, while susceptible to even rudimentary magic, would successfully hide them from any of the unsuspecting denizens of the forest, be they human or animal.

Cautiously he probed for signs of other spells. He found none but the faded remnants of sorcerous battles long past, little more substantial now than the carefully hidden trail that had led him here.

Irritably he withdrew and signaled Stakaster to follow him forward. He had wasted enough time with his baseless suspicions.

The gypsy encampment was precisely as his Sight had revealed it. A murmured phrase was all it took to shatter the flimsy concealment spells. The gypsies, a bare half dozen, sat around a campfire, as silent as they had been in the glass. One, a young woman with eyes as bright as diamonds, looked up.

"Welcome, Firan Zal'honan," she said.

And a chill descended over him, a chill even more powerful than the one that had gripped him at his death.

Suddenly Stakaster was laughing.

And the hundred men of Firan's guard were surrounded by a thousand in Nyrondese battle garb.

Magic crackled in the dark night air as shadows gathered, shadows the like of which he had not seen since the night of his death, and the hundred most trusted guardsmen of the Azal'Lan laid down their arms.

"So," Stakaster said as he drew his sword with loving deliberateness, "there are indeed illusions that even the great Azal'Lan cannot penetrate."

"So it would appear," Firan said, gathering his powers about himself in preparation for the coming attack. "As well as those traitors who can lie even when under the compulsion of truth."

Stakaster's smile was both amused and triumphant. "We will see whom history judges traitor and whom it judges liberator."

"And who is it that judges me now? Is your name truly Stakaster, or is that yet another lie?" Even as he spoke, Firan surveyed the advancing Nyrondese, his Sight searching for the weakest link. A dozen he could dispatch with ease, even a hundred, but a thousand . . .

"I am Stakaster, of the Clan Kirilarien. You may recall my great-grandfather, whom you slew together with two of his brothers and your own son three generations past."

Madness! Firan thought. But it was a familiar madness among the clans: to take vengeance for the death of an ancestor who had not only died a generation before the avenger's birth but had also richly deserved his fate.

"I cannot remember every traitor and troublemaker whose execution the law demanded," Firan said dismissively. And as he spoke, he saw the weakness he had been searching for in the ten-deep approaching ranks.

"Then we will remember them for you," Stakaster said,

raising his blade. The thousand surged forward, rightly expecting that hundreds might die but that, in the end, even Azal'Lan's sorcery could not defeat them all.

Firan wheeled his stallion about, directing his gaze at one of the approaching assassins, a boy no older than Irik at his death, a boy neither battle-hardened nor long separated from his family's superstitious bosom.

Tightening his mental grip on his mount, Firan urged it forward at full gallop. Simultaneously he removed all enchantments designed to counteract the effects of the aura that enveloped his undead body.

And removed all illusion.

In a single instant, the flesh melted from his face and hands, the fur-edged cape he wore fell to tatters, the polished boots suddenly became aged and cracking. And the ranks of advancing assassins suddenly found themselves facing not a cornered sorcerer but a creature from the pits of hell, hideous beyond belief, charging straight at them, preceded by a wave of sourceless terror that chilled them to the bone.

The boy directly in his path screamed, losing all control of himself and his whinnying, struggling mount. It reared violently, throwing the boy to the ground, slamming into the animals on either side.

Chaos rippled out from that point, sending mounts and riders into paroxysms of fear, instinctively and uncontrollably lurching backward, out of the path of the horror bearing down on them.

In seconds, a score of men were trampled or crushed beneath their rearing, falling mounts.

And Firan was clear.

But even as he plunged into the forest that surrounded the gypsies' clearing, he heard the sounds of the assassins regaining control of themselves and their mounts.

And then the thunder of a thousand sets of hooves.

His Sight gave him the advantage in the forest, but when he emerged, the clear, moonlit night was against him, and soon the muffled thunder of his pursuers' hoofbeats was growing steadily louder.

And then it was dawn, and despair was descending upon him. His stallion was steadily losing strength, battered as it was by the constant energy-draining conflict between its instinctive terror of the creature astride it and the oppressive spell that kept it from acting on that terror and expending all its energy in frantic, bone-jarring attempts to dislodge its rider and flee.

But then suddenly hope was restored.

Before him lay a valley, filled with morning mist that mortal eyes could not penetrate. A valley, his Sight informed him, that was more thickly forested than even the depths of Adri, a veritable labyrinth.

Without hesitation, Firan tightened his already mind-numbing hold on his whinnying mount and forced it to charge unhesitatingly into the valley mists.

If the mist covered the entire valley as thickly as it appeared to from the hillside, it would give him the respite he needed. It would allow him to regain the ground he had lost to his pursuers, and more. Unfettered by the limitations of human sight, he could continue through the blinding mists at an undiminished pace while his pursuers would either be slowed to a cautious trot or reduced to a mass of broken bones within a hundred yards.

And once he had gained sufficient distance, he could stop, tether his mount solidly, and concentrate all his energies on his pursuers, something he had not been able to do from the moment of their unexpected appearance. They were a thousand strong and well armed, and the gypsies' magic was indeed powerful. But the gypsies and their magic had been left behind in the forest, and the assassins alone were far from invulnerable.

And he need only delay them long enough to make his way back to Castle Galdliesh. He need not destroy them—yet. That could wait until he was safely ensconced in the castle. Then his undead armies would range forth and increase their number by at least a thousand.

Unerringly he guided the still-terrified animal through the maze of trees, both upright and fallen, and sinkholes and startling outcroppings of rock and sheer drops into hillside ravines. The morning sun, which even his magic could not slow, had already been within minutes of topping the hills on the far side of the valley when he had entered the mist. If only it did not burn away the mist too rapidly, he would have a chance. If only . . .

Overhead, the mist brightened.

This soon? Impossible! And yet the light continued to increase.

Cursing, he sent his steed leaping over a rotting log, then veering sharply around a small chasm that, even in the clearest air, would have been invisible to human eyes. At this rate . . .

The light began to fade.

Suddenly his senses screamed an incoherent warning, and he reined the animal to a lurching halt. The towering pine whose branches had been scraping against his fur-edged cape only an instant before was no longer there. The ground was no longer uneven and weed-choked but as featureless as the darkening mist. Even his Sight was blinded. The relentless sound of hooves approaching the borders of the mist was no more.

Instinctively he clutched the tiny golden dragon skull suspended from around his neck—and released it with a start. Its feel was not of comforting warmth, as it had always been, but of icy cold.

For the first time in decades, he felt fear.

The same fear he had felt the last night of his mortality.

The same fear he had felt when the voice of his long-dead brother spoke to him from the shadows of the crypt that only moments earlier had received the remains of his only son.

He listened, with both human and inhuman senses. There was only silence but for the labored breathing and nervous hooves of his mount.

Maintaining his mental grip on the animal, he lowered himself to the ground, holding the reins.

The moment his feet touched the ground, the reins fell limp in his hand. The animal, like the forest before it, was gone, and the light was fading to utter darkness, a darkness that even *his* senses could not penetrate. And out of that darkness came the muffled laughter of Quantarius, a sound not heard outside Firan's own mind for nearly a century.

Then total silence.

And total darkness.

How long it lasted, he had no way of knowing. He had no heartbeat to time the passing seconds, no breath with which to count the minutes.

Finally it ended, the mists reappearing around him but remaining dark, a sea of smothering gray.

Gradually they condensed into roiling tatters and vanished. . . .

PART III

BAROVIA

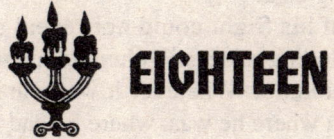

EIGHTEEN

542, Barovian Calendar

He stood in a forest, the detached reins still dangling from his hand.

But it was not the forest he had been fleeing through a moment—an hour? a day? a year?—before.

It was night, not morning.

At his feet, a steep, wooded bank dropped down to a swiftly flowing river. Overhead, lowering clouds blotted out the stars.

If this place had stars in its skies.

If it had a sky.

Cautiously he reached out with all his senses. The forest around him was dense with life, but most of it slept. And what little did not was frozen into fearful silence. Wherever he was, he noted with minor satisfaction, the reaction of the creatures of the forest to his presence was unchanged. Like his vanished stallion, they were instinctively terrified, whether he meant them harm or not.

But there was more. . . .

He turned slowly away from the river, his senses reaching . . . reaching . . . feeling. . . .

There!

Somewhere in the forest, at a distance as yet unclear, he sensed something: humans, such as he himself had once been?

Or something else?

Puzzled that his Sight could not reveal more, he wondered if the blinding mists still clung to his senses.

But it mattered not. Whatever it was, surely it would be able to tell him where he was, where he had been taken to.

Looking down, he saw that his appearance was still reality, not illusion: a decaying corpse held together by the invisible bindings of magic, a fur-lined cape in tatters, heavy leather boots dry and cracked with age, a broad metal belt tarnished and rusted.

Concentrating, he restored the illusion, brushing away a brief thrust of envy for the mortals who had pursued him. Their outward appearance was reality, not a mirage that would fade from sight without constant tending. But their reality was fragile and short-lived, whereas his . . .

The boots once again flexible and pristine, cape and belt restored, he marched into the forest, the branches and undergrowth parting before him.

* * * * *

From a distance, he studied the building and the grounds.

At one time, it had doubtless been a grand estate, but that time had been decades, perhaps centuries, in the past. Like himself, it was a rotting shell of what it had been. The stone fence that separated it from the rutted road was still standing, but the iron gates had long since fallen and now lay, half rusted through, almost invisible in a tangle of weeds and vines. The house itself was little better. The roof sagged dangerously, and most of the windows on all three floors were boarded over.

And yet a light burned within.

His senses told him that something tended that light, something that at least approximated humanity.

Soundlessly crossing the remains of the iron gate and passing through the weed-choked courtyard, he stood on broad, crumbling steps before a massive wooden door that hung crookedly on its hinges. Coarse laughter seeped through the opening.

Effortlessly he pushed the door aside. It scraped along the floor with a grating sound that echoed through the building, then crashed to the floor as the last rusting bolt of the hinges gave way.

The laughter was abruptly cut off. At the far end of a long hallway, where flickering light spilled out through an open door, there was the sound of scrambling footsteps. The light went out a moment later; at the same moment a woman's scream reverberated through the building. The sound of fist on flesh brought silence.

Their kind is everywhere. The thought came unbidden, as did the rising anger. But it was mixed with a shock of anticipation. He had not dealt directly with such rabble for decades, leaving such matters to his lieutenants.

Unhindered by the darkness, he strode the dusty length of the hall, letting his booted footsteps fall loudly. Stopping in the doorway, he saw a young girl, no more than fifteen, huddled, whimpering, on the filthy floor in the far corner of the room. Four men, three in rough peasants' clothes, the fourth and youngest in more respectable wear, stood scattered about the room, squinting unseeingly in his direction, an assortment of knives in their hands.

"Perhaps you would like some better light," Firan said,

gesturing. The candle they had snuffed out moments before flickered into life.

All four sets of eyes jerked toward the candle flame but swung back to the doorway almost instantly.

"Young lady," he said, his voice and thoughts dimming her terror, "you may leave if you wish."

The largest of the men, burly and heavily bearded, suddenly laughed. "And who are you to say who leaves and who does not?" The man stepped forward, and the others, apparently emboldened by his example, followed. Within seconds, they formed a semicircle around Firan.

The man laughed again. "Whoever you are, it seems *we* are the ones who have the say."

"Pay them no mind, young lady," Firan said, as if the four didn't exist. "Now begone. Tell your family your attackers will be dealt with."

Cringing, the girl scrambled to her feet, hugging her torn clothing about her. The youngest of the men, beardless and barely out of his teens himself, turned toward her. "We are not through—" he began, but his words came to an abrupt halt as he clutched at his throat and staggered backward.

The girl's eyes darted from the young man's distress to Firan's seeming tranquility and back, and then she was scrabbling past them all, her back pressed to the wall. With a last fearful glance at her attackers, she shot into the hall, her footsteps racing toward the collapsed door.

The young man, gasping for breath, staggered and fell. The burly leader, knife in hand, advanced on Firan. The other two, wide-eyed and shaken, tried ineffectively to help the one who was choking.

"No weapon, eh?" the burly one said with a guttural laugh. "Not that it would do you any good."

"I have all the weapons I require," Firan said quietly.

A moment later, the man lunged at him, slashing with the knife. Firan's right hand shot out, closing on the man's wrist while the blade was still inches from its target. There was a cracking sound, a gasping scream, and the knife clattered to the floor.

Picking the man up with seeming ease, Firan threw him toward the corner where the girl had huddled. The man hit the floor and came up hard against the wall but was struggling to his feet a second later.

"Get him!" he snarled, moving forward himself, his right hand dangling limply from the shattered wrist.

Firan gestured, and all four were gasping for breath. Another gesture, and they were flung backward into the corner, where they landed, arms and legs tangled.

Firan stood over them as they struggled to breathe.

"If you bother the girl or her family again, you will die—very slowly and very painfully. Is that understood?"

Abruptly their throats constricted even more tightly, cutting off all breath. For a full minute, they struggled until their faces were puffed and red, but not a trace of air reached their lungs.

Just as abruptly, their throats loosened and air rushed in.

"I would kill you here and now," Firan said, looking down at them coldly as they gasped for air and tried to untangle themselves, "were it not that I require the answers to some questions."

An hour later, he sent them staggering into the night, helpless and naked, while he tried to make sense of the answers they had given him.

Barovia, they had called this land, but where *was* it? How could there be a place so remote that no reports—not even *rumors*—of its existence had reached the Flanaess? It was inconceivable, and yet it was true, just as it was inconceivable but apparently true that no one here had ever heard of the Malachite Throne or the Great Kingdom or anything at all beyond the borders of Barovia itself.

And not all four of his unwilling informants had been ignorant peasants. One, the beardless boy, was a well-schooled if ill-behaved noble's son, whose wish for vengeance on the serving girl who had spurned his attentions had led him to fall in with the other three ruffians.

Could it be that the mists had taken him to an entirely different plane of existence? Mages in Knurl had spoken of such things, spoken with great solemnity and authority but also with, so far as he had ever been able to determine, a total lack of knowledge. It was almost a certainty that such planes existed, but equal was the certainty that no one had yet fathomed their secrets, regardless of the number who claimed otherwise and who so easily flummoxed peasants and nobles alike. He himself, in his early mortal years, had spun tales both dazzling and horrific, not a one containing a single grain of the revealed truth that he claimed for them. All he truly knew, all he had ever known, was that the powers he commanded, the creatures that he summoned, could not spring from nothingness. There had to be a source, but what that source was remained as much a mystery to him today as it had a century and a half ago. Obviously it was a reservoir of immense power and immense evil. His every encounter with the creatures he summoned up had proven that. And the creatures who had come unbidden: the shadows that feigned concern for his well-being and spoke in familiar voices of desires best left unspoken and then either snatched those desires away or granted them in forms that only added to his misery . . .

But this place—there was evil here, obviously enough, but to little greater extent than in the world he had lost, if the four from this night's encounter could be believed. Creatures walked the night, they claimed, though none of the four had until this night had the misfortune to encounter one, and even their wildest tales did not come close to matching the supreme horrors he himself was capable of summoning.

No, if this were another plane, it was not the one that served as source for his powers.

But whatever Barovia was, on whatever plane or world it existed, it appeared to be his new home—at least for now. And he had been put here with a purpose, he suspected, though he doubted that the powers that played so freely with his destiny would ever deign to say what that purpose was, other than to let him hear their hollow laughter whenever a new page was turned in the record of his existence.

But their purpose, whatever it might be, was not his.

When first he had encountered them, when they had given him his "heart's desire," he had naively taken them at their word and accepted their "gift." But in the long decades since, as one dashed hope followed another, he had come to realize the truth: that the powers delighted in his pain but most of all in giving him hope and then snatching it away. Time and again he had been seemingly on the brink of victory, and each time it had turned to crushing defeat.

Until this final time, when simply crushing his hopes of restoring his son to life had not been enough.

Until this final time, when they had robbed him of not only that immediate hope but of his entire world as well, his entire existence.

But they had not robbed him of his talent nor his determination, and he would never rest until his world was restored to him.

His world—and his son.

In the meantime, he needed to learn a great deal more about this world in which he found himself, this "Barovia." At first blush, it appeared that it could benefit from his powers and discipline, but he would have to tread lightly until his store of knowledge was far greater.

He would begin with Baron Latos, the unfortunate father of the young man he had sent screaming into the night with his brutish companions. He doubted Latos had the kind of political power the son had insisted he had, but it was a place to start.

And the son had mentioned, with peculiar pride, an extensive library of magical works and treatises. Perhaps there would be something among them that would be of use. . . .

 **NINETEEN**

542, Barovian Calendar (continued)

Angrily Firan swept the glossy, leather-bound volumes from the table to the polished study floor, some skidding dangerously close to the open fireplace. Baron Latos, middle-aged and obese, scrambled after them, a look of hurt and puzzlement on his florid face.

"Do you take me for a complete fool, Latos?" Firan snarled. "Those are worthless imitations at best, murderous frauds at worst!"

"But, my lord—"

"Silence! Unless you have something to offer that is not an open insult to my intelligence, something you have not chosen to destroy with your ignorance, keep silent!"

Barely able to control his anger, Firan stood waiting. The man was a fool! And apparently only the latest in a long line of fools that stretched back to whichever benighted ancestor had found the original volumes. Instead of carefully and meticulously preserving them or presenting them to someone who knew their value and their use, as anyone with even a modicum of intelligence would have done, this first in a long line of fools had elected to "improve" matters by copying everything into new and pristine volumes. At least once each generation, whenever the reigning fool grew tired of the existing copies, it would all start up again, until boredom or other matters intervened. Until now they were not only useless but also dangerous, filled with miscopied spells that, if one were careless or naive enough to follow blindly, could bring death or worse, not upon an intended victim but upon oneself.

His eyes widening in fear under Firan's stony gaze, Latos let fall the volumes he had been on his hands and knees to retrieve. "I—I have only one other, a volume recently discovered in—in the ruins of a small monastery in a remote corner of the Latos estate."

Firan's image scowled as he remembered his father's priests. "You are a religious man, Latos?"

Latos shrugged uncomfortably as he struggled to get his ample body back on its feet. An image of the hateful Ranald Zal'honan, the elder brother who had eaten himself into his grave a century ago, darted through Firan's mind.

"My many-times-removed great-grandfather allowed an obscure order to build it on his land," Latos said, eyes downcast, "but it has been unoccupied for at least a century. I suspect the order no longer exists."

"No matter. Where is this volume?"

Latos's Adam's apple, almost hidden by folds of flesh, twitched as he gulped nervously. "I have not had the opportunity even to clean it. It is still laden with the filth that—"

"Bring it!" Firan snapped. "Before you exhaust my patience entirely!"

Bobbing his head, Latos waddled to a polished oaken cabinet, unlocked it, and withdrew an ebony box with the Latos crest embossed on its side, as it had been on the leather bindings of the rejected volumes. Fingers trembling, Latos set the box on the table, lifted the lid, and stood back, as if ready to catch the box if its contents met the same fate as his other offerings.

Hope flared as Firan lifted the single volume from the box and laid it on the table. It could not have been more unlike the others. Dust and grime still covered it in layers. Its obviously ancient cover was cracked and curled. And when he opened it delicately, the brittle edges of the discolored parchment flaked away with alarming ease. The ornate script itself was blurred and fading.

But it was genuine. Of that he was instantly certain. Beyond the physical appearance, he could sense the age, and he could feel the power of the hand that had inscribed it.

Softly, ignoring Latos's worried stare, Firan murmured the words that would bring the deterioration of the fragile parchment to a halt, then those that would encase it—as his own decaying flesh was encased—in an invisible sheath that would shield it from damage and allow it to be handled without its being destroyed.

He turned to Latos and the flawed volumes that lay scattered on the floor. With a single gesture, he sent the huge tomes skittering into the fireplace. Latos lunged after them but stumbled backward an instant later, whimpering, as the flames billowed out and scorched his grasping fingers.

Dispassionately Firan studied the baron as Latos clasped his burned fingers to his chest and grimaced in pain. Only the uneasy desire to not yet draw further attention to himself kept Firan from gripping Latos's flittering, useless mind and consigning his porcine body to the flames along with the volumes.

Instead, with more than a slight tinge of regret, he wiped the evening from the baron's memory.

Replacing the seemingly crumbling but invisibly protected volume in the ebony box, he tucked it under his arm
and hurried back to the similarly crumbling but even more
strongly protected manor house that he had, for reasons he
did not fully understand, taken for at least his temporary
home. Every foot of the way, the one who had inscribed the
volume seemed to be calling out to him, as if anxious, after
all these centuries, to pass his knowledge—his gifts—on to
another.

* * * * *

For a few brief moments, Firan was as close to experi-
encing joy as he had been at any time since his mortality
had ended.

Here, in this ancient and tattered volume, was that which
he had sought for more than half a century: the means to
return the dead to true life, not to the travesty of life he had
briefly visited upon his tomb-bound son. It was the reality
to match the illusions the traitorous gypsies had created in
their glass. From the first moment he had touched the volume in Latos's study, he was overwhelmed with the certainty that the words inscribed on the fragile parchment
were those of an ancient sorcerer of far greater knowledge
and power than Firan himself. The imprint of that power
had outlasted the ages and was unmistakable.

But then his joy evaporated as he realized the spell was
useless to him in this world, in this "Barovia"! Irik's body
and spirit were still bound to the sarcophagus in Castle
Galdliesh, in a world now lost to him—the world that had
been stolen from him!

Stolen by his shadowy tormentors, who even now were
doubtless laughing at this latest joke, this latest example of

their wit and irony.

But they would not win! For them to win, he would have to surrender, and that he would never do! Someday they would overstep themselves, and he would be ready!

He would be ready!

With grim determination, he turned his attention back to the fading words on the discolored parchment and began to read, to memorize.

Finally satisfied, he made his way out of the crumbling manor house and into the encroaching forest. As always, it was dense with life, life that grew silent and trembling at his approach.

But it was not the living he was concerned with now.

He found what he was searching for in less than five minutes' time. Until a few days ago, it had been a rabbit, no different from one he might have found in Knurl as a child. But now it was the carcass of a rabbit, verminous slugs already establishing their claim. The otherwise undevoured body and snapped neck indicated it had been killed for sport or play, not food.

It would suffice as a small test of the treasure he had found, so that when he once again had access to Irik's body, there would be not one second's more delay than he had already endured.

Standing in the darkness, Firan focused his mind on the remains of the animal, bringing forth an image of what it had been in life, then visualizing the regression to that state—the slugs squirming and withdrawing, the rotting flesh filling in and firming beneath the fur, the eyes reforming and taking on the glint of life.

Finally he was ready to pronounce the words that would bring forth the power to match reality to his vision. The time would come when the process was as automatic as walking, as his countless other spells already were, but until that time, he would do it slowly, painstakingly, one precise step at a time.

He began forming the memorized words in his mind, then easing them carefully onto his tongue.

After a single word, he stopped in sudden shock. The remainder of the words were gone from his memory, as if they had never existed, and even as he tried desperately to dredge them up, the single word he had spoken was gone as well.

The shock turned to fear. Was his own mind betraying him now?

Or was it something else? A protection woven into the spell itself, preventing it from being learned and used? He had heard of such things but had never encountered them himself.

Scooping up the carcass and the sodden matt of leaves it lay in, Firan turned and stalked back to the manor house. In the study, he laid it roughly on the table opposite the open volume.

Rounding the table, he bent close over the fading words and began once more to read. It was as if he were seeing the words for the first time, each one new and fresh. The words had not changed, this he knew.

And yet . . .

The fear gripped him more tightly. Once again he lodged the words firmly in his mind. He looked up, focusing on the carcass less than two yards distant.

Once again, the moment the first syllables emerged from his mouth, the words vanished from his mind like evaporating mist.

For a third time, he repeated the procedure, with the same frightening results. The words were as clear in his mind as the carcass itself and the table on which it lay—until he strove to speak them. Then they were gone as if they had never existed. All that remained was the chilling memory that he *had* known them only moments before.

Cursing, Firan slammed his fist down on the table in frustration, making the carcass twitch as if it had actually been given a momentary flicker of the life with which he was so desperately trying to imbue it. Repressing the impulse to smash table and carcass alike against the wall, he turned once again to the ancient tome.

This time he moved the carcass closer, within inches of the text, and read the words aloud, never taking his eyes from the text.

But this, too, failed. For, though he had been able to painstakingly *speak* the words, one at a time, their collective *meaning* was lost. He could not, as he had done thousands of times in the past, simultaneously mouth the words and visualize the results he wished so profoundly to achieve.

And without that harmony between thought and tongue, the words, no matter how precisely or feelingly uttered, were nothing more than useless sounds.

It was good, he realized uneasily, that he had not given in to the temptation to deal with Latos in the manner the fool deserved. It would have attracted attention, and, as his repeated failures now demonstrated, widespread attention was far from advisable. Except for odd limitations on his Sight, he did not appear to have lost any of the powers he had possessed on Oerth, but until he found the reason for his inexplicable and repeated failure with this most important of spells, until he could determine just how vulnerable he was in this strange new land and who his enemies might be—other than the shadows and voices that had almost certainly brought him here—the fewer who knew of his presence, the better.

Carefully he lifted the brittle parchment page and turned to the next, where another spell awaited him. It was a spell of no import, unlike the one with which he had failed so many times, yet it was new to him. Perhaps . . .

Grimly, hopefully, he read and memorized, as he had thousands of times and more during his ninety-six years as a mortal and more than six decades since his resurrection. And when the time came that the words seemed engraved in stone in his mind, he turned from the fading script and tried to speak them.

But the words refused to come. Instead, they slid from his mind like water through a sieve, leaving behind only enough faint traces to remind him that, bare seconds before, they had existed.

But now they did not—not in his mind.

Grimly, with what little hope remained rapidly fading, he turned to yet another page and began again to read.

* * * * *

Firan closed the volume.

A dozen of the spells were new, and every one of that dozen was like the first. No matter how important or how inconsequential, no matter how complex or how simple, no matter how many times he memorized it, the words of the spell vanished from his mind the moment he tried to speak them.

For a long time, he stood over the ancient volume, silently cursing his tormentors.

No longer were they content to simply trick him, to take from him what he valued most. Now they dangled the ultimate object of his desire within his reach, then snatched it back the moment he tried to grasp it. But always they left it in sight, always seemingly within reach, their only purpose to tantalize and torment.

There had to be a solution. Someday, somewhere, he would find it.

Until then . . .

Until then, the spell whose existence most tormented him must never be separated from him.

Never!

Once again he opened the volume. The red glow of his eyes shone through the illusion some corner of his mind still maintained. His tongue and his mind spoke the words that would achieve his objective, words designed to hide a jewel or other precious object from covetous eyes by sealing it within another object of lesser value. He had seen it used more than once in Knurl to make gems or keepsakes appear to a marauder's eyes as nothing more precious than a lump of rock.

But here the objective was not to conceal but to join one object to another.

As the words were spoken, a single page arose from the ancient volume, the air shimmering and twisting around it like a panoply of invisible lenses. Slowly it shrank in on itself, never creasing or cracking, just gently folding and distorting, until it was a smooth-surfaced crystalline oval tinier than the golden skull suspended around his neck. Then abruptly, like a blunt dagger, it plunged toward his chest.

In an instant, it had penetrated and settled within a cavity of his unbeating heart. A moment later it was hidden from sight as the decaying flesh sealed the momentary wound and the illusory tunic re-formed over that.

The face of the illusion smiled. This wretched body might be worthless in all ways that gave worth to a normal human body, but for this it would suffice.

When his tormentors overstepped themselves and an opportunity arose, he would be ready.

He would be ready. . . .

TWENTY

542, Barovian Calendar (continued)

Count Strahd von Zarovich had been lord—and prisoner—of Barovia for nearly two centuries, and still the image of Tatyana haunted him. Not a night went by that the memory of her plunge from the parapets of Castle Ravenloft did not inflict new pain on his already tortured mind. He was not paralyzed by the obsession; he carried on outwardly with his duties and his work, and yet not a waking moment existed when some small part of him was not plagued by the twin questions: In what body does her soul now rest, and how can I atone for the pain she has suffered in life after unfulfilled life?

No conscious thought of her ever passed without the vain and tortured hope that, somewhere, someday, he would find the spell that would not only lead him unerringly to her but would also plant in her heart the seeds of the love that had always been denied him. And protect her from whatever power it was that pursued her from life to life, pursued and destroyed her each time love and happiness seemed within their grasp.

It was therefore with no little interest that he received the reports from Vallaki of the sudden appearance, and almost equally sudden disappearance, of a powerful wizard, one whose abilities, if the stories told by three of the thugs who had encountered him were to be believed, perhaps matched those of Strahd himself. He called himself sometimes Azalin and sometimes Zal'honan, and had spoken imperiously to the three of them of a land called Oerth, and when they had denied any knowledge of such a land, he had dismissed them as fools or worse and sent them screaming into the night. It was perhaps a measure of his own desperation that Strahd suspected that the mists that had kept him prisoner in Barovia for nearly two centuries were likewise responsible for this new arrival.

At first Strahd thought of summoning him, but a combination of discretion and the ever-present desire to escape the prisonous walls of Castle Ravenloft—though such escape led only to the larger prison that Barovia itself had become—was enough to set him thinking of going forth himself.

Weighing further in his decision was the fact that the reports had come from Vallaki, for it had been in the nearby village of Berez that first he had encountered Tatyana five decades after her death—her first death.

Marina, she had called herself then, remembering nothing of her former life and little of her present. He had patiently told her of that former life, less patiently begun the process that could have given them an eternity together, but she had been struck down before he could complete it, leaving him once again bereft, with nothing to comfort him but vengeance—all too brief a vengeance—on the monsters who, in their insufferable arrogance and ignorance, had taken from him more than they could ever imagine.

But it was the final report—that the mage had fallen

from public view and quietly taken up residence not in Vallaki but in the hills near Berez, apparently in the very same building in which Tatyana had been taken from him that second time—that took away all hesitation and sent Strahd forth, burdened neither by human form nor the encumbrances of normal travel.

It was, however, a cautious Strahd von Zarovich whose batlike form hovered silently in the rainy night outside what he had expected to be crumbling ruins, untenanted since that night a century and a half ago. But it was in no worse condition than it had been then—better, even, for then it had been through decades of bad times and ill repair, while now . . .

As he fluttered closer to the darkened windows—did this mage have no need for light at all?—he realized that this wizard's power was indeed remarkable. Not only was the manor protected by a spell Strahd had never before encountered, but its very appearance was also largely illusion, seamless illusion that left him barely able to detect the reality that lay beneath it.

Slowly, almost floating on an errant updraft, he drifted closer. Suddenly lances of pain shot through his tiny, fur-covered body, and his vision clouded.

Hastily he fluttered backward, settled to the rain-soaked ground, and resumed his human form.

Truly the mage's powers had not been exaggerated.

But there was something else—not a spell but a feeling, an *atmosphere*—that chilled Strahd's very soul. Only once before had he felt a chill the like of this: the last night of his mortal life, when the voices had spoken out of the darkness and had lured him into this half-life of eternal damnation.

"You are the one they call Strahd von Zarovich."

The voice stabbed into his mind at the same instant it

assaulted his ears. For a fleeting moment, he wondered if it were one of those same voices that had spoken to him nearly two centuries ago, but he discarded the thought almost immediately. Those had spoken only to his mind and had been voices from his past, voices made to speak words the ones to whom the voices belonged in life would never have spoken. This was a voice he had never heard, in either life or death.

And it had almost certainly come from the mage whose presence had been reported to him.

"You are the one who calls himself Azalin?" he asked.

"*Azalin is what some here have chosen to call me.*"

"But it is not your name?"

"*As some call you Count, some call me Azalin.*"

"A title, then."

When there was no reply, Strahd took a step forward, feeling once again the pricking of the beginnings of the protective spell.

He took another step.

And another. The pain was bearable and likely could do no permanent damage, but he stopped.

"*What is it you wish of me, von Zarovich?*"

"At the moment, I desire only to speak. I take an interest in my subjects."

"*You see me as your subject, then?*"

"All in Barovia are my subjects."

"*So I have been told. But not all subjects are given the honor of a personal audience with their master.*"

"Few of my subjects capture my interest. Those who appear out of nowhere, however, are an exception."

"*And what leads you to believe that of me? Are you so well acquainted with everyone in your kingdom that you know when even a single stranger enters?*"

"There are fewer arrivals than you might imagine. And I am indeed well acquainted with everyone possessing powers such as yours."

"*And are there many?*"

"Very few, I would imagine, though without knowing the precise nature and extent of your powers, I have no way of being positive."

The voice laughed. "*Their number is doubtless exceedingly small, else they would not long be your subjects.*"

"There is more to my rule than sorcery."

"*I would be the last to deny it. The willingness to use one's power is at least of equal importance.*"

Strahd frowned but did not flinch as the pricking of the protective spell momentarily increased. "I was told of your treatment of the ones you . . . ejected . . . from this house," he said evenly.

"*And you do not approve?*"

"On the contrary, I doubt that I would have been as merciful. I have little tolerance for those who take what is neither rightfully theirs nor freely given."

"*Even if the object in question is taken from those who are not worthy of its possession?*"

"And who is to be the judge of another's worthiness?"

"*He who is worthy. Yourself, for example.*"

"And *your*self?"

"*I will not deny it.*"

The pain once again ratcheted up a notch, but this time it did not return to its previous lower level.

"It is time we spoke face-to-face," Strahd said abruptly.

"*I think not.*"

The escalating pain sent Strahd staggering backward. A moment later, he dissolved into mist, and the pain vanished along with his body.

Tentatively he probed the strengthened spell and found it had virtually no effect on his vaporous form. He hesitated a moment, thinking it might be best to come back another night, when he had had time to study the situation from a distance, to get fuller reports from his agents. But the one called Azalin would then have had the same time to study, likely more, considering Strahd's diurnal limitations.

And there were his own vulnerabilities to consider. Against one with such obvious powers, would the protections woven around and throughout Castle Ravenloft be enough? Or could they be breached?

No, now that he had made himself known and had glimpsed the other's ambition and power, any delay would be to the other's advantage.

Wraithlike, Strahd flowed forward. There was modest resistance to the physical particles that made up the mist, but nothing more. Nothing touched the controlling essence that was Strahd except the chill that seemed to blanket the entire area, a chill obviously not of physical origin.

Likewise, the images that flickered through his disembodied mind as he drifted across the ruined courtyard were not of physical origin but sprang up from the depths within himself: Tatyana and her killer and the earlier degradations she had suffered at his hands when he would have made her his unwilling bride.

And the death, unsatisfyingly swift, of that killer.

The massive front door of the manor, seemingly whole as he approached, shimmered and became a fallen slab. The windows, at first appearing the same as they had a century and a half ago, were in reality blocked by rotting, sagging boards.

Illusion. All was illusion.

And the one who had created it? Was he an illusion as

well? An illusion created by whatever powers had kept Strahd prisoner here for nearly two centuries? The fact that this was happening here, of all places in the land, gave him no choice but to think that, illusion or not, it was in some way connected to those same powers and the never-ending torment they had apparently made his lot.

For a brief moment as he flowed through the gaping hole that had been the front door, he saw Ulrich, Tatyana's killer, his form as wraithlike as Strahd's own, and Tatyana herself in Marina's servingmaid's clothes, but they were again the result of his own mind's pained wandering, not the will of the one who waited within.

Inside, the faint resistance he had felt to his movement faded. Tentatively he assumed his human shape, but still shadowy and insubstantial, testing, feeling. When no stabs of pain brushed at the half-formed nerves, he moved further toward solidity, poised for instant retreat.

Still nothing . . . only the chill that apparently had no physical component.

Finally he stood, fully formed, in the dust and detritus that was the true state of the manor house. As he had expected it to be.

Silently he looked about. And listened. Not a sound but the faint sighing of the wind through the unprotected door behind him.

Nor were there even, he noted with some relief, the darker shadows within the darkness itself, shadows like those that had visited him before.

Then a sound: a faint scraping, immediately pinpointed to a room along the hall. A century and a half ago, it had been the chamber in which Lazlo Ulrich had displayed his wares, the decrepit trunk filled with even more decrepit and ancient magical tomes.

Of course. There was a pattern to all things, even though its meaning more often than not eluded him.

Silently he moved down the hallway, the ghosts of that other time still haunting it.

In the darkened room, a man seemed to stand at a broad table, his back to the door. On the table lay a single ancient volume, even older and more fragile-appearing than those Ulrich had provided Strahd a century and a half ago. On the floor, in one corner, lay an ebony box, thrice embossed with the Latos crest.

Strahd remembered the crest well. Latos's grandfather, like others through the decades, had heard of Strahd's interest in thaumaturgical matters and had offered certain "magical volumes" for sale, not for money but for favors. The volumes themselves had proven worthless, elaborately made but dangerously inaccurate copies of older volumes containing nothing Strahd had not long possessed. The Latos lands were subsequently far smaller and poorer than they had previously been. Had the current Baron Latos already thrown his useless lot in with this newcomer? If so, the Latos lands would soon become even smaller, perhaps no larger than would be needed for a grave.

"I see you have made the acquaintance of Baron Latos," Strahd said, stepping into the room.

The figure spun about, startled, the fur-lined cloak swirling out with the movement.

Like the house, the figure, too, was illusion, Strahd saw, but unlike the house, he could not penetrate this illusion. It was too tightly held, shielding whatever lay beneath from even his senses.

"I see I underestimated you, Strahd," the figure said warily, no longer speaking to his mind as well as to his ears.

"It is a common mistake," Strahd said evenly.

The figure—the illusion the figure presented—smiled. "Now that we are speaking face-to-face, as you wished, perhaps you would be willing to answer some questions."

"If you would be willing to do the same."

"Of course. What would you wish first to know?"

Strahd studied the figure in the darkness. "How did you come to Barovia? Was it the mists that brought you?"

"You know of the mists, then?"

"I know of them. For two centuries, they have surrounded my land and held it hostage, held its people, and myself, prisoners. What do *you* know of them?"

"Far less than you, apparently. I entered what I thought were morning mists waiting to be burned away by the sun, but when they cleared, it was night. And I was here, in a land so distant it is unknown in my own, as mine is unknown in yours."

The illusion shrugged, an oddly human gesture, and continued. "I have come to suspect your land of being on a different plane of existence. Are you familiar with the concept?"

"I have heard mages speak of it, but none have offered evidence to bolster their words."

The illusion nodded. "It is the same on Oerth," Azalin said, as if with the words he had abandoned the thought that the two lands might exist in the same world. "I have feigned similar knowledge, admitting only to myself that it was wildest speculation."

"Such candor is rare. Does it extend to other matters? Your reasons for establishing yourself here, for example, in the remnants of this particular manor house?"

"It is of significance, then?"

"I will perhaps know that when I know your reasons."

The illusory figure shrugged again. "It was the first

structure I came upon after my puzzling arrival. And my need for shelter is not great."

"The mist deposited you nearby?"

"Quite nearby. I was able to detect the presence of those four fools and their victim. I intended merely to question them, but the situation I found upon entering demanded my actions. But tell me, of what significance is this place to *you?*"

"One very dear to me was slaughtered here many years ago. It has not been occupied since that time. I am surprised that, beneath the illusion, much of the structure still stands."

"You can see the truth beneath illusions, then?"

"In many cases. The one you wrap so tightly about yourself, however, is, as yet, beyond my abilities."

Once again the figure evinced momentary surprise. "You would not wish to be privy to my reality. I often wish that I were not."

"You are more than mage, then?"

"And less."

"And your plans?" Strahd's eyes swept over the ancient tome. It seemed to radiate power.

"My only desire is to return to my own land."

"And if you cannot? I trust you would not then try to steal mine."

"I would not steal what is another's."

"But to challenge that other? Is that acceptable in your eyes?"

"To challenge openly is always honorable. That is not, however, currently my intent."

Strahd nodded. "I see. But in the future?"

"Whatever happens, it will be dictated by circumstance and necessity."

"You do not rule it out, then?"

"I rule out nothing. Nor, I imagine, do you."

"It would be the height of foolishness to do so."

"As it would be for me."

Strahd studied the figure, still trying to see beyond the illusion, to get at least a hint of what this Azalin's true form was and what sort of powers, beyond the obvious, he possessed.

But whatever he was, wherever he was from, he was here now, in Barovia, and it was here he had to be dealt with, and carefully. Used, if possible. Controlled, no matter what the cost.

But dealt with. In that, there was no choice.

* * * * *

Firan eyed the tall, caped figure before him. Strahd von Zarovich, he called himself, and he was obviously more than the simple sorcerer Latos thought him to be. Only one with substantial powers could have penetrated the defenses enclosing the manor house so easily.

And he was familiar with the mists, perhaps even the shadows and their voices. Perhaps, despite his seeming denial, he was their master.

Had Firan still been mortal, he would have shivered at the thought.

But whatever Strahd was, this was his land—had *been* his land, if he could be believed, since half a century before Firan's birth.

If anyone knew how to escape this land, even to reach beyond it and pluck another in, it would almost certainly be Strahd. Therefore, even if it were possible to destroy him— and that was seriously in doubt in any event—it would be ill-advised.

At least until he learned a great deal more. A very great deal.

No, this was someone with whom he must deal, and deal with exceeding care. In that, he had no choice.

 **TWENTY-ONE**

542–579, Barovian Calendar

Thus was an uneasy alliance formed. For nearly four decades, it continued, neither prospering nor entirely withering.

Early on, Firan decided that, though Strahd possessed this land—or was possessed by it—to a far greater degree than Firan had ever possessed Knurl or any of the lands he had conquered, Strahd was far from being in control of his own fate. He was certainly not, as Firan had alternately hoped and feared, in control of the mists and the shadow voices that appeared to be their true masters. Strahd was as much a prisoner as Firan was, and equally frustrated at his powerlessness to escape.

Twice a new incarnation of Strahd's obsession was found, and twice she was lost, despite Firan's earnest efforts to aid him. Olya, she was named once, and Tanya the other, as if something were taunting him not only with her face and soul but her name as well. Each time, though Strahd vehemently—perhaps too vehemently—denied its presence, Firan heard the shadow laughter that he had come to expect whenever another hope was dashed.

A score of times, they seemed on the verge of achieving their mutual goal, the piercing of the mists that bound them both to this land. A score of times they failed.

A score of times, each found reason to lash out at the other, placing blame for the failures or cursing the other's trickery and deceit.

A score of times, the shadow laughter ate at what remained of Firan's soul.

Another score of times, spells and rumors of spells reached their ears—spells that, if not capable of providing them with passage through the mists, would allow them to reach through and pluck back the objects of their desire from the lands beyond. All but one were proven to be frauds, and that one, like the summoning that had long ago destroyed a beloved brother, brought forth something that neither of them could control or countenance. Only their combined efforts—one of the few times they had truly worked together without each diverting at least a small part of his attention and strength to keeping watch on the other—made it possible to banish the creature and ward off even greater disaster.

Every day, while Strahd lay in his secret and impenetrable resting place, Firan spent at least a few moments in what had from the first days become a ritual: attempting to commit to memory a spell, *any* spell, that he had not known before the mists had deposited him here. Every day he failed. Every day he heard the shadowy laughter, though he suspected that, in these instances at least, his own mind was the culprit, as Strahd insisted it was in all. There was surely a limit even to the shadows' appetite for witnessing his repeated failure and humiliation.

And yet he did not surrender. He would not break the vow of constant defiance he had sworn that first night.

More importantly, he would not take the chance that the one day he failed to make the attempt would be the one day the shadows would choose to relent.

Still, there were many hours left in which to contemplate the fate of the land that had been taken from him.

And the fate of Irik, his son, whom he had, no matter the reasons, failed, both in life and in death.

And his own fate, over which he seemed to have less control with each passing day.

And so it went, his frustration and despair growing greater with every defeat and every disappointment.

Until . . .

* * * * *

The long-abandoned monastery stood on the banks of the Luna, within sight of where the river disappeared into the mists that marked the Barovian border. After more than an hour of searching through its crumbling interior, Firan emerged with a single scroll.

Strahd, though he could have entered without undue effort or danger, had chosen to remain with the open carriage outside the grounds on what, perhaps a hundred years ago, had been a narrow supply road through the surrounding forest. Impatiently he held out his hand for the scroll as Firan approached and climbed onto the seat beside Strahd.

"This is all?" Strahd eyed the single scroll suspiciously.

"You are welcome to enter and conduct your own search, von Zarovich!" Firan snapped.

Strahd only grimaced and carefully uncurled a small portion of the scroll, then grimaced again. "Protection against the depredations of the undead. I have seen a hundred like it and have had half of them directed against me"—a dark smile curled across his face— "before I turned them on the wielders."

Abruptly the vampire stood, dropping the scroll onto the seat beside Firan. "Do with it what you will," Strahd said. A moment later, his human form folded in on itself like a dark flame drawn backward into its source. Briefly it floated amorphously in the air before wings billowed out and began to lightly churn the air.

The creature's tiny eyes locked with Firan's for a moment, and then it flowed away, taking a brief circle through the monastery grounds as if to prove that it could, then rising toward the treetops and setting off to the west and the Balinok Mountains. It would flutter down from the peaks and into Castle Ravenloft well before dawn, while Firan would be lucky to have found his way back to the Old Zvalich Road and reached Vallaki by then.

But it mattered not. After nearly forty years of powerless imprisonment in this land, little mattered. In *his* world, *everything* had mattered. There had been a thousand tasks and decisions that demanded his attention. There had been tens of thousands of his subjects and all the problems that entailed. There had been lands beyond the borders of Knurl, lands that provided a constant threat and a constant challenge, both of which he had been more than capable of meeting.

There had been new spells to be found and learned. There had been hope. But here . . .

Here his only goal was to escape, to return to that other world, the *real* world.

And he was no closer to that goal now than the moment he had been deposited here.

Or perhaps he was farther from his goal. There was no way of knowing, no way to judge his progress—when there was no progress.

The horse shifted nervously in its harness. Now that Strahd, whose rapport with animals almost counteracted Firan's opposite influence, was gone, he would have to strengthen the spell or risk the creature's bolting. His constantly maintained illusion of humanity, while it might fool the eyes, could not beguile the animal's inner senses. Nor could it trick Firan's own, no matter how hard he wished he could achieve total forgetfulness. An image of the decaying corpse that was his true form always lurked just below the surface of his thoughts, ready to spring forth and remind him of his true nature if ever he had the great good fortune—the audacity—to succeed in his constant effort to force it from his consciousness.

Murmuring the requisite words, he held the reins tightly as the animal gradually calmed, at least externally. Inwardly, Firan knew, it was still a coiled spring ready to explode the moment the spell was lifted.

His eyes went to the swirling wall of mist barely a hundred yards beyond the remnants of the monastery. The almost invisible cart track they had followed through the forest disappeared entirely where it passed the fallen iron gate to the grounds. At one time, before the mists had cut Barovia off from the outside world, the track had doubtless continued on, paralleling the riverbank toward some distant sea. But now? The river still flowed, its waters disappearing into the misty border, but if he were to leap into the river and let himself be carried along by the current, he would be enveloped by the mists for a few seconds, even a minute, only to emerge, completely disoriented, where another river entered the land, sometimes miles away, sometimes tens of miles. Strahd had warned him, but he had tried anyway, not once but a dozen times in a dozen rivers.

As he had tried the roads, and the fields, and the mountains.

As Strahd had tried before him.

He had tried every spell that he knew. He had even taught those same spells and others to Strahd, in vain hope that the vampire lord, more in tune with this land in which he was both ruler and prisoner, could accomplish what Firan could not.

But it was all to no avail. There was nothing more to try, nothing more to do but wait.

And curse the day he had fled into the morning mist rather than stand and fight. He might have been defeated, his existence brought to an end, but even that would have been preferable to the eternity of frustration to which he had apparently been condemned.

From out of the darkness came the sound of hooves, and all else fell silent except for the nervous shifting of his horse in its leather harness.

It wasn't the muffled thunder of his long-ago pursuers—though he would have welcomed them!—but a slow and rhythmic tapping, not unlike that of his own horse barely an hour earlier as he and Strahd had moved cautiously along the nearly invisible cart track.

His Sight, still blunted after all these years, pierced the nearby darkness of the forest, but there was nothing.

The sound of hooves grew louder. A moment later it was joined by the murmur of voices, the muffled bark of a command.

And the unmistakable creaking rumble of wagon wheels.

The mists! The sounds were coming from the mists! For the first time in three decades, Firan felt hope.

Fearfully, instinctively by now, he looked about for the

shadows, listened for their laughter.

But there were only the sounds of the approaching wagons.

Leaping down from the carriage seat, he raced to the edge of the mist. Like a wall of roiling smoke, it towered over him, stretching as high as his senses could reach.

The hooves couldn't be more than a dozen yards in, so close he could feel the vibrations in the ground itself, and yet he could see nothing.

Still closer the sounds came, certainly no more than half a dozen yards now. He could hear the rustle of the harness, the fluttering of a horse's muzzle as it exhaled, could almost feel its breath.

But it came no closer. The sounds continued, not getting louder, remaining at the same level, as if the very ground beneath their hooves was sliding backward as they trod forward.

Yet still nothing emerged. He could hear the voices now, several talking at once, individual words still unintelligible. Behind him, his own horse whinnied and bucked weakly against the harness and the spell that held it.

Suddenly he realized that the sounds were beginning to fade. It was as if the wagons had turned and were moving away, yet there had been no sound of turning, no grating as the wheels shifted direction, no barked commands to the horses.

And yet the sounds were fading.

He shouted, "Come back! Whoever you are, come back!"

There was no response, only the still-fading sounds of the wagons.

He shouted again, a wordless scream of anguish, and raced into the mists, not slowly and cautiously as he had done so often before but full speed and recklessly.

But the sounds of hooves and wagons came no closer.

He ran, shouting, "Wait! Wait for me!"

The rough floor of the forest vanished from beneath his feet, replaced by a featureless plain. The sound of the Luna River was gone. There was only the sound of the hooves and wagons, somewhere ahead.

Still he ran.

Suddenly the sounds were growing louder. Without warning, the mists vanished, and he was crashing headlong into the side of a wagon, a round-roofed, brightly colored gypsy wagon.

Vistani! They who traveled the mists.

Strahd had spoken of the gypsy tribes a hundred times, spoken of how they seemed tied to no one world but could travel through the mists to any world they chose. But he had also spoken of his own inability to grasp their ways and their inability—or unwillingness—to help him.

And of their long absence from the land. When Strahd had been mortal, before the mists had enclosed Barovia, the gypsies had been a common sight. For many years after, while Strahd sought vainly for a means of escape, they had been, if not common sights, far from rare. Strahd had spoken with different tribes dozens of times, had sought their help, had begged and bargained with them to explain their abilities in ways he could understand and make use of, but to no avail.

And then, in a fit of frustration and temper, he had lashed out at one tribe, taking their patriarch prisoner, vowing to free him only when they gave up the secret Strahd sought.

The very next night, a fog had rolled inward from the borders of Barovia, blanketing the entire land, from deepest valley to highest mountaintop.

When the fog burned off the following morning, like the

most natural of morning mists, no Vistani wagon or camp-fire could be found within Barovia.

And the patriarch Strahd had held prisoner in Ravenloft's deepest dungeon was gone, his bloodstained shackles empty.

From that day to this, more than sixty years had passed, and if Strahd could be believed, not a single Vistani had been seen in Barovia.

Disoriented, Firan looked around. The brightly colored wagon had stopped, the pair of sturdy horses that pulled it standing motionless except for the flick of a tail, the flare of a nostril. Beneath its wheels there was no path, not even so much as the remains of a cart track. A second wagon was halted a dozen yards behind the one Firan had crashed into. On all sides was forest, with few openings wide and tall enough to accommodate the wagons. Somewhere beyond the wagons, a river whispered past, but not the Luna, Firan realized with a start.

It was the unnamed river by which he had been deposited four decades ago! The forest had changed and thickened, but he knew it was the same spot.

A luxuriantly mustached man, gypsy bandanna tight about his head, billowing silky shirt above silver-belted breeches and mud-stained boots, jumped down from the front of the lead wagon, glaring at Firan. A pair of similarly dressed, similarly scowling men sat on the driver's seat of the second wagon.

"Who are you to interfere with our movements?" the man demanded. "To bring us *here?*"

"I brought you nowhere!" Firan said, returning the anger. "I merely followed the sounds of your wagon into the mists in order to speak with you."

"If not you, then who? Has Strahd found new magic to

work against us?"

"Against *you?* What magic works against *you?*" Suddenly the years of pent-up fury exploded. "It is *I* who have been trapped in this benighted land for nearly four decades! It is *I* who was delivered here and held prisoner by the very mists that you so blithely travel! It is *I* whose kingdom was stolen! It is *I* whose son has been forced to endure an eternity of torment while I have in my hands the power to release him, if only I were allowed to use it!"

"Do not take offense, my Lord Zal'honan," a vibrant new voice advised, "but do you yourself have no responsibility at all for any of these misfortunes?"

Turning sharply to face the new speaker, Firan momentarily suppressed his angry retort as he saw that the door at the rear of the lead wagon had opened, and a woman—an ancient woman, seemingly bent and frail despite the power in her voice—was haltingly descending the steps. Her gypsy dress was not colorful but dark, in keeping with her age, while a jeweled comb, almost a tiara, glittered in her black and silver hair. The man at the front of the wagon broke off his glaring at Firan and hurried to steady the old woman, but she waved him away.

"I recall that Barovian nights were cold," she said. "A warming fire would be welcome."

"This is not a land where we are welcome," the man said, scowling.

"Perhaps not," she said, "but there are things to discuss." Her eyes, Firan could not help but notice, were oases of youth in her parchment face.

The man lowered his own eyes and hurried to do her bidding, joined quickly by the two from the second wagon.

A fourth man, perhaps the first man's father, had climbed down from the front of the lead wagon, patting the nearer horse lightly, as if to calm it.

"It would be best if you kept your distance from the animals, Zal'honan" the old woman said. "Vistani horses are well trained and accustomed to many things, but even they have their limits."

As if to illustrate her point, one of the horses whinnied and reared up in its harness. Frowning, the older man turned back to the animal and laid a calming hand on its flank. A fifth man, no older than the first, had appeared at the rear of the lead wagon, a steadying hand on the old woman's arm, a lightly made three-legged stool in his other hand.

When Firan started to speak, she raised a hand. To his own surprise, he remained silent as she crossed the few yards to where the three men already had the beginnings of a fire going and were laying on larger slabs of wood that also caught with unnatural ease.

The one who accompanied her set the stool close to the fire, and she lowered herself onto it, her black skirt surrounding it, giving the impression that she floated rather than sat.

"I would offer you similar accommodations," she said, her startling eyes looking up at Firan's face, "but I am given to understand that your kind does not set great store by creature comforts."

All five men, now gathering behind her, exchanged puzzled glances but said nothing.

"What do you know of 'my kind'?" Firan asked warily. "And how do you know my name?"

"The mists hold few secrets, my Lord Zal'honan, from those who will listen."

"If you know my name—and my nature—then you know my plight. And you must also know that only your kind can return me to my rightful domain." Hope was once again beginning to seep into him. Perhaps, after four decades, his tormentors' interest in his disappointments and humiliations was flagging. Perhaps they were looking elsewhere for their diversions.

Perhaps . . .

" 'Rightful domain . . .' " the old woman said, smiling faintly. "By what right do you assert dominion, Master Firan?"

"By *all* rights!" he flared at the seeming challenge. "But most of all by right of strength and justice! I brought my land back from chaos! I drove out the vandals and brigands who preyed on its people, and I gave them more than a century of peace and stability and justice. Even my enemies cannot dispute those claims! My subjects prospered, and all were treated fairly and equally."

"Except for those you tortured and those you executed."

"*Especially* those! None were so treated that I did not personally determine were deserving of their fate!"

"As you determined the fate deserved by your son?"

"His above all others! In his weakness, he betrayed me, betrayed his *country!* Justice demanded his death, as it did the deaths of his fellow conspirators!"

"And yet you would abrogate that justice, were you given the chance."

"Never!"

The old woman smiled again. "Would you not? What, then, is this desire to give back to Irik Zal'honan the life that your own justice took from him? Where is the fairness in that?"

"There is a higher justice demanded of those whose destiny it is to rule."

"And that higher justice demands what? That your son

be returned to life while all others remain in their graves?"

"The others can rest easily in their graves! Theirs was not the responsibility to lead! Their failures were small by comparison, and unsurprising. Before my son can rest easily, he must be redeemed! Before he can rest, the weakness that overtook him, the weakness that others fostered in him, the weakness that led to his betrayal must be overcome and expunged!"

"And if he does not wish to be redeemed?"

"The choice is not his!"

"If not his, then whose?"

"*Mine!* It is my *duty* to see that he is redeemed, that he can finally go to his rest!"

"*Your* duty, Master Firan?"

Under her prodding, a thousand memories flooded Firan's mind.

A thousand failures bred by a thousand weaknesses of his own.

A thousand instances of when his discipline of the boy had not been thorough or harsh enough, his reasoning not cogent enough to convince the boy of the rightness of the course his father had chosen for him.

And for the last six years of Irik's tragically short life, Firan had, he realized now, completely abdicated his responsibility to the boy. Despite the suddenness of the boy's seeming awakening to the harsh realities of life, despite his unexpected acceptance of his father's edicts, Firan had taken the boy's word for his conversion. He had not used his magic to determine its truth or falsity, as he would have with any servant or ally. He had not ferreted out the truth, as he surely could have done, and then faced it and fought it with all his might.

And that had been the greatest failure of all: It had

allowed Irik to become a traitor. It had enabled him to ferry secrets and warnings to his so-called friends for six long years.

And it had sent him to a traitor's death at his father's hand.

"*My duty!*" Firan grated. "Can't you see? It was *my* failure that allowed this weakness to take root within him! It was *my* failure that led directly to his death!"

"And if you were given a second chance, you would, for his own good, remedy those failures? Is that your true heart's desire?"

"Of course it is! What father could say otherwise?"

"What father indeed. Certainly not one who slew his son with his own hand."

"*It was necessary! That was my duty as well!*"

"Only you can be the judge of where your duty lies and what form it takes. Likewise, only you can determine your own heart's desire."

The old woman stood, the movement so smooth it was as if she had levitated. As she turned, her black skirt billowed out like a shadow in the firelight. The men who had stood guard behind her parted as smoothly as she had risen. The youngest picked up the stool and followed as she made her way back to her wagon, offering his arm as she reached the steps.

"It is time to continue on our way," she said. At the top of the steps, she turned to look at Firan. "It is time for you to move on as well."

Then the colorful door was closing behind her, and the men were climbing into the drivers' seats. A mist was rising from the nearby river gully. Shadows seemed to gather high above the campfire, which was dying, though it had been only minutes since it had flared into life.

"Wait!" he shouted, but the wagons were already moving, the mist billowing out from the gully, enveloping them.

And the shadows . . .

Suddenly he was alone, the mists blotting out everything but the sound of the wagons and the quiet commands of their drivers.

"You have been given a second chance to achieve your heart's desire, Firan Zal'honan, Azal'Lan of Knurl," his long-dead father's voice rolled out of the mists. "Few are granted such a privilege. I certainly was not, when my sons were lost to me. Do not squander this opportunity as you have squandered so many in the past."

And his memories began to disappear.

Like the forgotten spells, they vanished one by one, leaving in their wake only the terrible knowledge that he *had* known something moments before, something that was now hidden, perhaps gone forever. His last memory was of two young boys, racing recklessly through the back alleys of a city he couldn't remember, on an errand he couldn't comprehend.

And then that, too, was gone.

For a moment, a wrenching dizziness struck at him, and he was confronted by a hideous figure in shrouds of the grave. For another moment, the figure's eyes, glowing coals deep in hollow sockets, bored into his, and then it was retreating through the mists, fleeing.

And he was alone, shivering and helpless.

PART IV

DARKON

 **TWENTY-TWO**

579, Barovian Calendar

On the cold stone floor, the shattered fragments of the golden dragon skull stirred, as if touched by a gentle whirlwind. Glittering in the near darkness, the shards circled like a swarm of tiny golden insects, first dusting along the floor itself, then rising slowly into the air to form a whirling spiral.

Even more slowly, the spinning cloud of particles drifted over the hideous thing on the floor. For a long time, it hovered over the body, then slowly descended, swirling about the head like a grotesque crown.

It brightened, almost sparkling.

The body twitched in its blood- and dirt-encrusted burial shroud. The eye sockets, black and empty until now, began once again to glow redly as consciousness reluctantly returned.

The swirling motes brightened again, grew thicker, and then hovered about the pedestal on which the skull had rested. All around the room, shadows stirred and muffled voices murmured.

And the dragon skull began to re-form out of the motes.

And to expand.

Like a glittering cloud, the skull took shape, growing larger and more ominous by the second.

Finally the motes took on solidity and fused into a massive whole.

Hundreds of times the size of the original skull that Firan Zal'honan, long ago on Oerth and then in Barovia, had worn on a chain around his neck, it rested imperiously on the pedestal. The horns, bare fractions of an inch before, were curving, foot-long daggers. The almost invisible depressions in the top of the skull were now deep, graceful indentations.

And in the mouth, flickering behind teeth whose living counterparts could rip a man to shreds, burned a flickering light that could never be extinguished, a light that cast a baleful glow on the paintings and carvings that stretched completely around the room. The one depicting the execution of Irik Zal'honan was back in its place, the stoically impassive face of the executioner plainly visible now.

Muffled laughter replaced the murmuring voices as consciousness returned to the creature—to the undead thing that Firan Darcalus Zal'honan had long ago become and had now become once more—and Azalin, whole again, lurched to his feet.

And the memory of what he was and what he had done and how he had been tricked descended over him like the poisonous fog that surrounded Strahd's castle.

"You played false with my memory!" he raged at the voices murmuring from the shadows. "The choice you offered was meaningless! The whole charade was just another of your endless, vicious tricks!"

"You were given the chance to achieve your true heart's desire." Irik's voice, laden with sarcasm, emerged from the shadows. "You were given the chance to forgive yourself for my death."

"Forgive *myself*? What madness is this? I need no forgiveness for meting out justice, least of all from myself!"

"There is no other from whom you will accept it," Irik's voice continued relentlessly. "You will not accept it even from me, though I have offered it endlessly."

"Nor will you accept it from me," his younger brother's voice, unheard in reality for more than a century and a half, spoke from the shadows.

"More tricks! You are not real, any of you! You are the voices of my tormentors, nothing more!"

"Your torment is of your own making," his son's voice said sadly. "Only you are capable of ending it."

"This is insane! I desire for you—I desire for my *son*—to have the chance to redeem himself for his weakness! That is *all* I desire!"

"Is that why you torment us both?" Irik's voice continued. "Is that why you refuse to allow my spirit to move on? So I can be redeemed? In whose eyes? In yours?"

"In his own!"

"To have acted in accord with my conscience is redemption enough, Father. As it should be with you."

"It is! My conscience is clear!"

The shadows stirred. "Then we will leave you to face it," his father's voice said. "You are what you are, Firan. It was always beyond my power to change you, and now it seems that it is beyond your own."

And the shadows were gone, allowing for no final reply.

For a long moment, he was silent, remembering, hardening. He would not allow his tormentors to win, to make him doubt himself. He would remain strong, as he had for over a hundred and fifty years.

His only error had been those moments of weakness when he had fallen prey to his own despair and wished for some indefinable surcease. That was when the powers that had long ago deposited him in Barovia had once again exercised their sadistic sense of humor. They had sent him once again through the mists, this time not as a single being but as two. They had given independent existence to the mortal body he had long ago abandoned and to the rotting shell he had grown to hate, and they had given each its own set of distorted and treacherous "memories."

A "second chance," they had called it, and they stood back and laughed as he made the inevitable—and correct!—decision.

Forgiveness!

No more! He would not again play into their hands by displaying weakness. He would play the hand as dealt, and damn the consequences! Let them do their worst!

His glowing eyes raked across the paintings, acknowledging their reality, denying their power over him. To prove to himself—*to them!*—that he could, he settled his gaze on Irik's image, then let it drift upward to the face behind the descending blade, the face of Firan Zal'honan, the mortal he had once been.

No weakness.

I was right then, and I am right now. I had no other acceptable choice. None. As I have no choice now but to continue searching for a way to give my son a chance for redemption.

Turning abruptly, he strode from the room, barely noticing that the bloody, dirt-encrusted burial shroud that had wrapped his decaying flesh had been replaced by the glistening ebony finery he had seemed to wear when "Lord Darcalus" had welcomed the guests to Avernus. And the rotting wreck of his face and body were once again being transformed into the illusion of humanity.

But not the golden-haired illusion he had presented then. Now that he was whole again, he was done with such vanity and foolishness. *You are what you are*, the shadows had said through his father's voice, and that is what he would be, at least for the rest of this night.

As he flowed down the stairs, his feet brushing against only an occasional step, the hawklike features of Firan Zal'honan formed and solidified. The illusion smiled grimly as he thought of Firan's companions of the evening and imagined their reaction to this development.

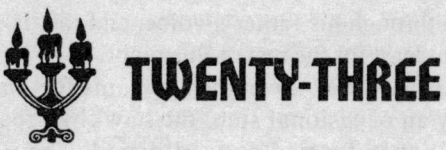

TWENTY-THREE

579, Barovian Calendar (continued)

"Where have you *been?*"

The anger in Balitor's voice was betrayed by the concern in his eyes as Oldar approached him through the milling crowd in the ballroom. There was no such concern in Lord Karawinn's face. The deliberate humiliation of having to stand by like a common servant while Aldewaine and the other nobles and their ladies gorged themselves and prattled on inconsequentially had long since drained his limited ration of forced good humor. Even Lady Karawinn, taking the place of the nonexistent Lady Aldewaine, had found a seat and seemed to be enjoying herself immensely despite her husband's increasingly obvious discomfiture.

"More to the point, Oldar," Karawinn snapped, brushing Balitor aside, "where is that fool who calls himself a wizard? Has he accomplished anything? Has he even *learned* anything, now that we have risked our lives gaining him entrance to this place?"

"He will have to tell you himself, my lord," Oldar said, lowering his eyes. "It has been a stranger time than I could have imagined, and I have understood none of it. He has told me I should leave Avernus as soon as it is possible. If it indeed will be possible."

The frowns of both questioners deepened, Balitor's in concern, Karawinn's in renewed annoyance. "What have you done that would prevent you—or any of us—from leaving?" Karawinn demanded.

"We were guided, I know not by what, to the nether regions of the castle, where I was possessed by a spirit claiming to be Master Firan's son. He sent me away when the spirit released me, so I know not—"

"What madness is this?" Karawinn hissed. "My cousin and I have virtually laid our lives in his hands, bringing him into Avernus under our protection, and you talk of possession."

"I know we were led to a place Master Firan wished to find."

"And what place was that?"

"I do not know. I know only that it is in the upper reaches of Avernus, high in a tower that must touch the sky. Master Firan seemed to recognize it, as he recognized the spirit of his son when it spoke through me. It meant me no harm. I was frightened, but only because of the utter strangeness of the experience, not because I feared the spirit might wish me ill."

"How very considerate of this wraith!" Karawinn's whisper was laden with sarcasm. "What of me? What of my cousin? Did this spirit—"

"*I would have your attention, my lords and ladies.*"

The cavernous rooms were filled with a sternly commanding voice, a voice that spoke not only to their ears but directly to their minds as well. Karawinn and a hundred others winced and fell silent, as if a needle prick had accompanied each word. Oldar and Balitor, eyes wide but otherwise unaffected, exchanged startled glances and looked up to the balcony, where, hours earlier, Darcalus had appeared to welcome them.

But the balcony was empty.

And the voice was coming from everywhere.

"My lords and ladies, your meal is at an end, and your presence is required in the ballroom."

Around the banquet table, the few who had continued to eat after the first words had been uttered were caught in paroxysms of coughing, spewing out showers of half-chewed delicacies.

When the coughing and choking finally subsided, there was total silence. Even the sound of breathing was subdued.

"I apologize for neglecting my earlier promise—Darcalus's promise—to speak individually with those with whom I had business, but the events of the evening have been such that those discussions are no longer required."

The disembodied voice paused to let a collective and uneasy sigh of relief rise from the assemblage.

"With a few exceptions," it went on, *"you will be free to be on your way to your lands before the night is over, and those exceptions will be dealt with here and now, for all to see . . . and to be instructed by."*

Dozens paled, none more so than Karawinn, his eyes filled with fear and fury as they sought out Oldar, but he somehow maintained his silence. Along the length of the table, there was the sound of a hundred chairs sliding backward simultaneously, snatched away by invisible hands. Some of the occupants crashed to the floor; others managed to lurch to their feet. Not a few grasped at the table covering and still fell, bringing the remains of their meals down upon them.

First one, then another began a lurching, marionette-like walk from the dining hall to the ballroom. Others, taking their lesson quickly, were suddenly trampling each other in an effort to reach the ballroom before they, too, were taken in hand.

As the last of the stragglers, Aldewaine and Lady Karawinn among them, had cleared the dining hall, the air above the balcony at the far end of the ballroom, almost directly above the tiny, drapery-hidden door through which Oldar had led Firan, shimmered, setting the wall behind to wavering like a distant desert mirage.

When the shimmering stopped, a figure stood there, a figure clad in deepest black, the same as Darcalus had earlier appeared in. But the face was not the handsome, boyish one they had all seen only hours before, nor was it topped by the equally illusory golden curls.

It was a leaner face, middle-aged and hawk-nosed, its hair dark and straight, its glittering eyes stern and hard.

"Firan!" The harsh whisper of the name emerged unbidden from Karawinn's throat. For a moment, his face was a model of confusion and puzzlement, but then he grinned, barely able to suppress a shout of glee.

"He did it!" The hiss of his whispered words could not have carried a dozen yards, and yet the diamond-hard eyes of the figure in black turned immediately to Lord Karawinn.

A faint smile, as unforgiving as the eyes, slithered across the parchment-thin lips.

"Lord Karawinn," the figure acknowledged, the words now spoken normally, even quietly, no longer projected simultaneously into the minds of the listeners. Even so, the words reached every corner of the massive, crowded room. "I take it you are pleased with my new appearance."

The grin that Karawinn had struggled to control faded,

not because of the words but because of the icy tone. His eyes darted questioningly toward Oldar, who could offer no counsel.

"It—it seems you have achieved your goal," Karawinn stammered.

"In a manner of speaking," the figure agreed. "But there is more to be done this night." The eyes left Karawinn and focused on the crowd near the door to the dining hall. "Bargains to be discussed. Is that not true, Baron Aldewaine? Lady Karawinn?"

"There was an agreement made, Master Firan," Aldewaine's voice, wary but not yet as uneasy as Karawinn's, agreed.

"There was." The figure smiled again, its lips like razors. "Unfortunately for you, the one you knew as Firan was not in full possession of the facts when that agreement was made. But now that he is . . ."

"But *you* are Firan!" Aldewaine's voice protested.

"Again I must say, 'in a manner of speaking.' I am and I am not. I was and I may be again. I choose now to be addressed as Lord Azalin. The events of this night are likely beyond your comprehension, as certain aspects are yet beyond my own. Therefore I will deal only with matters that are clearly understood by all involved."

"As you wish," Aldewaine agreed.

"As I wish, indeed. And what of *your* wishes? Your fondest wish, as I recall, was to live the rest of your days here, in Avernus."

A collective gasp rose from the crowd, but Aldewaine remained silent.

"Was that not your wish, Baron Aldewaine?" the figure prodded.

"As it would be anyone's," Aldewaine finally said, the

wariness in his voice edging over into uneasiness if not fear.

"Perhaps. But no others have been prepared to go to the lengths that you and your cousin were willing to go. Is *that* not right, Aldewaine?"

There was a long silence before Aldewaine spoke again, his voice tight. "No further than you yourself, Master Firan."

The figure nodded sagely. "No further than Firan," it said musingly. "Quite right. But as I have already pointed out, Firan was not in full possession of the facts, and I am not entirely he. But that is unimportant now. Is it not time for you to be given a better view of your new home?"

Without waiting for an answer, the figure gestured beckoningly. A moment later, Aldewaine let out a muffled scream. The press of other nobles surrounding him suddenly loosened as they backed away, gasps and curses escaping their lips.

Slowly a visibly struggling Aldewaine rose out of the crowd into the air, as if gripped by an invisible hand. Gasps and screams filled the ballroom for a moment, followed by total silence as Aldewaine continued to rise and then drift, no longer struggling, toward the figure on the balcony.

"Surely you wish to invite your cousin and his lady to share in your good fortune," the figure said, its eyes going briefly to Karawinn and Lady Karawinn before it twice repeated the earlier gesture.

Karawinn screamed and grabbed at Oldar's clothing, but his fingertip grasp was torn free as he lifted slowly from the floor. Across the room, Lady Karawinn, tight-lipped and silent, was rising also.

"And while you observe your new domain, Lord Aldewaine, we must think what to do with that which you are leaving behind." The figure smiled, this time in seemingly genuine amusement, as the three continued to drift toward the balcony. Then it looked down, its eyes fastening on Balitor.

"My friend Balitor, you have been within Aldewaine's estate. Did it strike your fancy?"

Balitor gulped. "It is far too grand for the likes of me."

"As it was for the likes of its previous owner," the figure said. "Nonetheless, you strike me as both intelligent and pragmatic, just the characteristics required of one who would govern Il Aluk."

"I would not presume—"

"There is no need. It is my decision . . . Baron."

Another gesture, and the golden chain that held Aldewaine's medallion of office about his neck jerked sharply upward, tugging at his hair, the medallion scraping roughly against his face. Then it was free, floating tantalizingly over Aldewaine's head like a twisted halo. His eyes wide in terror, Aldewaine flailed the air, grabbing for the medallion as it floated gracefully out of his reach.

"Your badge of office, friend Balitor," the figure said, "and the deed to your estate." As he spoke, the medallion, its chain trailing like the tail of a comet, swooped through the air. Balitor cringed as it came to a stop, hovering above his head. Gently, not so much as brushing against his unkempt hair, the chain settled around his neck, the medallion centered perfectly on his liveried chest.

"You are most generous, my lord," Balitor managed to say.

"To those who do not offend me," the figure said in seeming agreement.

Aldewaine's journey through the air was coming to an end. Approaching the balcony, he had ceased struggling except to raise his arms before his face as if to shield himself from the sight of the waiting black-clad figure.

Then he was hovering a yard above the balcony. Slowly he was turned until he faced the crowd.

The figure nodded minutely, and Aldewaine was released.

Arms flailing, he landed with a thud a few feet from the figure, staggered backward, almost falling, and came up hard against the wall.

And stayed there, legs bent, arms akimbo, as if frozen.

The figure turned back to the crowd, its eyes, now glowing very faintly, coming to rest on Oldar.

"And you, my young friend . . ."

"There is nothing I desire, Master Fir—Lord Azalin," he said quickly.

"Is that true, young Oldar? Did the Vistani woman not speak of your father? And of your desire to return to the land he still tills?"

"If I am permitted, I will leave Il Aluk before daybreak."

"And you and your father are pleased with Baron Cauldry? His laws, his tax levies, have not been too burdensome, his decrees too onerous? You would not wish to take his place, as your friend Balitor has taken Aldewaine's?"

"I would not rule over others," the young man said, his voice trembling. "It is neither my nature nor my desire."

From somewhere in the crowd, a voice was raised in nervous protest, but a gesture from the figure restored silence. "Do not presume to question my words, Cauldry. There are others who would accept your medallion gladly."

While the figure had been speaking to Oldar, Karawinn and his lady had followed Aldewaine's path and now floated above the balcony. Without looking toward them, the figure gestured minutely, and they were released, crashing to the balcony floor, stumbling and lurching backward until they were frozen in place on either side of Aldewaine. All three faces were chalky white, the beauty marks and paint on Lady Karawinn's face standing out like a parody of her original intent.

The figure turned back to Oldar. "Very well, young Oldar. By your dispensation, Cauldry can remain . . . for now. You shall have the estate of those who would have murdered you. Your father can come and live out his years in the luxury he doubtless deserves."

Oldar's eyes went to Balitor, who was nodding vehemently, urging him to accept. But he could not.

"He would not come," Oldar said, his voice steadying slightly, though his heart still pounded thunderously in his ears. "It is not in his nature to endure luxury, least of all in Il Aluk, as it is not in mine to rule others. Most assuredly, he would rather perish than come to this city, and if he were forced to come, he *would* soon perish."

"Then what *do* you wish, young Oldar?" The figure's eyes had hardened once again, and a trace of annoyance had entered its voice.

"Only one thing, Lord Azalin: to be allowed to do as you yourself instructed me when we parted only minutes ago."

"But that was before—" The figure broke off, and Oldar suppressed a wince, half expecting to be hoisted into the air like the others.

"I did not mean to offend, Lord Azalin," he said.

The figure shook its head. "Rest assured, you did not. And I remember well that advice. My word will not be broken. You shall be on your way by daybreak, if such is your desire."

"It is, Lord Azalin."

"Very well. But you shall not go empty-handed. I myself

will purchase the estate of which you have recently become owner."

The figure gestured, and a shower of gold coins appeared in the air before Oldar. A moment later, a leather pouch appeared, not unlike the ones that had held the vials, but larger. As if falling through an invisible funnel, the coins slid into the pouch, its drawstring tightening after them.

Briefly it hung motionless, then fell. Oldar, who had himself stood motionless throughout, suddenly and jerkily reached out and caught the pouch.

The figure's eyes swept across the crowd. "Let it be known," it said, and the voice became stentorian, as if issuing from a hundred-foot giant, shaking the very walls, "that this young man is under my personal protection. Should anything untoward occur, should he be harmed in any way, should a single coin be taken from him without his freely given consent, the offender will answer to me!"

The figure turned toward the three who stood trembling against the wall beside him. "As these three shall now answer for their own misdeeds!"

The figure gestured once again, and three crystal goblets appeared before them. At first they were empty, but as the three captives watched, a blood-red liquid bubbled into existence until all three goblets were filled to near the rim.

Already ashen pale, the three struggled to press themselves backward into the very stone of the wall against which they stood.

"A toast," the figure said, its voice returning to normal as a fourth goblet appeared in the air before it. The goblet filled as the others had, and the figure reached out and plucked it from the air, then held it out toward the three.

The figure smiled, its lips razor thin, its eyes once again diamond hard. The three still cringed against the wall, their eyes focusing on the goblets as if they were snakes about to strike.

"It is both impolitic and impolite to fail to join one's lord and master in a freely offered toast," the figure said, swirling the blood-red liquid in its own goblet. "Perhaps you require assistance."

Oldar opened his mouth to speak, but Balitor clamped a hand on his arm. "Hold your tongue," Balitor hissed, leaning close, "before your overly forgiving nature costs both of us our lives! Those three deserve whatever happens to them, and even if they didn't, it is no business of ours!"

Balitor winced and clamped his lips tightly together as the figure's eyes darted momentarily in his direction.

Your friend counsels you well, young Oldar. The words appeared in Oldar's mind, apparently in no other's. *Do not raise your voice in protest lest you exhaust my patience.*

Reluctantly Oldar held his silence, and the figure's attention returned to the three frozen on the balcony. The goblets had been drifting slowly toward them, and now three right hands came up, trembling violently, to grasp them. The goblets shook as fingers closed about them, and yet not a drop of the blood-red contents escaped, though time and again it splashed well above the rims. Slowly their bodies straightened from the awkward positions they had fallen into when they had been dropped onto the balcony.

Once again the figure held the fourth goblet out toward Aldewaine and the Karawinns at almost eye level. This time, each of the three took a lurching step forward, their goblets extended stiffly before them. Slowly, deliberately, the figure touched the fourth goblet to each of the three in turn.

"To the new baron of Il Aluk," the figure said, placing the goblet to its lips, "and to his long and successful rule."

And as the fourth goblet was drained, the other three, held in hands that trembled even more violently than before, were brought toward tightly clenched lips below glazed and terror-filled eyes. Then the goblets were pressing against those lips, gently at first, then with greater force.

A trickle of blood appeared in the corner of Aldewaine's mouth.

The goblet shattered, the shards stabbing into his lips, but the blood-red liquid did not spill. Instead, it mixed with Aldewaine's blood and formed a mask that covered both mouth and nose.

"No!" Oldar's voice shattered the silence. "Even they do not deserve such as—"

A gesture by the figure brought Oldar's words to a halt, though he continued to strain to speak through lips that were suddenly numb and leaden. Balitor gripped the young man's shoulders, pleading with his eyes for him to be silent.

"They receive only what they would have dealt the two of you and the one called Firan Zal'honan," the figure said, its voice as hard as its eyes. "I deal in justice, nothing more and nothing less."

Clawing with bloody fingers at the smothering, poisonous mass, Aldewaine suddenly spasmed backward, slamming once again against the wall, jarring loose the last vestige of control over his starving lungs. The blood-red liquid, mixed with his own blood and shards of the shattered goblet, vanished into his mouth and nostrils, only to be spewed out a moment later amid a paroxysm of coughing.

But even as it sprayed into the air, it halted and turned back like a grisly tide, and this time it covered Aldewaine's entire face like a bloody hangman's hood.

And was absorbed, the liquid as if through his pores, the shards of glass making their own portals in his flesh.

With a gurgling scream, he fell.

And the Karawinns, whose goblets still pressed against their lips but as yet less viciously than Aldewaine's, exchanged a final glance and let their lips fly apart and the poison flow in.

Soon, their features still whole but locked in grimaces of agony, they joined Aldewaine on the floor.

The figure turned once again to face the shocked silence of the crowd below.

"Thus ends this night's lesson," it said. "Take it to heart, my lords and ladies. Take it to heart."

A gesture, little more than a raising of the fingers of its right hand, and the massive door to the outer bailey lumbered open to reveal a cluster of waiting carriages. By the time it was fully open, dozens had already scurried through to search for their conveyances, and the balcony was bare except for the three bodies.

 **TWENTY-FOUR**

579, Barovian Calendar (continued)

Azalin—for he had finally assumed that corruption of his title as his name, not just in his words to the fawning barons but in his own thoughts as well—watched from the highest parapet of Avernus as the antlike carriages scurried along the moonless road toward Il Aluk. The tatters of his grimy burial shroud fluttered in a breeze he had not bothered to still. Gone was the illusion of the shimmering black garments that so matched the mood of his unbeating heart. Gone was the hawk-nosed Zal'honan face he had worn for so many years in life. Gone was the face his Darcalus fragment had worn, the face that had never been in life, the bright-eyed face of what could have been, what *should* have been, except for the horrors of that night more than a century and a half in the past, in a land that might itself no longer exist.

Here stood the reality of Azalin, his only reality: hideous, decaying flesh clinging to ancient bones, kept from disintegration only by forces he had long ago realized he did not understand, even though he had wielded them with his own tongue, with his own thoughts. But that wielding had been unknowingly done under the guidance of beings whose nature and purpose he understood less with each passing year.

What would the preening fools he had instructed this night think if they were made privy to this reality? Would they be even more horrified than by the object lesson he had delivered? Would they be cowed by the powers that were obviously required for such a reality to exist? Or would they, like the ones in that other world who had maintained a vendetta down through the generations, gather courage from the truth and rise up in sufficient numbers to drive him out? To destroy him, even?

And if they did . . .

If they did rise up against him, brandishing their mortal weapons, perhaps finding a mage foolhardy enough to join them, would he resist? Would he destroy them as he had Aldewaine and his sniveling cousin? Or would he yield himself up in the hope that they would succeed, that his existence—not his life, but his existence; his life had ended nearly a century past—*could* be ended?

If tonight were that night, if the hordes were to come clambering up the stairs and walls this very minute, would he fight or yield? Despite his vow never again to give in to weakness, he could not be certain what his decision would be.

For in this night's obscene reunion, he had come finally to realize, fully and viscerally realize, the true nature of the bargain he had struck that long-ago night. He had come finally to realize what he had given up: life itself, and everything that entailed.

For all those years—six long decades in the world of his birth, more than half as many more in the accursed land of the thing that called itself Strahd—for all those seemingly endless years, he had, to an increasing extent, deluded himself. He had, unconsciously but methodically, forgotten what it had meant to be *alive*.

But now he had been reminded: In those brief days and nights when the mortal man he had been, Firan Darcalus Zal'honan, had been called into existence once again, independent existence, he had once again experienced what it was to be alive. He had also experienced to the fullest the horror and hatred of what he had become—and what he had done. No matter that it was all a deception, no matter that all his actions had been right and just. For those few days and hours, the life and the hatred and the revulsion had been real, and his memories of that time could not be conveniently wiped out, nor even blurred as the decades had blurred the memories of a century ago. They were sharp and vivid and verged on intolerable.

It mattered not that his magic allowed him to detect a million things that human senses could not. It mattered not that he could cast a spell that would create the illusion of virtually anything he desired, from the pleasures of an exotic meal to the release of a sexual encounter. It mattered not, because none of it was *real!* The only thing that was real was this rotting body, held together by invisible forces he could neither control nor understand, and *it* experienced nothing.

No, that was not entirely true, the Darcalus memories told him unexpectedly. There was, they said, one sensation this body *could* experience: pain. It *had* experienced pain, relentless and excruciating, again and again, whenever . . .

Forcing the unwanted memory aside, Azalin saw that the last of the carriages had straggled onto the road to Il Aluk, and he was once again alone in Avernus.

Except . . .

An image of Aldewaine and the Karawinns sprang up in his mind, their bodies still crumpled on the balcony overlooking the ballroom.

If not for their treachery, none of this would have occurred, he thought. If they had not sought out the weapon of cowards and weaklings . . .

They had perished far too quickly, far too easily.

But that could still be remedied.

Turning from the parapet, he flowed into the tower and down.

*   *   *   *   *

Alone inside the ornate carriage they had ridden atop bare hours earlier, Oldar and Balitor sat uncomfortably on the velvet cushions. Uneasily Oldar leaned out the window and looked back at Avernus, a dimly visible hulk against the night sky.

Shivering, he fell back into the seat, occupied on that last trip by Lord Karawinn.

"Will I really be allowed to return to my home, do you think?" he asked, his voice a mixture of nervousness and earnestness.

Balitor laughed sharply, not altogether comfortably. "You will or you will not. Idle speculation will have no effect on the reality. However, if you would care to enlighten me as to what actually transpired between you and Master Firan while you were strolling the passages of Avernus, I might be better able to provide an educated guess."

The young man shook his head, not in refusal but perhaps in bewilderment. "I suspect I was possessed, but never having had such an experience before, I can hardly vouch for the truth of it."

"So you said before our mutual enrichment. You also said that whatever spoke through you laid claim to being Master Firan's son. Was this true? Or some demon's trick?"

"How can I know? Master Firan appeared to believe it was his son, though it may have been more his desire than his senses that prompted his belief."

Balitor snorted. "You ask me to define your future, yet you yourself cannot even define your past. Do you take me for one of the Vistani?"

Oldar flushed. "Forgive me. I did not mean to—"

"Do not be constantly begging forgiveness, young Oldar, not with me, at least. Now, may I assume that you will at least keep me company my first night as Baron of Il Aluk? I would be most pleased to have a familiar and trusted face at my side."

"You—you wish me to stay the night in Baron Aldewaine's manor?"

Balitor grinned and shook his head. "Not at all. I wish you to stay the night in *my* manor!"

"You are going to accept these riches, then?"

Balitor laughed. "It was Master Firan's wish. Or Lord Azalin's wish. In any event, you saw what happened to those who defy the wishes of—of whoever now rules Darkon, did you not?"

"But surely that was different." Oldar shuddered at the memory. "They had plotted to kill him. We had no such plans."

"To one with such powers, there is probably little difference between us. Would you distinguish between a mosquito that merely whined around your head and one that landed and supped upon a drop of your blood? Would you swat the one and not the other?"

"But we are not mosquitoes!"

"Are we not? To one such as Azalin, I daresay we are less. But you have not answered my invitation, young Oldar. Will you stay the night or not?"

Oldar glanced once again out the window. Though he could not see it, he could still feel the looming presence of Avernus.

He let his breath out in a whoosh. "Very well, I will stay, but only the night. I must be on my way at daybreak."

Before Firan, or Azalin, or Darcalus, or whoever he is changes his mind, he thought with a shiver.

* * * * *

Once more cloaked in the Zal'honan image, Azalin looked down at the bloody, crumpled bodies.

He reached out with his mind for their spirits and found them, gibbering in the same voiceless fear they had been drowning in at their deaths.

He smiled, unsurprised. He had not expected that the shadows—or whichever of their unknown brethren watched over Avernus—would have let these souls slip from their influence so quickly or so easily. He himself had been under their watchful eyes, if they had such mundane organs, for close to a century with no end in sight. There was no reason to think that others who attracted their attention would fare better.

Murmuring the same words he had pronounced so precisely over Irik's sarcophagus in that other world, he watched as the bodies, one by one, began to twitch with a form of life. They were the same words he had subsequently used a hundred—a thousand!—times to create the armies of the dead that had so often fought his battles. But those times, the spirits had already moved on, leaving the bodies mindless husks that would blindly do his will. Now, however. the spirits were being returned, were being imprisoned in those husks.

As Irik would have been imprisoned in his own decayed body.

As he himself had been imprisoned for a hundred years in *his*.

They would serve him. Their bodies would do his bidding while their imprisoned souls could offer no resistance, only undergo whatever degradations he chose to visit upon them.

They would, as they had wished, live out their "lives" in Avernus, but not in quite the way they had hoped. And not nearly as quickly as their swift deaths might have led them to expect. Their "lives" would continue until the time came that he deemed their punishment sufficient.

He could not, at this moment, imagine that time would ever come.

He looked down into their bruised and bloody faces and saw not the blank stares of undead, mindless slaves but the terrified eyes of a trio of souls who were finally beginning to realize what lay in store for them.

Father! Surely they have suffered enough!

Irik's voice lanced through his mind. The shadows once again. What new torment were they offering now?

"Enough of this charade!" Azalin snapped. "If you wish to speak to me, speak with a different voice!"

I have no other voice, Father. I am Irik, your son.

"What sort of fool do you take me for? Now, begone! No torment can add to what has already been visited upon me this night!"

I am not one of those you call your tormentors, Father. I

am truly your son.

Azalin looked up sharply, as if to face his tormentors, though he knew that such an act was itself a charade.

But the air in the massive ballroom was clear. In the lights from a hundred sconces, no shadows hovered in the corners nor billowed over his head. And the voice, he realized, unlike the others, spoke directly to his mind, not to his ears.

Unexpectedly, hope flared within him. Could it be true?

"Was it truly you who spoke through Oldar earlier this night?"

It was. Your mind was closed to me then, but his was open, a kindred soul.

"Why did you not tell me the truth, then?" he asked suspiciously, remembering.

I did not lie, Father.

"Perhaps not, but you couched your words in a manner meant to deceive. And there was much you did *not* tell me!"

I told you all that I was allowed, as clearly as I was allowed.

"Then you *are* under their control!"

No more so than are you, Father.

"No! No matter how much they may torment me, they do not control me!"

Then how is it that you are here? How is it that you do not still rule in Knurl? How is it that, for a time, your very memories were not your own?

"That was trickery, not control! As were the half-truths you spoke through Oldar!"

Would you have believed the full truth, Father? Would you? Or would you have thought it merely another trick designed to thwart your plans for vengeance?

"Enough!" he thundered, the hope of moments before drowned in directionless anger. "I will hear no more of this! If your purpose is still only to add to my torment, begone!"

To be gone from here is my fondest wish, but I am no less a prisoner than you. You who bound me to my tomb know that as well as I.

Suspicion flared brighter. "If you are bound to your tomb, how come you to be here? Your tomb lies not in this place but in Knurl, on the very spot—"

Does your memory still play you false, Father? Do you not remember even that?

Suddenly he did.

Suddenly he did remember.

TWENTY-FIVE

579, Barovian Calendar (continued)

Memories that had lain dormant in his mind since the reunion were awakening and demanding the attention he had been denying them.

Memories of the thing that had called itself Lord Darcalus, memories of the days and years since the part of him that had *been* Darcalus had emerged from the mists and found itself in Avernus. The days and years the part of him that had been Lord Darcalus had ruled Darkon while the part of him that had remained Firan Zal'honan still wandered the mists.

Upon his emergence from the mists, Darcalus had been burdened with even fewer memories than Firan. As Firan had remembered nothing of the undead creature he had once been, the emerging Darcalus had remembered nothing of the mortal *he* had once been. Nothing consciously, at least, though the golden-haired mask he had hidden behind indicated that memories of his long-dead brother had still operated at some level.

For those years, Darcalus had occupied himself exploring the limits of his powers and learning of this strange land he had apparently been given to rule over. Unlike Firan, he had accepted his situation without question, not seeming to care that, like Strahd in Barovia, he was prisoner as well as ruler. He had, his dregs of memory told him, once ruled in another land now lost to him, and once, even further back in time, he had himself been like those he now ruled: pitiable mortal creatures subject to precious few pleasures and countless miseries, many of the latter of which were visited upon them by their lords and masters, beings of power such as Darcalus himself. The massive granite sarcophagus he found high in one of the towers had at first seemed naggingly familiar, an indistinct reminder of something he didn't want to remember, something from those lost years, but he had soon been able to push it from his conscious mind.

His only desire, sterile though it was, had been to safeguard and enhance his powers and his position. For both had their limitations. And limitations meant vulnerability, the possibility of defeat, even the possibility of being returned to that former powerless existence he had long ago escaped in a manner he could no longer recall and certainly could not duplicate.

That quest for greater power had eventually lead Darcalus to a room high in Avernus, not far below the parapet from which Azalin had earlier this night looked out into the darkness toward the hovels and mansions of Il Aluk. And not far from the room in which the half-forgotten sarcophagus still lay.

In that room, Darcalus had discovered, to his muted amazement, his powers were enhanced. Spells ineffective anywhere else were quick and powerful there. Spells of limited range elsewhere, if cast from there, could touch the farthest corners of the land. The spells that shielded Avernus from its foes, mortal and magical, when cast from there became truly impenetrable.

But there was, he had quickly learned, a price: pain.

It started as a thousand pricking needles, a feeling Azalin now remembered dimly from his mortal days when he had lain too long in a cramped position. But instead of dissipating, as his long-ago mortal affliction had, the pricking grew into an invisible flame that burned deeper and deeper into his unchanging flesh. What the next level of agony might be was yet unknown, for Darcalus had never had reason great enough to remain in the room to discover it. The few experiments, the few protective spells he had cast, had been completed before that next level was reached.

But now . . .

Now, if Darcalus's muffled memories were true . . .

And if this voice that claimed to be his son were not simply another trick to torment him . . .

Aldewaine and the Karawinns forgotten despite Irik's repeated pleas for their release, Azalin sped through the maze that was Avernus, following Darcalus's reluctant memories.

The room he sought, he realized as he came to a stop in the narrow stone stairway short minutes later, was the same one Firan and Oldar had been passing when the boy had been possessed by Irik's spirit. And a dozen yards below the spot where the pain had, only moments later, reached out and took Firan in its grip.

The door to this level was an unadorned slab of discolored timber, hung from massive iron hinges. No spells protected or sealed it. No lock barred entrance, only a simple latch that could be lifted from either side.

Under his touch, the door swung back, its hinges creaking loudly.

He stepped inside.

Like the room he had entered short hours ago, it filled virtually the entire breadth of the tower. Unlike the other room, with its scores of paintings, the walls of this room were hidden behind dusty, moth-eaten tapestries of ornate but meaningless design, barely visible in the dim light from a single ceiling sconce.

Directly beneath the sconce stood a massive granite sarcophagus, its every surface elaborately carved. A faint mist hovered over it, as if to protect it.

Or as if struggling to escape.

Within the sarcophagus, his senses told him, lay the time-ravaged body of his son.

It was true, then. Or perhaps it was yet another trick, another illusion to be snatched away at the last minute.

But it didn't matter. He had no choice but to continue as if it were real. His vow to his son demanded it. His own sense of duty demanded it.

A gesture, and the massive cover of the sarcophagus began to slowly grate to the side. The mist fluttered helplessly. Irik's pleading voice, no longer concerned with Aldewaine and the Karawinns but with his own fate, clamored at the gates of Azalin's mind.

No, Father! it said again and again. *Do not subject us both to this madness any longer!*

But he knew what he must do. He must restore the life he had taken, and most importantly, he must then give his son the strength he needed to use that life to achieve redemption, not succumb once again to weakness.

But first he must recover the parchment on which the necessary spell was recorded. Murmuring the words he had waited four decades to utter, he watched eagerly as the front of his illusory tunic shimmered and parted, as the decaying flesh of his own chest writhed and dissolved.

And then, from the chambers of his unbeating heart, a crystalline oval emerged, glistening and bloodless. As his flesh became whole again, as the illusory tunic sealed itself seamlessly, the crystalline oval darkened and expanded, the air around it shimmering and warping the light like a twisting sphere of misshapen lenses.

With a faint hiss, the distortions vanished, and a sheet of parchment hung in the air before him, its faded script as tantalizing as when he had made it a part of himself nearly forty years before. At the same moment, the cover of the sarcophagus grated to a stop, on the verge of crashing to the floor.

Despite himself, Azalin shuddered as the skeletal body of his son began to rise into view. Only shreds of flesh remained on the hairless skull, none at all on the fingers that gripped the edge of the granite coffin as the corpse struggled to lift itself upright.

The mist that had hovered and fluttered above the sarcophagus arched upward, as if trying to avoid contact with the emerging thing, and the litany of pleading for release reached new heights of intensity in Azalin's mind.

"When we have both redeemed ourselves," he murmured as the figure of his son climbed from the coffin and lurched to the floor, the remnants of the body mercifully hidden by the burial shroud, "you will be free. We both will be free."

The now fully formed parchment in his hand, Azalin took control of the empty husk and walked beside it to the door and up the steps. He braced himself for the onset of the pain as the darkly glowing, bronzelike door came into view.

But it did not come.

With growing suspicion, he continued up the steps, the

thing that had been his son plodding mindlessly at his side. Still there was no pain.

Were the Darcalus memories false, then?

No, it had not been Darcalus but Firan who had—

"If you are impatient to experience pain, Zal'honan," the voice of the Nyrondese traitor Stakaster said, "do not be timid. We await your pleasure."

And with the words, a billowing shadow appeared out of nowhere and dimmed the door's already faint glow as it swung open in utter silence.

Do not enter, Father! Irik's voice flooded his mind, but even as it did, there was an echo of laughter—Irik's laughter, and then his father's, and then Quantarius's.

And all the while Irik's voice, seemingly independent of the others, continued to plead in his mind.

Finally he was at the door.

There were no sconces, no individual sources of light, but a soft greenish-yellow glow seeped from the walls themselves. Except for a bare plank table in the center of the room, it was empty, barren of all furnishings and life.

As Azalin stepped inside, the walls of the room seemed to waver, twisting and shifting with his slightest motion, as if the light itself could not decide, from moment to moment, what path it would take.

But the dizzying distortions were forced from his consciousness an instant later. The moment he was fully within the room, his entire body was drenched in pain—not the pins-and-needles prickling he had been expecting from the Darcalus memories but the agony of skin being peeled from flesh, of every square inch of his flesh being seared by open flames.

Involuntarily he jerked backward toward the door, but the echoing laughter of the shadows halted the movement.

It was, he realized abruptly, a test of his resolve, the first step in his *own* redemption. He had failed his son during Irik's brief life, and when faced with that failure, he had surrendered, albeit briefly, to weakness, and now he must prove his strength anew.

But would the spell, even here, be torn from his mind as he tried to mouth its words? The constant fiery pain would be distraction enough, under normal circumstances, to break his concentration, to render all but the simplest spells useless.

But now, with Irik's resurrection and both their redemptions at stake . . .

Through the agony, he gestured the tattered remnants of Irik's body into the room. There was no hesitation, no reaction as it stepped inside.

Azalin made his way through the invisible sea of fire to the table at the room's center, the searing pain growing worse with each step. He laid the parchment on the table and gestured the thing that would be Irik to lie next to the parchment. The mist that *was* Irik fluttered in the doorway, his pleading voice half obliterated from Azalin's mind by the constant pain.

Silently, meticulously, he read the faded words on the parchment.

He lifted his eyes to the burial shroud and the bones and shreds of flesh that protruded from it. He visualized his son as he had been moments before his death: standing behind the block, head unbowed, looking out over the crowd that had assembled to watch and savor a dozen violent deaths.

He looked down at the remnants of his own body and wondered: If Irik's body can be restored, perhaps mine can be restored as well.

The pain escalated a notch, though he hadn't thought that

possible, and he gripped the edge of the table to steady himself. A warning? Or the natural progression?

Quickly he turned his eyes back to the parchment and began to read aloud, focusing on the faded script, seeing in his mind the body once again whole.

And the reading of the spell *was* possible!

Somehow, in spite of the added distraction of the invisible flames that ate at his flesh, he was able to simultaneously speak the words and hold in his mind both their meaning and an image of the intended results.

And the body began to change.

A shred of scarlet flesh showed where, moments before, only the white of the skull could be seen. The bones of one finger twitched as tendons appeared and spasmed momentarily. The burial shroud shifted as the bones beneath it were slowly enveloped in flesh, as organs long fallen into dust began to re-form. Noisome fluid bubbled up in the eye sockets of the skull and slowly took shape and color.

And all the while, the unseen flames continued to sear and the words continued to be spoken, until finally it was the face of his son, not a hundred-year-old corpse, that stared unseeingly, mindlessly at nothing.

One step remained, but it was not a step that required he stay in this room. Already this night he had performed it on others.

Releasing his grip on the table edge, he gestured at the now perfect body. Slowly it raised itself into a sitting position and turned to set its feet on the floor and stand. At first its motions were erratic and uncertain, as if it were a marionette in the hands of an untrained puppeteer, but with each move, it seemed to grow steadier, until, as it neared the door, its gait was sure and graceful despite the blank, unseeing eyes.

As it reached the door and Azalin took his first step to follow, he was struck by the next level of agony: nausea. He doubled over uncontrollably as the stomach that had felt neither food nor water in nearly a century, the stomach whose last contents had been the vile, poisonous brew that had ended his mortality, heaved and churned and the desiccated throat spasmed like an imprisoned serpent.

But only dust spewed forth as the shadows laughed.

Staggering, unable to fully control his wretched body for the first time in a century, Azalin lurched across the floor, the distortions in the air around him growing greater, adding to the nausea with each step. The door, square and massive one second, was oval the next, then shrinking to a pinpoint before momentarily returning to its true size and shape. The walls, their yellow glow pulsing now, alternately receded and closed in on him, bending and twisting like ship's sails in the wind until . . .

As if vomited from the belly of some carrion-eating monster, Azalin pitched from the room and crashed to the grimy stone of the stairway landing, inches from the feet of Irik's body. As he lay there, crumpled, the nausea faded, and then the pain receded like a befouled tide flowing back into the sea.

Strength returning, he lurched to his feet.

Irik—Irik's body—stood waiting, the only imperfection a faint scar that ringed the neck.

He had won! Despite every obstacle the shadows had thrown in his path, despite every trick, every deception they had worked, *he had won!*

There remained but the final step.

Triumphantly he reached out with his mind, as he had for the cowering spirits of Aldewaine and the Karawinns, and touched the spirit of his son.

And drew it to him.

As if knowing further protests would be to no avail, Irik offered only token resistance. The body, standing rigidly in its ancient burial shroud, trembled for a moment as the mist that was Irik Zal'honan gathered in the surrounding air and let itself be absorbed.

The dead eyes came alive, not with the terror he had seen in the eyes of the three traitors but with resignation, even sadness. The body—*Irik*—drew himself up, pulling in a deep breath, as if to savor, in spite of himself, the first breath that had entered his lungs in a century.

"You will come to see I was right," Azalin said, though in that moment he thought of himself only as Firan Zal'honan, father of Irik.

"You were wrong then," Irik said, "and you are wrong now. Nothing has changed except that we have both undergone a century of torment because of your actions. I would do the same again if offered the choice."

"As would I!"

"Then this hideous thing I see before me is your chosen form, Father?"

"It is the price I pay! I have the strength to bear it."

"And is it the only price?"

"Whatever the cost, it is mine to bear."

"And what of the cost you have forced me to bear, Father? But for you, my spirit would have been free to move on, not bound to a decaying body in a granite tomb. I would—"

Irik broke off with a choking sound, his hands going to his throat.

A hair-thin ring of blood had appeared where the scar had been moments before, and now the blood began to trickle down onto the ragged folds of the burial shroud that still covered him. When he tried to speak again, only a guttural rasping emerged, and the trickles merged to become a sheet of red.

What have you done? Irik's voice screamed in Firan's mind, echoed by his own scream at his tormentors.

Within seconds, the blood had dried, but the face had grown mottled in those same seconds, and now it began to shrivel, flesh falling away in chunks that clung briefly to the shroud and then melted and vanished, leaving behind only a hideous stain. The skull was showing through now, and the fingers were once again little more than loosely connected shards of bone.

Azalin plunged back into the room, grasping at Irik's burial shroud, but a patch of the rotting cloth came free in his fingers.

The searing pain enveloped him again.

And even as it did, even before he retrieved the parchment and began once again to read aloud the faded script, Irik's body ceased its deterioration and began to restore itself. By the time the crippling nausea struck at Firan, the body was almost whole again. Only the trickle of red that ringed the neck remained.

And then that was gone as well, leaving the faint ridge of scarring that could not be erased.

Prepared this time for the wracking nausea, Firan was able to remain upright, essentially in command of his body despite the convulsions that shook it and threatened to tear away his control.

And he realized the truth. He realized the nature of this latest torment forced upon him. As long as he remained within this room, within whatever nexus of power existed here, Irik's body would remain whole. The moment he left, the moment his strength failed him and he surrendered to the agony and withdrew from that nexus, that which he had accomplished within began to be negated.

Irik's body would crumble before his eyes.

So. His tormentors had won after all. Even he could not withstand this magnitude of torture forever.

And even if he could, he would be trapped here, unable to rule this land or any other, unable to watch over his son and stiffen his spine and do all the things he had failed to accomplish with the boy in Knurl.

He had lost.

Unless . . .

The face of the one called Oldar, so like Irik's own, flashed before his pain-clouded eyes.

"His mind was open to me, a kindred soul," Irik had said. For several minutes, Irik had spoken through the young man, had virtually possessed him.

A kindred soul . . .

An exchange was possible between two such.

Surely it was fate, not simple coincidence that the first person Firan had seen when he had emerged from the mists was this young man. Surely it was not accident that Oldar had remained close, had provided the channel for that first contact with Irik.

A kindred soul . . .

Suddenly the nausea overwhelmed Firan, and he stumbled from the room.

Blocking Irik's angry pleas from his thoughts, he reached out and gripped the minds of his newest minions, Baron Aldewaine and his cousins, and sent them on their way.

TWENTY-SIX

579, Barovian Calendar (continued)

No matter how hard he tried, Oldar could not fall asleep.

But he had not really expected to. For one thing, his urgent desire to be on his way out of Il Aluk at dawn made his nerves taut with both expectation and apprehension. For another, the luxury of the bedclothes and the size of the bedroom Balitor had given him, instead of making him comfortable, made him feel even more out of place. Such things were not for the likes of him, who was used to open ground or straw pallets, and neither were the closets full of finery Balitor had offered him. In the end, much to Balitor's amusement, he had donned the woolen trousers and shirt he found in a departed gardener's closet along with worn coat and boots.

Worst of all, though, was the knowledge that servants waited in their quarters, ready to be roused from sleep to answer his summons at a moment's notice. If Balitor had not forbidden it, he would have sought them out and apologized.

And the fact that he was here only because the former owner and his cousins had been killed in cold blood only

hours before made Oldar want to grab Balitor by the scruff
of the neck and drag him from the manor and get as far
from Il Aluk as possible before Firan or Darcalus or Azalin
or whoever he was changed his mind yet again, and the two
of them ended up in a another bloody heap like the one that
probably still lay on the balcony in Avernus.

But Balitor would have none of it. "If you wish to offend
him by refusing his favors or by openly doubting his
word," he said, "you do that, but don't ask me to put my
head on the block next to yours."

And so Oldar, fully clothed but for his boots, the leather
bag of coins in his coat pocket, lay on top of the luxuriously
quilted covers on a huge canopied bed, waiting for the first
indication of dawn. Balitor, between silken sheets in an
even larger bed in an adjoining room, snored blissfully,
doubtless intent on enjoying his situation while it lasted,
however long or short that might be. At the very least, he
had told Oldar gleefully, he would root out a few of Il
Aluk's citizens who had in the past been less than charita-
ble toward him and return the favor with interest.

Though he still considered Balitor a friend, Oldar was
glad he would not be in Il Aluk long enough to see what his
friend did with his newfound power, or what he became as
he used it. If he indeed had the chance to use it. If he did
not himself fall victim to—

Footsteps in the hall beyond the bedroom door sent
Oldar leaping from the bed, his spine tingling with apprehension.

"Balitor?" he blurted. "Is that you? Is dawn finally
coming?"

But there was no reply, and as Oldar listened more
closely, he could hear Balitor's snoring, faint through the
doors to the other bedroom. Hastily he slipped his boots on

and waited as the footsteps halted just outside the door.

The latch turned, and the door swung open.

Oldar gasped. Stepping stiffly through the door was Baron Aldewaine—the *body* of Baron Aldewaine, for the parts of the face not covered by blood only now beginning to dry were the dead white of a corpse. The only sign of life in the face was in the horror-filled eyes.

"Balitor!" Oldar screamed, and he heard the interrupted snort of a snore as his friend was jerked from sleep. "Help me, Balitor!"

But Aldewaine's hand was already on Oldar's arm, its grip as iron-hard as that of the creature in the marsh grasses outside Avernus. And as the door to Balitor's room was fumbled open and a dazed Balitor lurched through, Lord and Lady Karawinn, similarly corpse-white, appeared and took up positions on either side of Aldewaine as he dragged a struggling Oldar out of the room.

Balitor lunged forward, and for a moment it seemed he was rushing to Oldar's aid, but he lurched to a stop in the doorway, as if belatedly realizing what he was doing, what it was that moved away down the hall of his newfound home.

As it was, he could only stand and watch, motionless except for the sudden trembling that gripped him as he wondered if similar creatures would be coming soon for him.

And if there was anywhere in all of the land he could hide.

*   *   *   *   *

No, Father! You cannot force this upon me!
Irik's voice—his son's true voice—persisted in Firan's

mind as he waited for his minions to return, but it was almost drowned out by the voices of the shadows as they clamored and laughed.

"Have you abandoned even your honor?" his father asked in a voice of shame. "Does your word now mean nothing to you?"

"Do you not remember your vow?" His brother's child-like voice was filled with disbelief and disappointment. "Bare hours ago, you promised Oldar he could leave Il Aluk at dawn, that he could be reunited with his father."

"You do not understand," Stakaster's voice, laden with sarcasm, replied. "For those as exalted as your brother, for those with motives and duties as noble as his, words are more flexible than they are for others."

"That is true," Quantarius's voice took up. "Oldar will indeed be allowed to leave Il Aluk and be reunited with his father—if he still so desires. The fact that he will be wearing a somewhat different body is of little consequence."

"But, Son," his father's voice cajoled, "you vowed that if anyone stole so much as a single coin from him, the thief would answer to you. And yet now you yourself propose to steal his very body?"

"But Firan Zal'honan *will* answer to himself," Stakaster's voice intoned, "and he will no doubt deal as sternly with himself as he does with others. You must be aware of his unflagging fairness. Family and friends are dealt with as harshly as are total strangers. Surely his wife and son can testify to that."

And so it went as the minutes and hours dragged by, until . . .

Heavy footsteps grated on the narrow stone stairs, and Oldar appeared short moments later. He no longer struggled in Aldewaine's unbreakable grip. Stoically he climbed the steps under his own power, having long since realized resistance was futile.

Irik, his body reduced once again to a living skeleton with tiny, clinging shreds of flesh, had fallen silent and now stood waiting, as if in resignation in the face of something he could not prevent. Even the voices, as if grown weary of their taunts—or of their victim's lack of response—had been reduced to an indistinct murmur.

Oldar flinched involuntarily as a sickly yellow light from the open door fell on the landing and he saw for the first time the burial-shrouded reality that lay behind Azalin's illusory self. And the even more grotesque creature that stood next to it.

But still he did not struggle, not even when he was brought to stand beside the almost fleshless skeleton himself.

And Firan began.

In his mind's eye, he saw the exchange, saw the mist that was the essence of Irik Zal'honan emerge from the tattered remnants of its body, saw it meet and mingle briefly with the lesser thing that was Oldar's essence and move on, surrounding and seeping into that other body that would now be its own.

He began to speak the words.

And as the words formed, Oldar felt a tugging, gentle at first, then more powerful, and each tug was accompanied by a dizzying feeling of disorientation, a sensation of rapidly shifting double vision.

Then words began to appear in Oldar's mind, in the same way they had appeared when Irik had spoken through him. But now there was no impulse to speak the words aloud, only to listen.

He must not succeed. You have only to resist, as I am

resisting.

But I am not versed in his magic, Oldar responded silently. *I know no spells or counterspells.*

You have no need for such things. All you require is your will. Hold tight to yourself and do not let go, no matter how savage a pull you feel. Natural bonds are not easily broken, nor unnatural ones easily forged.

For a moment, the world seemed to spin around Oldar, and he saw his own body below him. But he reached out instinctively, and he was whole again.

Hold fast! The words appeared in his mind. *Hold fast, and the natural bonds will endure!*

And Oldar did, in the only way he knew how, wrapping his arms tightly about himself and closing his eyes and folding himself into a ball the way he had as a child when the night had been dark and cold and the bedcovers had offered the ultimate protection.

And the phantom grip gradually faded. The peculiar, nausea-inducing tugging lightened and finally disappeared. And he could feel only the cold stone floor beneath him even through the coat he still wore.

For a long time, he lay there, shivering and afraid, until light penetrated the narrow slits in the tower wall and filtered dimly through his still-closed eyelids.

The light of dawn.

He opened his eyes. He was alone. The horrors of the darkness were gone. And he was still whole, still clad in his own body.

Quickly he uncurled and lurched to his feet, his young muscles stiff and aching. The only sound was the faint sigh of the air as it moved throughout the castle, almost as if the entire structure were breathing.

Or sighing.

Taking the steps two and three at a time, he raced down the tower stairs, then retraced his steps through the maze of Avernus. To his utter surprise and relief, every door yielded to his touch. Even the massive courtyard gate, which he had been certain he would have to scale, silently yielded just enough to let him slide through.

He didn't look back as he pounded down the crooked drive to the main road and continued running until sweat and exhaustion erased the tingling chill from his back.

Finally he slowed to a heavy-breathing walk.

Il Aluk and Balitor lay directly ahead, but the images he held in his mind as he continued to walk were of a freshly plowed field and his father's weathered face.

* * * * *

Firan watched from the parapets with a peculiar mixture of emotions as the distant figure cast a final brief glance over its shoulder and continued on its way.

Once again he had been thwarted, but this time not by his tormentors but by his own misguided son, who had clung so tightly to the hideous thing that had once been his body that even Azalin's magic could not pry him free. He had even somehow lent some of his strength to the other, the one called Oldar, and the attempted exchange had been an utter failure.

And he had been shamed.

For once, the shadow voices had been right in their baiting. To play word games in order to break a promise while pretending to keep it was unworthy of him. He would never give them that opportunity again, no matter how many obstacles they threw in his path, no matter how many worlds they saw fit to exile him to.

But he had also been encouraged, for the boy *had* shown strength, exceptional strength, and courage, no matter how misguided. Someday, when he escaped or defeated his tormentors and was able to truly restore the boy to life, he would finally be able to channel that strength in directions worthy of the son of Firan Zal'honan. Until then . . .

Until then he had a land to rule and to learn about and to explore.

A prison to escape.

A son to watch over . . .

* * * * *

His imprisonment would never end. Of that, the spirit of Irik Zal'honan was finally convinced. His father's obsession was beyond reason. Even the disaster that this night had become had taught him nothing, neither the pain nor the shame.

Irik's body, little more than a skeleton wrapped in a tattered burial shroud, was once again shut from sight in the elaborate sarcophagus that Firan Zal'honan's guilt and magic had created nearly a century ago. The spirit, tethered by an invisible cord that even Irik's will could not break, hovered helplessly in the air and stone of the sarcophagus and the room that now held it.

He waited, aware of every second that passed, with only his memories of long-ago times to occupy him. Now and then, as if he were unconsciously trying to return to those times, the form he had held in life would take wraithlike shape and drift aimlessly about the room that was his prison. His existence was as empty as it had been for nearly a century and would continue to be for another.

And yet another.

But slowly, as another unseen dawn broke outside Avernus, he began to realize that this time something was different.

This time he was not alone. Something watched him, something unseen even by him.

Are you the force that brought me to this place? he asked the silence. *Are you that which brought my father here to torment?*

There was no answer, but the presence remained, skirting his senses, growing closer.

What are you? You speak to him with familiar voices, but they are not yours.

The same muffled laughter that had taunted his father echoed through his mind. *Are they not?* The words appeared soundlessly in his thoughts. *Were they not given to us by Firan Zal' honan?*

Surely you do not speak for my father!

More than either of you can ever know.

And the presence began to fade. *Wait!* he cried, but there was no longer a response.

But as they faded, he felt a growing lightness, what in life would have been a feeling of giddiness.

Suddenly he could feel the invisible cord that bound him to this wretched place loosening.

And a figure was forming, a wraithlike figure with features that were identical to his own.

Slowly it drifted toward the sarcophagus, as if drawn to it to take his place.

You are free, the soundless voice whispered in his mind. *You have been held prisoner far too long for sins not your own.*

No! he screamed, pulling violently back, resisting, as he had resisted the theft of Oldar's body. Whoever this wraith might once have been, he did not deserve to take on this burden any more than Oldar deserved what had almost been done to him.

But as he watched, as the insubstantial figure passed by—passed *through* his own, their essences touched.

And he knew the truth.

This form was not real. It was just another illusion created by whatever had spoken to him, a mindless ethereal puppet controlled by whatever power it was that held his father—held this entire godforsaken land!—in its grip, now and forever.

Irik knew not why he was being released, any more than he knew why he had been summoned here in the first place. He knew only that he had no reason to stay, now that he was finally being set free. He owed nothing to a father who long ago had slain his son simply because the son would not—could not—bring himself to slay and torture others. He certainly owed nothing to the thing his father had become, which he now knew would continue with its mad obsession forever unless a merciful true and final death at last reached out and took him.

With a last look back at the sarcophagus and the simulacrum that would now inhabit it and continue to provide false hope and torment for the creature that had once been his father, Irik let go.

And moved on.

If you enjoyed reading *King of the Dead*, you may also be interested in the following books, all set in the grim gothic horror world of the RAVENLOFT® campaign setting.

Lord Azalin himself makes an appearance in *Tower of Doom*, by Mark Anthony. The book also concerns a hunchbacked bell tender and a personal agent of Azalin's, as well as a certain monster who occupies the bell tower. . . .

If you wish to learn more of Count Strahd Von Zarovich, be sure to pick up P. N. Elrod's *I, Strahd*, the personal memoirs of the notorious vampire lord. Strahd is also featured prominently in *Vampire of the Mists*, by Christie Golden, which transports a certain gold elf from Evermeet to the nightmare world of Ravenloft, where he confronts the evil Strahd.

Ask for these and other exciting titles from TSR, Inc., at fine book and hobby stores everywhere.